THE SECRETS OF WILLOW BAY

PHILLIPA NEFRI CLARK

Storm
PUBLISHING

ALSO BY PHILLIPA NEFRI CLARK

Temple River

The Cottage at Whisper Lake

The Bookstore at Rivers End

The House at Angel's Beach

A Travelling Celebrant Mystery

Of Marriage and Murder

Rivers End Romantic Women's Fiction

The Stationmaster's Cottage

Jasmine Sea

The Secrets of Palmerston House

The Christmas Key

Taming the Wind

Martha

Detective Liz Moorland Series

Lest We Forgive

Lest Bridges Burn

Lest Tides Turn

Lest Nobody Lives

Lest Angels Weep

Last Known Contact

Charlotte Dean Mysteries

Christmas Crime in Kingfisher Falls

Book Club Murder in Kingfisher Falls

Cold Case Murder in Kingfisher Falls

Plans for Murder in Kingfisher Falls

Festive Felony in Kingfisher Falls

Bindarra Creek Rural Fiction

A Perfect Danger

Tangled by Tinsel

Doctor Grok's Peculiar Shop Short Story Collection

Simple Words for Troubled Times

PROLOGUE
29 JANUARY 2000

The first few seconds are the worst.

A shock of cold water. Sea water stinging my eyes and filling my nostrils. Legs kicking as I force my body down and away from sight as fast as possible.

Where I can't be seen in the blackness of the sea.

There's little visibility, just a murky mix of sand and water disturbed by the movement of the boat. Something touches my hand and I almost scream until my brain identifies it is only seaweed. I'm close to the sea bed and swim as far as I can along the bottom before my lungs are ready to burst.

Somehow I surface slowly, cautiously, but my gasps for oxygen sound loud and I send out a silent plea that he won't hear and find me.

That's if he isn't too badly hurt. He'd been in a heap at the bottom of the steps when I escaped.

The air crackles with electricity and the water swells and swirls.

I rotate slowly, paddling on the spot to get my bearings.

Dark shadowy hulls surround me. Other yachts moored in this small bay. His boat is further than I expect. I can't be complacent. He's also a good swimmer and will track me down one way or another after I saw... found, his terrible secret. The beach is in sight. After a few more deep breaths, I swim again.

The water tugs at me as the tide rapidly rises. Lightning flashes across the sky and thunder rumbles. My energy is almost drained yet I have no choice but to swim. Nobody is around to save me if I get caught in an undertow. My dress weighs me down and for a moment I contemplate stripping it off but another flash of light propels me forward.

At last there is sand beneath my feet and I stagger into the shallows.

My body heaves and shudders as I suck in air. The shock of what just happened sends my brain into overdrive, going over and over the last few minutes. Not just the swim but the awful moment on the boat when he realised I'd uncovered the truth.

The storm is close and a hot, blustery wind pushes the waves further up the beach. On shaking legs I part-walk, part-crawl to the safety of the dense forest abutting the bay. I lean against a tree, water dripping down my face from soaked hair. My handbag and shoes are still on the boat. Well, I'm not going back for them, not after what just happened.

It wasn't supposed to have been like that.

But I'm alive and for now, that is enough.

A fork of light illuminates the boat and I'm sure I dimly can see him there, standing on the bow. Looking out over the water.

My heart is pounding.

I have to keep moving.

I have to get to safety.

ONE
NOW

Aromas drifted from the kitchen through the open living area, winding their way outside to the covered entertaining area. Delectable aromas of freshly baked bread rolls and garlic prawns marinating on the counter, the latter waiting for the guests to arrive before they'd be cooked and served on a bed of vermicelli noodles. The earthy smells were among her favourites, right up there with rain after a hot day, jonquils at the beginning of spring, and sea spray.

There was no sea spray here although the canal water was saline. The surface was presently flat and the depths unmoving, at least from Joanna Johnson's vantage point. She'd come out here for a few minutes' peace before the dinner party began. Precious time to centre herself and summon the perfect hostess from somewhere deep inside. She sipped herbal tea and pushed away the nerves which always showed up when her home was open to these guests.

Joanna leaned on the top rail of the fence between her garden and the canal. On the other side was a narrow strip of artificial grass where one could walk, but only in single file because there was a drop of a metre or so into the murky water just a step or two away. She'd fallen in once, misjudging the distance at night, possibly after a drink too many. Being in the canal, night-time or not, was a terrible idea. There were all manner of dangerous creatures lurking down there, but thank goodness her dad was with her and had fished her out. It was the first week they'd been living next door to her and he swore if she did it again they'd move into what he called an old people's home.

A boat filled with merrymakers went by at the top end of the permitted speed limit, laughter and music trailing them as much as the wake which slowly splashed its way to her side of the waterway.

But no sea spray.

For that, Joanna needed to walk a couple of kilometres from here to the long sands of Broadbeach. It was a fine beach. Beautiful enough to be included in many tourism ads. And sometimes overcrowded, thanks to the Gold Coast being such a popular tourist destination.

But even on a windy day in the middle of winter, with only locals jogging the tideline or walking their dogs, the sea spray wasn't the same.

After close to twenty-five years' absence and travelling all over the world, nothing had ever matched the scent or freshness of the sea spray as the Southern Ocean crashed into the rocks around Rivers End beach, where she'd grown up.

Her watch beeped. And kept beeping until she gave in and tapped it. Ten minutes until the guests arrived, assuming they were on time. With a small sigh, Joanna finished her tea.

A sudden downpour before dessert moved the dinner party indoors, although the table was well protected. When the boss's wife complained her hair would be ruined, one did what was prudent to keep her happy. Ted and Hazel Grey picked up their glasses of wine and left everything else for the other guests to bring in.

There were only four other guests; two who also worked for Ted's company, and Joanna's parents. The Gold Coast – particularly Broadbeach Waters – was a small world and her parents had become friends with the Greys years ago at the golf club they all belonged to.

Hazel Grey wasn't directly involved with the company but she insisted all senior members of staff hosted dinners on a regular basis, inviting them and other team members for what she called 'team morale' evenings. She even had a roster she'd email out every six months. Joanna's one attempt to miss hosting had resulted in a long phone call from Hazel, reminding her how much Ted did for his employees and what it meant to be a team player. She even mentioned, twice, how she deliberately left Joanna off the roster during the busiest time of the year to make sure she wasn't under pressure. Other than Hazel's interference, the company was a good place to work, even during the busiest times. It just wasn't worth the angst of arguing, and if Joanna was honest with herself, it wasn't as though she had a good excuse.

No husband or kids. Not even a pet, thanks to attending international fashion shows each year. At forty-four years of age, Joanna had given up on the dreams of a younger woman. Even as she put the finishing touches to a dessert of chocolate mousse with strawberries, Joanna wished she was wearing her comfy shorts and T-shirt, bare feet, and working on a design upstairs in her sewing room.

'Pity about the rain, love.' Dad had a tray piled high with dirty plates and stood looking around the kitchen.

'There, Dad. Just near the sink is fine. I think we could have stayed where we were. Don't you?'

He settled the tray where she'd gestured then leaned over to whisper. 'Can't have someone's hair getting all frizzed up, now can we?'

Joanna giggled and he winked. She was close to her parents, technically her mum and step-dad though she always thought of Malcolm as Dad, and after they retired they'd moved next door, making all of their lives a bit easier and less lonely. They'd downsized from a few acres up Tamborine Mountain way, where they'd lived for more than twenty years. Like Joanna, Dad loved kayaking and when the house next door went on the market, everything fell into place.

'Would you carry these out to the table?'

As Dad left, Ted wandered in holding an empty wine bottle. 'This wasn't half-bad, even for a Victorian wine.'

'I'm not going to bite, boss, so don't waste your breath teasing me about my home state.'

'Yeah, yeah.' He leaned against the counter. 'You never do. But that's what makes you such an asset, Joanna. Not much ruffles your feathers and that's saying something in our line of work. Fashion is tough.'

Fashion *was* tough. Being a buyer for global brands was challenging and consuming and Joanna earned every cent of her admittedly decent salary.

'Thinking I might retire in a year.' Ted gazed at her. 'Maybe you'd like to buy me out. Be your own boss.'

Barely managing to catch the spoon which almost slipped from her fingers, Joanna took a minute to breathe. She'd wanted that for years. Even quietly looked around for other jobs with a clear line of progression, which was something not obvious with Ted. He'd begun as a buyer himself, but had quickly seen a need for an agency who provided experts to the big companies to save them having their own staff. Now his business was a go-to in the industry.

'Thought you'd die in the job, Ted.' She placed coffee cups on a second tray and gave him her full attention. 'I'm listening.'

'Still little more than an inkling of an idea. Hazel wants to cruise the world on one of the big liners and we were looking at brochures the other day. Realised I rarely take a proper holiday and got me thinking. For that matter, you hardly stop. When did you last take leave?'

'Me? I get to visit Paris and Italy and Japan every year.'

He snorted. 'I might not be a buyer these days but can't recall ever stopping to look at the scenery on those trips.'

Ted was right. International trips were less glamorous than they sounded, with a huge amount of ground to cover in a short time. Besides meetings with brand managers there were shows and networking events to attend. Joanna usually slept all the way home.

'No need for holidays. I live on the Gold Coast.' Joanna smiled. 'Shall we have our dessert and a brandy?'

The evening, and the rain, wound down toward midnight. As the guests left, Ted kissed both of Joanna's cheeks and told her to think about her future plans.

'Just about everything is in the dishwasher,' Mum said. 'I left something on the breakfast bar for you.'

'No need to leave me a tip.'

'My tip is to open it.'

Her mother's face was unusually serious. She suddenly took one of Joanna's hands.

'What's wrong, Mum?'

'Probably nothing. And normally I'd have just returned it but your Aunt Beryl included it with a covering letter and said it was important you read it. Thank you for a lovely dinner.'

Thoroughly confused, Joanna waited until her parents had locked themselves in their own house before closing the door. She turned off lights as she walked to the kitchen. The only thing on the breakfast bar was an envelope. Her name was handwritten on the front, just the word 'Joanna', no address. It wasn't Aunt Beryl's writing but with a sinking sensation, Joanna recognised it. Only one person ever turned the 'J' in her name into a little tree.

Dropping onto a stool, she stared at it.

Aunt Beryl was the last of her family living in Rivers End. She flew up for visits every couple of years and always said she'd eventually move to be closer to her sister. And Aunt Beryl knew that Joanna had a rule in place for every member of the small family.

Don't talk to me about Rivers End. Especially, never mention Roslyn.

So why would her aunt – who'd never once mentioned Joanna's former best friend – be passing on a letter from her after all these years?

Glaring at it with suspicion, Joanna wanted nothing more than to throw it away. Unopened. But her aunt thought it important enough to risk upsetting the person she called her favourite niece, even if she was her only niece. Her mother had suggested she open it. Had something bad happened to Roslyn?

She snatched it up and slid a fingernail under the flap, sliding along until it opened.

What happened was all in the distant past of course. But the habit she'd built up of not reopening the wound was hard to overcome. More than half her lifetime. They'd been so young. She and Roslyn. Best friends forever. Until they weren't.

Joanna didn't open the envelope. She poured a glass of water and took both upstairs, to her sewing room. This was her haven. The place where she could be herself with nobody to impress. The mannequins against a wall were bare apart from the one she was currently fitting for a range of outdoor wear she had spent the past year developing. Affordable, made from natural fibres, comfortably cut to fit any-shaped woman. It was only a hobby. The dream she'd shared with Roslyn had stayed in Rivers End the day she'd left her hometown. And if Ted truly wanted her to buy him out in the future, then this would have to stay a hobby, because his company only dealt in high-end fashion.

She flicked on a lamp above a worn armchair she'd picked up years ago from a garage sale. It fitted the room. Fitted her old-fashioned personality.

Joanna sat and after putting her glass on the floor, pulled a single sheet of paper from the envelope. She didn't unfold it. Her hands were trembling and that annoyed her. Whatever Roslyn wanted, Joanna would deal with it without emotion. There was nothing on earth important enough to make her respond to the letter.

Dear Joanna,

Hoping like heck this reaches you. Beryl promised to try.

Something happened this week.

Parts of an old boat washed up on the beach. A shipwrecked yacht. There's talk of an investigation to find the rest of it. The thing is, I'm certain it's Trent's yacht and I think you need to come home. Even if you don't want to see me, you need to find out for yourself.

Come home, JoJo. Please.

X

Roslyn

PS I have never forgotten our friendship.

She read it twice before she understood. Her stomach churned as she crushed the paper into a tight ball and threw it across the room. This couldn't be happening. Not after all this time and a whole lifetime of burying the events of that night. Roslyn was mistaken and anyway, why did she even care? It was the one thing Joanna had never spoken of, not even to the friend with whom she'd shared every dream and heartbreak. Almost every heartbreak.

'I don't want to go home,' she whispered. The words were a lie. Joanna had never wanted to leave Rivers End. She'd planned to live her life there. For an instant she could taste the sea spray on her lips and then she covered her face with her hands and wept.

TWO

Midnight ticked over on the digital clock on the dashboard. The car was stationary, the motor idling while Joanna took a moment to gaze at the town where she'd grown up.

The spot she'd chosen to pull over was partway down the hill leading to Temple River and its namesake bridge, and gave a spectacular view across it, all the way to the distant hills which eventually led to the Otway Ranges. How often as a teen had she stood in a similar place to admire Rivers End, but always during the day? In the darkness it was a whole other world with street and house lights spreading out further than she remembered.

Rivers End was the opposite of the Gold Coast. No tall apartment buildings or endless strip shopping. No tourists from all over the world, let alone the business conventions and group tours. And here it was so quiet, so still, that one might be looking at a painting, unlike the constant movement and sound which had become a backdrop to her daily life.

Window wound down, Joanna inhaled, savouring the crisp air with a touch of saltiness. She was tempted to park the car and run beneath the cliffs to the beach. She could let the

Southern Ocean tickle her toes and finally smell the sea spray. Would it be as wonderful as she remembered? Her heart skipped at the vision in her head. Feet in the water, breeze in her hair, a myriad of stars the only witness as she laughed aloud like a child.

But it was two minutes past midnight. She still had to get to Aunt Beryl's and find the key hidden in the pot plant near the door to sneak in without waking her.

Nosing back onto the road, she wound up the window of the hire car. Her sudden request for a month of annual leave had shocked Ted, but she'd reminded him of their conversation in her kitchen and he'd agreed. Being late November, her workload was more about planning for the start of the fashion season in February anyway, and she said she'd work on that during her time off. It was likely she'd be home within a week, but at least she had a buffer if anything held her here. And she'd be back in time for Christmas with her parents.

Nothing will. It's a false alarm.

All she'd thought about on the trip from Queensland was that yacht. Where exactly had pieces washed up? Willow Bay seemed the most likely, yet how, and why?

Joanna skirted around the outside of the main shopping area then passed Palmerston House, the gracious old property on the right. If she took the sharp left here, she'd find herself on a dead-end road on a cliff. It was a beautiful spot but not her current destination. Instead, she accelerated up a hill and at its peak, turned onto a narrow road on the left. It was so well hidden that most people drove by without noticing it was a street. Along here were only a handful of houses, all nestled behind bushland. Aunt Beryl owned the one closest to the water and had lived here for as long as Joanna could remember.

It was impossible to miss the house because it was at the end of the road. A dirt driveway led between gum trees to a carport with an empty space beside a hatchback, and as Joanna parked, a light came on. By the time she was out of the car, the back door of the house had swung open and Aunt Beryl was hurrying down the steps.

'My darling girl!'

With a sudden rush of happy tears, Joanna held her arms out to her aunt and they embraced, gripping onto each other and rocking side to side.

'Two years is too long, Joanna. Let me look at you.' Aunt Beryl stepped back. 'Too skinny and far too stressed and over-worked. Let's get you inside and off your feet.'

'Is it two years since you visited us?'

Between them they collected her two suitcases, laptop bag, and a rather gorgeous carry bag with goodies for Aunt Beryl that Joanna had selected at one of her airport waits.

Once inside, the smell of herbal tea brewing almost brought more happy tears and Joanna figured she was exhausted from travel to be so emotional. Aunt Beryl led the way to one of the bedrooms which had a sliding door out to a balcony. It was open, allowing a sea breeze through the screen door. Waves crashed nearby.

'The bed is almost new and I put fresh linen on this morning. If you need another blanket there's more in the cupboard in the hallway but the weather's lovely right now. Take a moment then come and get some tea. Have you eaten?'

'Only on the first flight.'

With a roll of her eyes, Aunt Beryl disappeared in the direction of the kitchen.

The bed was inviting, with plump pillows and a lightweight dressing gown draped on the end. Joanna pushed the suitcases out of the way, dropped her laptop bag on a small table, and took the carry bag to the kitchen. Aunt Beryl – who Joanna finally noticed was wearing a dressing gown and slippers – had the stove on and was cracking eggs into a bowl.

'Pour some tea, darling, and sit. I'll have an omelette in front of you in minutes and that will help you settle for the night. No point trying to sleep hungry. The tea is my own blend.'

'And it smells divine. But why are you still up? I thought I'd be sneaking in.' Joanna part-filled the two cups which were near the teapot. 'Are you having some omelette?'

'So many questions. Good to know some things don't change.' Aunt Beryl smiled. 'I might have a little. And some toast. Sourdough from my own starter and I'm rather proud of it. Now sit.'

Waking up in Rivers End was surreal, and Joanna took her time. The sound of the sea woke her, that and daylight which told her it was at least mid-morning. And an unexpected hunger.

She lay on her side for a while to stare out through the sliding door. She'd left it wide open, with only the screen door between her and the outside world, and it felt so natural and safe. Not something she'd do in the Gold Coast. There weren't even any security cameras here, in stark comparison to the half dozen around her house.

Her hand reached for her phone, which she'd left on the bedside table and switched off before she'd climbed into bed. She turned it on and quickly sent a message to her parents.

> Safely here with Aunt Beryl. Sorry not to message last night but it was after midnight.

A tap on the door was followed by Aunt Beryl's head appearing. Her eyes lit up seeing Joanna awake.

'Brunch in fifteen minutes. We might sit out on the main balcony and get some sun onto your skin.'

With that she was gone again.

Joanna held her arm out. It was pale because she was careful to protect her skin. Dad had sun spots which were periodically removed when they began to change into something more sinister and he was constantly on at her to wear a hat and apply sunscreen. Even at her age.

Her phone vibrated.

> Have a lovely time, kid. Mum and I will keep an
> eye on your house.

After a quick shower, Joanna threw on shorts and a tank top and joined her aunt outside. This balcony came off the living room and like the three bedrooms in the house, overlooked the Southern Ocean.

'Oh, my.' Joanna couldn't help herself, going to the railing and gazing at the gorgeous deep blue sea in front of her. 'I'd forgotten about your views.'

'They are special and I shall miss them.'

'Miss them?'

'I've poured a coffee for you, so please fill a plate.'

Joanna sat, eyes still on her aunt. 'Where are you going?'

'In the short term, I'd like to visit your parents. I miss Molly and I'm giving some serious thought to a permanent move closer to her and your dad. And you. Darling, this might sound sudden seeing as you just arrived, but with Christmas around the corner I realised I'd struggle to get a reasonably priced flight until after the school holidays next year. I've booked a flight up tomorrow, so I hope you don't mind being here on your own. And when I get back in a few days we will properly catch up.'

Aunt Beryl began to serve herself and Joanna followed her example. A person would never go hungry around her aunt, who was a passionate baker and all-round great cook. She loved foraging for ingredients and had a good working knowledge of using indigenous plants to enhance any dish. The brunch included savoury muffins, mini quiches, homemade croissants, fruit, and yoghurt. Joanna's mouth watered.

'I can't imagine you not living here. This house reflects you and your personality.'

'Nutty as one of my fruitcakes?' With a laugh, Aunt Beryl deftly sliced a fat peach. 'That's sweet of you though. And I've had a good life here, Joanna. A happy one. But I'm almost seventy and my walks to the beach are restricted to days when my hip co-operates. Sometimes I'm driving to Willow Bay to swim rather than go down the track along the cliff.'

'I'm so sorry, Auntie.'

'No need. I'm fit and active apart from that and have had my eye on a life like Molly has for a while. Much as I love Rivers End, there's a definite appeal to living on the canals and the much flatter landscape around Broadbeach. And no more freezing winters.'

I love the winters here. The wind whipping up the waves. The colours of the ocean.

For a while they ate and sipped the delicious coffee, the sun creeping across the balcony to warm Joanna's toes. The rest of her was in shade but before long, it would become too warm to sit here. From the balcony the sea looked calm and only in the far distance was there any sign of life as a container ship moved along the horizon. If she were to wander to the end of the sprawling garden, near the track down to the beach, there'd be rocks below and probably people swimming or fishing, all within a short walk.

'Is your career still fulfilling?'

Interesting choice of words.

'I still enjoy it, at least most of the time. The hours are a bit exhausting and in a couple of months I'll be back in Europe.'

'Is it enough though?' Aunt Beryl asked. 'You always loved it here.'

'I love the sea. This sea.'

'And the town. And the community. And your plans. And your friends.'

Deciding that avoiding the question in her aunt's statement was better than struggling to explain, Joanna bit into a quiche.

'Good, you keep your mouth full so I can talk.' Leaning back in her seat, Aunt Beryl crossed her arms. 'I've tried to hold my tongue for far too long. Not interfere in your choices. Watched you throw away a perfectly good friendship – a once-in-a-lifetime friendship. I reckon I know why, and it would have mattered a great deal at the time, but it could have been repaired. Seen you turn your back on your dreams. Even your mum and dad don't understand why but they were happy you followed them to Queensland and I don't blame them. And now you're back. All because of a letter which you probably didn't want in the first place.'

'Jeez, Auntie. I've never heard you talk like this.'

'Put more quiche in your mouth. Followed by some muffin.'

Unsure if she was going to be able to swallow because her emotions were halfway between laughter and tears, it only took a glance at her aunt's set face to obey, as if she was still a child.

'I thought you'd go and get your design degree and return once the heat of the moment cooled. But as the years have passed by you made it clear this place wasn't for you anymore. I'm sad because I miss you but I understand you've made a good life for yourself. The thing is, child,' Aunt Beryl said, her voice softening, 'whatever drove you away had no right to keep you away. Not if your heart belongs in Rivers End. And for all your overseas travel and luxury home and status with your job, I sense you still are the same sweet country girl who longs for a simple life in her hometown. Maybe being back here will remind you of your dreams because it isn't too late to start over and finally follow them. Just think about it.'

With no idea how to respond, Joanna swallowed, then finished her coffee.

Aunt Beryl must have felt she'd said her piece, getting to her feet and collecting both cups. 'I'll make us another. Keep fattening yourself up on my wholesome food.'

· · ·

They took their second coffees to the edge of the garden. It was exactly as Joanna remembered. From here ran a track, wide enough for one person and at times perilously close to steep drops, crossing the front of the cliff in the direction of Rivers End beach. It met up with a similar path from further along, not far from the dead-end road she'd passed in the early hours. Most who lived along Aunt Beryl's road accessed this track at some point.

But partway down was a fork and a walker might brave much steeper conditions for the reward of a tiny beach – which only appeared when the tide was low – where few people visited. That was where Aunt Beryl loved to go but now struggled, thanks to a hip replacement operation which made most tasks manageable but not the difficult terrain.

'You should go down there, darling.'

'I might. I probably will, another day.'

'It was so strange. The wreckage washing up like it did.'

Joanna's stomach lurched. Aunt Beryl seemed unaware as she pointed in the direction of Rivers End beach.

'Between this cliff and the jetty. At first people were in a big panic, thinking it had just occurred, and a search was mounted. The coastguard and local boats were all out searching for a yacht gone to ground. There was a near-tragedy a few years ago with a local yacht. *Jasmine Sea*. No wonder the community was on edge.'

'But it wasn't? A yacht gone to ground?'

'Nothing to suggest it. No missing boats within five hundred kilometres. No mayday calls. And then some expert took a look at what washed up and they estimated it was in the sea for a while.'

Don't ask about it. Let it go.

But this was why she was here. The only reason. She had to reassure herself that this shipwreck had nothing to do with her.

It couldn't possibly be the same yacht because that one had sailed away as expected and never returned.

'How long? In the sea?'

'Hmm... think they said at least twenty years. Not more than thirty. Funny though, because there's only so many places it could have come from, given tides and the time and most of the areas I've heard about are within ten kilometres of here. Makes you think.'

'Think? What about?'

Aunt Beryl tossed out the dregs of her coffee. 'About what yachts were around this area twenty, twenty-five years back. Weren't a lot, and most were moored in Willow Bay. Might go and clean up.'

'I'll be right there.'

As soon as she was alone, Joanna stepped to the very edge of the cliff and her eyes turned in the direction of Rivers End beach. Her fingernails dug into the flesh of her palms. A yacht once moored in Willow Bay, now apparently a shipwreck.

The past forcing itself onto now.

Onto her.

THREE
5 DECEMBER 1999

I'm first on the beach and I wish Roslyn would hurry up because all I long for is to run into the surf until it is waist-high, then dive beneath a wave. The sand is hot after such a warm day and I've kept sandals on for now. With evening approaching, it should cool down by the time we've had our swim.

Our first swim here in months.

About to toss my bag and towel as close to the tideline as I dare, I change my mind and step onto the jetty. No errant wave will wet our things up here and diving off the jetty is just as much fun as playing in the surf. I go right to the end. My eyes close for a minute and I suck in the air like this is my final breath. Salty freshness tingles inside my nostrils and my lungs and it is all I can do to not laugh aloud.

I love this place.

My home.

Rivers End.

Most of the kids I went to school with couldn't wait to leave. They crave excitement and think a big city is their future.

Me? I'm stuck in Melbourne for weeks on end studying

fashion by day, socialising and making garments by night, and dreaming non-stop of being home. Roslyn feels the same and neither of us could wait to finish the semester. We got off the bus three hours ago for our long summer break. And swimming was in our top five things to do once we got here.

- Hug the whole family
- Eat Mum's food
- Unpack quickly and fill the hamper with clothes
- Give everyone who is home a rundown on how fantastic Melbourne is
- Swim

All in no particular order.

'I'm he-re!'

A blur of arms and legs speeds past, launching herself off the end of the jetty and hitting the surface hard enough for a giant splash to send water high into the air. Before the ripples stop, Roslyn's head pops up, seawater streaming down her face which is filled with a silly grin.

I can't wait another second and toss off my sandals. And because I'm not uncouth like Roslyn, I dive with a graceful arc.

Warm salty water envelopes me like an old friend and I kick to keep my momentum downward until I am deep enough to touch the sandy floor of the sea. I slowly let the water lift me back to the surface. This is heaven.

Roslyn splashes me, laughing, so I submerge and grab her ankles, tugging her down a bit. We chase each other through seaweed and around the pylons of the jetty.

Two mermaids wouldn't have more fun.

It's ages before we climb out. Roslyn collects the bag she'd dropped earlier and we lie on our beach towels on the timber boards. The sun is beginning to set and there's such a feeling of peace here with the water splish-splashing against the jetty and seabirds cawing as they check out whether we brought any food for them. I roll onto my front and rest on my elbows.

'I didn't notice you're wearing your own design.'

Roslyn sits up and pushes her curly brown hair – made even curlier by the water – to one side. 'No better way to test it out.' She fusses with a strap. 'This isn't as comfortable as I expected now it's wet.'

'So the fabric tightened too much? There's marks on your skin, up on your shoulders where it is digging in.'

The bikini is in a pretty material with a wave pattern over a deep blue background and the cut allows for lots of movement without showing more than it should. Our major project this semester was designing one piece of beachwear. A lot of the other students chose wraps and shorts but Roslyn and I wanted to create swimwear. After all, it will be a big part of our business when we open our own boutique.

I help Roslyn adjust the strap. 'We might need to make this from a different fabric. What if the straps were a bit wider?'

'But then I'd need to change these to match.' She touches the side of her hip where similar straps connect the front and back of the bikini bottom. 'These aren't too bad and a bit tighter is better than looser.'

'Right. Falling off would be bad.'

'Oh, I agree.' She gets to her feet and wiggles her hips. 'Unless there was a cute guy around.'

'Roslyn!'

'Joanna!' She mimics my tone. 'How'd I get such a prude for a bestie?'

Deciding there's enough time for another quick swim, I stand as well but without the hip wiggles. 'I'm not a prude. And you're lucky to have me. To keep you from straying from our business plan should some *cute guy* come along.'

After rolling her eyes, Roslyn pinches her nostrils and jumps off the jetty.

I wait for the water to settle to see where she is before getting in again but instead of my friend, a triangle of fabric drifts to the surface, followed by another, and finally Roslyn. She paddles and grabs at the bikini top while I burst into laughter.

'Not funny! The whole thing fell apart and there's not even a boy to impress. Just you!'

As she climbs up the ladder I hold out her towel so she can keep her modesty. 'Good thing the elderly fisherman isn't here. He'd have a terrible shock.'

'We both would.' She wraps herself up then hands me the pieces. 'Back to the drawing board.'

Both of us are busy with family stuff for a couple of days because with Christmas only three weeks away, there's plenty of planning to do and presents to arrange. We live in the same cul-de-sac and every year there's a street party for everyone. My mother and Roslyn's started the tradition when we were little kids and it grew to become an evening people look forward to. If the weather is nice then the party is held outside, with trestle tables and music and games and we all make paper lights to line the roadside. There's about ten houses and as the street is a cul-de-sac, it has few cars and we all watch over the children.

Every family in the street puts in an amount of money anonymously because not everyone can afford much and Mum won't have people feeling embarrassed or judged. But once all the money is counted there's always enough to cover things like a lucky dip for the kids, a few luxury food items, and enough cold drinks – all family friendly. On the night we all bring extra food or drinks.

Roslyn and I have been sent into the town to scout for prizes and for an idea of Mum's – a new lucky dip for all the grown-ups in attendance.

'What about this one?'

This is the third time Roslyn's said that since we got here. We'd decided to walk down each side of the shopping streets first and make a list of shops to come back to. It isn't the day to buy the goodies but we come up with solid ideas. The 'committee' of our mothers will have the final say.

'What about it?' I walk back to where Roslyn is peering in through the window of an empty shop.

'Well, for us, silly.'

'Okay, let's check it out.' I join her, hands either side of my face, nosed pressed against the glass. 'Definitely empty. Wasn't this a fast food joint? I'm sure this was a weird attempt at burgers.'

'It was. They offered about twenty types and I must have tried three before I realised they were all awful. And the chips.'

'Ew. I remember now. Soggy or solid. No in-between. But no, look at all the work it would take.'

The interior is set up for take away. Long counters and a lot of deep fryers and ovens.

Roslyn steps back. 'Well, that's three out of three you've rejected.'

We start down the street again and I tuck my arm through hers. For such close friends, we're quite different. Roslyn gets impatient quickly. I like to think things through and plan. She's impulsive and takes risks but I prefer to stand back and assess. And she has so much courage and such a love of life. Sometimes I don't understand why she hangs around with me, yet for most of our nineteen years, she has.

'This isn't something we need to rush into,' I say. 'Next year our lives will be nuts with study and portfolios and working out exactly how we want to go forward.'

'Yeah. But isn't it fun to dream? Our own boutique to start with. Filled with our designs and made by us. At least at first. Then we take on the world. Fashion shows in Paris and Milan. Buyers coming from all over the world, jostling for our creations. Rivers End inspired, natural fabrics wherever possible. And ours. Joalyn Designs.'

When she says it like that, I totally get the dream. Our dream.

'You can do all the fashion shows, Roslyn. I'll stay and run the shop.' The idea of dealing with all those clever and rich people is scary.

'You are such a small-town girl,' Roslyn says. But she is smiling. 'Sure you don't want to marry some local boy and use your talents to make clothes for all the children you'll have?'

Before I can turn bright red, I change the subject by directing us both into one of the shops we came to see.

One day I will marry and have a big family. I love kids and wish I'd had siblings but there's only me. Roslyn is as close as a sister and she can tease all she wants but nothing will ever make me mad with her. Finishing our fashion degrees is just the first step to creating our business together. Marriage and kids can come later because we're following our dreams and I cannot wait to see what happens next.

My aunt lives a little bit outside Rivers End but close enough to walk, and she lets Roslyn and me use her sewing room. She has a decent sewing machine and because she makes her own clothes, a mannequin and big cutting table. Mum doesn't like craft so much but Aunt Beryl taught me to use the sewing machine when I needed an art smock for primary school and I've never stopped.

Today she's not home but as long as we lock up, she's happy for us to be at her house and we spend hours redesigning then sewing another bikini. It fits Roslyn even better than the last one and all we need now is to test it in the sea.

Aunt Beryl's home is surrounded by bushland and sits just above a tiny beach. It is only safe during low tide and after a quick look shows almost no sand in sight, we decide to head to Willow Bay, which is about a kilometre in the opposite direction of Rivers End. It is a deep harbour where boats are moored, not heaps, but those locals who own them keep them here. It's a safe beach for swimming and boating, with the main danger being some of the rocks further out.

The water is lovely and we swim without any mishaps with the new bikini. There's a pontoon we sit on for a while counting the yachts. Ten in total and I recognise a few which are always here.

'That one's new.' Roslyn points at the furthest yacht. There's a man sitting on the side deck with his legs dangling over the edge. He's too distant to see his features but when he notices us looking, he raises his arm and waves.

Roslyn waves back.

'You don't know him.'

She pokes me in the side. 'Do you think he's going to kidnap us and sail to some tropical destination? Actually, that kinda sounds nice.'

There she goes again.

I drop back into the sea and swim to shore. Roslyn follows slowly and I'm sure she is checking out the person on the new boat. There's more people on the beach now, I recognise people we knew at school including Salina, whom I used to be on a swimming team with.

'We're having a beach bonfire tomorrow night. You should come,' Salina suggests.

'And me!' Roslyn jogs up, wringing her hair. 'Here or at Rivers End?'

They get into the details while I pull on shorts and a tank

top. Most of the group run down to the shore leaving the three of us and a guy I hadn't noticed. I don't know him. He seems a bit out of place. Shy.

But then he looks directly at me and smiles and I swear my heart flip-flops as I gaze into the bluest eyes I've ever seen.

FOUR

NOW

Joanna's bare toes curled into warm sand at the highest point of the beach. At her back was bushland and ahead, a small, picturesque cove. The tide was low and there were no real waves – more a gentle lapping, reminiscent of a lake. Willow Bay was protected from the strongest variations in tides and the worst of the wind by cliffs and high rocks which surrounded all but a wide channel. The water here was deep and only ever stirred up during storms. It made a safe harbour for yachts to moor. A couple of dozen yachts.

So many. This is far from the little sanctuary I remember.

It was late in the day and the small beach felt crowded as groups of teens descended, much as she and her friends had decades ago. Several people were dragging dinghies to the water to head out to their boats for an evening sail. A few families were taking advantage of the low tide to have fun in the shallows.

She didn't want to go to the water's edge, although her heart longed for the chance to dive into the sea.

Not here where her last memories of the bay were a chaotic jumble.

Her heart thudded painfully as she returned to the car, sliding her sandals on before climbing in. It was Aunt Beryl's hatchback and currently was blocked into its parking spot by a big ute with jet skis on a long trailer. The owner waved and called something about only being a minute.

It was ridiculous to let herself react so strongly to a place she'd once loved. Willow Bay was a favourite haunt from the time she and usually Roslyn were old enough to be off alone. Probably too young for the world of today. But the two girls had explored lots of the coastline, from the little beach up past Rivers End all the way to Driftwood Cove, although that was by catching the bus. They'd get ice creams from the little shop facing the sea then sit at the park beside the beach to eat them before swimming the day away.

The tension drained away with the happier memories. The ute moved and Joanna started the engine.

Aunt Beryl's flight was early tomorrow morning from Melbourne and she'd suggested that Joanna return the hire car and use the hatchback. The closest return point was Green Bay, which Aunt Beryl declared was ideal because they could both drive there and then she'd catch the bus to the city where she'd spend the night. Joanna couldn't argue with her logic. A big hug and then waving goodbye had come too fast until the emotions which Joanna had battled with since the letter arrived threatened to bubble up, yet again. So she'd planted a smile on her face and kept it there until the bus disappeared from sight.

On the drive home she'd reminded herself how much her auntie missed her own sister. They only saw each other every year, taking turns with Mum flying down for a week then Aunt Beryl going to the Gold Coast the next time. It was selfish of Joanna to want her to stay when she was the one who'd run away in the first place. Instead of turning into the road to the house, she'd driven a little further until she'd reached Willow Bay and found herself in the carpark.

Maybe it was better to have the house to herself and be able to work through this crisis alone.

It is hardly a crisis.

Over the years, Joanna's sense of logic and order had only solidified. By nature she wasn't a free spirit. She was calm and sensible and always had been the one who would take a step back to assess a situation. Almost always.

She'd gather information about the shipwreck and judge for herself whether this was as big a worry as Roslyn's letter suggested. It seemed unlikely this was anything more than dots being joined where none existed and if so, Joanna would spend a few days on the beaches in the area until Aunt Beryl headed back. She could be a tourist and get some sunshine and her fill of the Southern Ocean and not ever worry about the past again.

Without her aunt here, the house had a distinctly empty feel. Its owner was a woman with a big personality who'd created a warm and happy home. Aunt Beryl spent her working years as a local school teacher, eventually becoming principal of the primary school. She'd never married and was the only person in Joanna's life who completely supported her choice to stay single. Mum and Dad wanted grandbabies and on occasion would nudge her in the direction of what they called 'nice, single men. Gentlemen'. And although she'd dated and had a couple of long relationships, there'd never been anyone who understood she wasn't giving up her career to suit theirs. Selfish it might be, but it was her choice for her life.

Her stomach growled and she laughed aloud and rubbed it. Hunger wasn't something which usually bothered her because her body was accustomed to being fed erratically, thanks to odd work hours. She'd normally placate her stomach with water or coffee and carry on until she had time. But this was different. Joanna peered into the fridge. This was her first real holiday in ages and she could eat at regular hours for once.

Aunt Beryl had already warned her there were only the basics in the fridge in anticipation of flying to Queensland. She'd made some meals up and frozen them for Joanna to use if she wanted, or she was welcome to have anything from the vegetable garden and glasshouse and pantry. Joanna closed the fridge, smiling. The generosity of her aunt filled her heart. But she was too tired to be creative with what was in the fridge, and too impatient to wait for a dinner to defrost.

Grabbing the car keys, she headed back out.

'So here I am in my home town, alone, and hungry. What should I do?' Joanna muttered.

After parking on the street, she stood on the footpath trying to orient herself with patchy memories of where each shop was. Could it really be almost twenty-five years?

The dining options she remembered included a couple of cafés which always closed by mid-afternoon, the bistro attached to one of the pubs, a Chinese takeaway, and a fish and chip shop. Not much else.

Joanna went for a walk.

The Chinese takeaway was still there, looking exactly as she recalled. Sadly, the fish and chip shop was now a real estate agents. A pang of something made her pause... regret? Old memories? How often had she and Roslyn bought dinner from there and eaten on the beach? Surely Rivers End needed its own fish and chip shop. Perhaps it had moved. Her mouth watered at the idea of salty chips with tangy vinegar.

She stopped outside a gorgeous wine bar. Rivers End Food & Wine Co. This was new and if the decor was a guide, vibrant. Through the window was a piano, a long bar, heaps of seating options, and enough room for a small dance floor. This was her thing. Of all the restaurants she'd eaten at over the years, piano bars were her favourite. Sadly, this didn't open for half an hour.

Another new eatery was an Italian restaurant with red and white checked tablecloths on a multitude of square and round tables. It was filling up quickly and a sign outside said 'bookings advised'.

Well, there was the bistro. Joanna wandered along the windows of the old building – here since the second half of the eighteen-hundreds. Her memory of eating there was less than exciting. Basic meals. Noise and the smell of beer wafting in from the public bar adjoining it which overpowered the whole bottom floor of the grand old building. This change was the biggest.

Somebody loves you now.

She pushed the door open. Inside were nice tables and booths and bright colours rather than the dull previous decor. The background music was modern and not overpowering and it smelled of food, not beer and sweat.

'Good evening!' A woman about her own age hurried from behind the old bar, which was also transformed with a lovely new timber top and a row of stools at one end. 'Meal to go or a table?' She glanced around the almost empty room with a wide grin. 'Might have trouble fitting you in.'

Joanna warmed to her. 'Would you mind trying? To fit me in?'

'Hmm, let me see. I do have one window table left.' Still smiling, the woman led the way, collecting a menu as they passed a stand. 'How about here?'

'Thank you. I can't believe how nice the bistro is now. New owners?' Joanna settled on a seat which gave her the best view of the bistro and she smiled at the woman. There was some-thing vaguely familiar about her. She wore a name tag saying *Tessa*, which didn't help.

Sliding the menu onto the table, Tessa nodded. 'Yes, me.

And thanks for the kind words but they also tell me you've been here prior to the upgrade. Beryl's niece, right?'

Joanna wasn't sure she liked being recognised, she hadn't meant to draw any kind of attention to herself. 'That's right. I lived here a very long time ago and remember having lunch or dinner in here with my parents and... and friends. What do you recommend from the menu?'

If Tessa knew she was being redirected she showed no offence, running through the specials of the day and suggesting locally caught fish with beer-battered chips and hand-cut coleslaw. That sounded perfect and made up for the missing takeaway shop, at least for tonight.

Alone again, Joanna sat back and gazed out at the street. There'd been a few changes. The intersection used to have the jewellery store, the café, and two real estate agents on opposite corners. One of the two had moved to where the fish and chip shop used to be and its building was now a bookshop. No doubt Aunt Beryl was a regular customer there with her great love of reading. Another thing they shared was an enjoyment of mystery fiction, particularly Australian and British crime. These days, Joanna mostly read on her Kindle because it went everywhere she did and was ideal for long plane trips, but she had a decent collection of paperbacks at home. Perhaps she'd visit this bookshop tomorrow and buy her aunt a few new releases to thank her for the use of the car and home.

And what else tomorrow? When will you face why you're here?

Ignoring her inner thoughts, Joanna checked her emails on her phone, pausing long enough to thank the server who brought her a small cob loaf of garlic bread and a diet soda. But her mind wouldn't rest so she assigned the worries to a note, a trick she'd taught herself as a child. By writing down the crux of a problem, she was usually able to set it aside until the time was right to address it.

*I'm here to assure myself that the shipwreck has nothing to do
with me or anyone I know. I'm here to keep the past in the past.*

Writing that was easy. Reading it back... her heart was
pounding.

Dinner was delicious. Even after paying the bill and heading
toward the car, Joanna was still thinking about how much the
bistro had changed, and for the better. It had begun to fill up as
she'd eaten, particularly with families. The staff were attentive
and the food was well priced so no wonder it was busy.

By now most of the shops were shut, but it was still light
and as the air cooled, people were out and about. It was like this
at home on the Gold Coast, with the residents often staying
inside their air-conditioned homes until the humidity and heat
dropped in the evening. Then the canals would fill with small
craft and dinner boats and kayaks and the beaches were a
popular place to cool off. The difference was that here, in Rivers
End, people also said hello as they passed. There were smiles
and groups stopping to chat and the feeling of community
almost overwhelmed Joanna.

She climbed behind the wheel and sat there for a while
without turning the ignition.

Coming here was risky on a level she hadn't considered.

It took all of one conversation to show a stranger she was –
at heart – a local. Now she was watching people who lived here
enjoy the fresh air as they walked the streets with their children
or their dogs or on their own.

A couple wandered by, their golden retriever off the lead
and trotting ahead of them. The dog's tail never stopped
wagging and he was obviously well-known as he was petted by
everyone he came across. Joanna smiled. She loved dogs. One

day, when she retired from the rat race of fashion, she'd fill her home with rescue dogs.

Why wait?

Joanna swallowed to push down a sudden lump in her throat. She was a long way from retirement. Getting all emotional was probably natural with the stress from the letter and saying goodbye to her aunt so soon. Memories were expected. The powerful feelings of loss were a shock. She was tired, that was all. A good sleep would sort it all out.

FIVE

Sleep still evaded Joanna by the time midnight came around so she threw off her sheet and got up, sliding her feet into slippers but not bothering to dress. She'd gone to bed in a sleeveless satin slip and still she was overheated.

It was her own fault for closing up the house. Every window and door was shut and locked, purely by habit. She'd not thought to put on the overhead fan in her bedroom and after a long warm day, the heat had nowhere to go. She opened the sliding door in her room, locking the screen door, then repeated the process with the living room, putting on the fans as she went. There was the remainder of a jug of orange juice in the fridge and after pouring a glass, Joanna let herself out onto the main balcony.

The air was still warm but far cooler than inside.

Relentless waves whooshed and crashed against the base of the cliff. The only other sounds were nightbirds and something climbing through the branches of a tree next to the house. It was a possum, which stopped and stared at Joanna with huge eyes as it chomped on whatever delicacy it had found.

'Hello, beautiful.'

Aunt Beryl sometimes left fruit and other goodies out for the possums and birds so the local wildlife probably was unworried by humans. Much better than the stingrays, jellyfish and even occasional sharks which hung around the canal at her Gold Coast home. Joanna thought it a bit funny that she was unafraid of the sea creatures inhabiting the coast here, but would never risk a swim in the canal outside her back door.

Standing out here with the salty air carrying the scent of the sea, the concerns and feelings of the day – of the last few days – dropped away, replaced by a sense of calm. This was exactly where she needed to be to take a long look at her life and consider pursuing Ted's suggestion she buy him out in the future. The unexpected break from her normal life might turn out to provide much-needed thinking time once she dealt with the contents of the letter.

It was nice to be back in Rivers End. Alone with her thoughts. And safe.

Something touched her bare shoulder and she squealed and jumped, orange juice splashing out of the glass over her hand. A golden orb spider had descended from the roof on a thread and was now perched on the edge of her shoulder. Carefully putting down the glass, Joanna slid off a slipper.

'Hey, little dude. Can't let you sit there so will you play nice and let me move you?'

She held the slipper against her skin and nudged the little creature, who complied and crawled on. Not waiting for a change of mind, Joanna gently tapped the slipper on the top of the railing until it was spider-free.

'And that is my cue to go inside.'

Joanna took her sticky hands into the bathroom and washed them. She was smiling and hadn't realised. A little thing, literally, had lightened her mood even further. And when she yawned, she settled back in bed and this time, was asleep in seconds.

. . .

Awake before dawn, Joanna donned shorts, T-shirt and her running shoes and was out of the door before she could make up an excuse to avoid a run.

Rather than take the road, she cut through the garden to the path down the cliff, careful of her footing where it was steepest and using the flashlight on her phone to avoid the worst parts. The sky was lightening and by the time she reached the bottom, Joanna was able to see through the gloom.

She ran a few times a week and preferred this time of day. It was the best way she'd found to clear her mind. Running was portable, too; all she needed was the right shoes and some time to herself. From city streets to lonely forests, she'd run all over the world at one time or another. But here was a first. Running was something she'd taken up after leaving Rivers End.

Joanna was on the sand at the bottom of the cliff. She'd been up and down that path hundreds of times, taking the fork toward Rivers End beach rather than the one closer to Aunt Beryl's house. But that was years ago.

More than twenty-five. You were a young woman then. Unstoppable. Fit.

Pushing the negative self-talk away, she retied her shoelaces to account for the sand and limbered up. Long stretches and little jumps until her body was ready and her mind couldn't wait. One glance down Rivers End beach to plan ahead and she was off.

The hard sand close to the water was incredible beneath her feet. Firm and supportive unless she strayed to the edge of the waves. Then it became slippery and unstable and she'd move a little higher up. Her breath came quicker as her lungs sucked in air and the first twinges of protest from her muscles were ignored. She knew how to push through.

Joanna ran all the way to the far cliff and back without stopping or slowing. That was about two kilometres and a decent start. After a sip of water, she began her second loop but this time paid attention to her surroundings, with the coming of dawn. Unlike Willow Bay with its heavy vegetation lining the beach, here it was a long cliff which formed a gentle curve around the sand. To her right was the jetty and ahead and to the left was the lagoon. This was where Temple River pooled into a wide, shallow body of water with a couple of narrow rivulets to the ocean. A meeting of river and sea. The river flowed to its final destination through a natural arch beneath the limestone with a footpath running alongside. Joanna powered through the rivulets, enjoying the splash of water on her legs. Once she reached the far cliff, she slowed to a walk and then stopped, squatting to catch her breath and drink more water. Steps were carved into the limestone cliff going all the way to the top. Up there was a graveyard and a carpark and beyond was the road to Melbourne.

There was access to another small beach around the base of this cliff but she'd only been there a couple of times. The tide had to be low to safely go around and she'd never been sure if the beach was public. The only other safe access to it was through a large estate housing an artists' retreat and it felt a bit rude to simply cut through a private property.

Joanna had run enough. She still had the climb back up to the house and her legs were a bit jelly-like, thanks to the extra effort of running on sand. As the first rays of sun peeked over the cliffs, the sky displayed a riot of colour which was reflected by the surface of the ocean in long fingers of pink and orange. She stepped onto the jetty, regretting not wearing swimwear underneath. A swim now would be perfect.

How many times had she dived from the end? Or shared fish and chips with Roslyn, their feet dangling into the water as they watched the sun set? Beneath her the boards creaked and water swirled around the pylons. The jetty was as old as the town. But something was different. Joanna stopped short of the end and took a proper look. The last few metres of the timber were new, with wider boards and a waist-high fence on the left and the end, while the right was open with a ladder down almost to the bottom of the corner pylon and a little landing with posts to tie up a boat further back toward the beach. Perhaps over the years the wood had deteriorated and needed replacing. But why add the fence? Had someone fallen off?

At least she could sit on the boards and slide her legs through the space beneath the first of three horizontal rails. She could even lean her arms on the second, so this wasn't too bad after all. But nobody could run along the jetty and jump off the end now.

Roslyn would hate it.

She couldn't help smirking at the image in her head of Roslyn barrelling along to build momentum only to come to a screeching halt. Roslyn only ever did things full on. Or had.

For a while she leaned on the railing watching the sky turn to day. A fisherman settled on the landing after a grunted, 'morning'. Surfers and early joggers appeared along the beach. The world was waking up and the spell was broken. Joanna got to her feet and took a last look out at the horizon.

From somewhere out there, debris had washed to shore from a sunken yacht.

There were eggs in the fridge and they were yummy poached with homemade bread from the freezer and a tomato from the veggie garden. While the water boiled, Joanna made a list of what she needed from the supermarket to supplement the contents of the fridge and a few perishables in the pantry. Before Aunt Beryl returned she'd restock both.

After eating she cleaned the kitchen and then tidied her

bedroom and eventually ran out of reasons to keep avoiding the elephant in the room.

She took her laptop bag outside and sat at the table, glancing up first to make sure her little spider friend from last night wasn't planning to visit again. As the laptop woke up, Joanna removed more items from the bag and lined them up. A notepad with a hotel logo at the bottom – one of many she had from various buying trips. Two pens, one black and one red. A diary, old with a plain black cover but loads of stickers all over it. She'd gone through a long phase of adding stickers to anything she could and sometimes looked longingly at her work ones, but never followed through.

The final thing was the letter from Roslyn which she'd retrieved from where she'd thrown it the other night. It was relatively flat but still criss-crossed with lines from her silly moment of crumpling it into a ball.

Deciding she needed a coffee, Joanna used the few minutes of the coffee machine heating to talk herself into a more productive state of mind. Getting emotionally involved would turn this into a long and uncomfortable event. No, she'd be better off treating it like a game... which didn't sit well. She settled on it being a work problem but without the fashion.

Except fashion has everything to do with this.

If not for her love of sewing and then designing, her friendship with Roslyn would eventually have drifted into something less intense, without the connection of their shared interests and plans. If she hadn't been so close to Roslyn, then the bad stuff would never have occurred.

Coffee in hand, she sat at the table and sipped, staring at the letter as if expecting it to do something. Get up and leave. Vanish into thin air. Or morph into an entirely different letter from Roslyn. An apology. A plea to make things right. But nothing happened and Joanna put down the cup and picked up the letter to reread.

Dear Joanna,

Hoping like heck this reaches you. Beryl promised to try.

Something happened this week.

Parts of an old boat washed up on the beach. A shipwrecked yacht. There's talk of an investigation to find the rest of it. The thing is, I'm certain it's Trent's yacht and I think you need to come home. Even if you don't want to see me, you need to find out for yourself.

Come home, JoJo. Please.

X

Roslyn

PS I have never forgotten our friendship.

'Well, I *have* forgotten it.'

Even as the words left her lips they sounded like the lie they were.

Some things were impossible to forget. For years she'd shut the memories in a mental box and now it was open and there was nothing Joanna could do to stop them escaping.

SIX

A search of the local newspaper's website was a good start, with several articles over the course of a week or so on their online portal. Joanna hoped she could pick up some paper copies in town but for now was cutting and pasting details into a blank document.

The first article took up the front page of the paper that week, with an alarming headline and a photograph of unidentifiable pieces of timber scattered on the beach.

Desperate Search for Missing Yacht and Crew

There were more photographs. Long planks of timber with flaked paint and one with a metal rail attached. Pieces of a mast. No wonder people imagined a disaster had occurred out at sea.

The next day's report had images of coastguard boats and a helicopter scouring the water in different locations. Small local craft were out in force to help search and speculation was rife. Which yacht did the wreckage belong to? Was anyone missing in the area? More photographs of a marquee set up against a cliff where a community group had created a place to itemise each piece.

'So what about the police?'

Joanna had no idea who would respond to this kind of thing. Coastguards would be there during the search phase. If the rest of the yacht was located then possibly there'd be salvage companies brought in to retrieve it, but she really needed to speak to someone who understood this better. The most recent entry on that website was from yesterday morning. It reported the water search was no longer under way and with evidence pointing toward this being a wreck from many years ago, investigations would likely turn to historical missing boats in the area.

A familiar chill went up her spine.

He was alive. I'm sure he was alive. Why would his yacht go down?

She opened a new tab and searched for a map of the region, quickly narrowing it down to a marine map.

Willow Bay had always been considered a safe mooring place and it was clear from the sheer volume of boats there now that it was even more popular than it had been back then. Joanna had spent plenty of time on different yachts thanks to friends of her parents and that included sailing out through the rocks on either side and into the open sea. She had a vague memory of being told that it wasn't the rocks you could see which were dangerous but the clusters beneath the surface, which were to be avoided at all cost. They were somewhere around the narrowest part of the channel and along the cliffs.

Her finger traced the route out on the map. Once clear of the rocks and cliffs, a yacht could continue forward into the open sea or, more often, go right toward Warrnambool or left in the direction of Green Bay, passing Rivers End, which yachts rarely visited because it offered little protection from the wind or tides.

I need someone to help me.

She dialled her dad's number, tapping the end of her pen against the table as it rang, before going to his voicemail.

'Hi Dad. Just checking in. No rush. Talk later.'

The minute she hung up, she changed her mind. Dad would have some ideas about tides and the coastline here but he'd want to know why she suddenly had an interest in them. Neither of her parents had any knowledge of the events of that night so long ago. Even Aunt Beryl didn't know that it was the shipwreck which brought Joanna back to Rivers End and wouldn't even remember the people she'd hung out with back then.

Joanna pushed her chair back and began pacing. Not the kind she did sometimes while thinking through a problem, but one borne of sudden deep agitation.

The biggest mistake she'd made was not going straight to the police when she was safely back on land. But she hadn't spoken to the police or anyone and was left with nobody she could talk to about what she'd seen on the old yacht that night or what she'd done to escape.

Not then and not now.

By leaving Rivers End she'd lost almost everyone from her childhood and teenage years. Her parents had moved to Queensland shortly before she did and she'd never said a word to them. Nor to Aunt Beryl. All the friends her own age had drifted away. Or betrayed her.

She stopped pacing and gripped the back of the chair.

Being honest, only one friend betrayed her. Roslyn. But it might as well have been the entire Rivers End community, so deep was the hurt at the time. A lifetime of friendship gone in a matter of weeks. Her future plans and dreams with it. Joanna's stomach turned and her throat tightened. *This* was why she'd stayed away.

The phone rang and she answered with an abrupt, 'Hello.'

'Bad time, kid?'

'Dad. Sorry, no. Not at all.' She sank back onto the chair, holding on to his voice like it was a way back to her normal life. The safe, controlled one she'd engineered for more than two decades. 'Has Aunt Beryl arrived yet?'

'Flight lands in another half hour or so. We're about to head to the airport but thought I'd call quickly while Mum finishes the last lot of flowers she's been making pretty in vases. Think this last one is heading for your auntie's bedroom.'

'She could have had use of my house if that was easier?'

He laughed. 'As if your mother would allow Beryl out of her sight for so long. Those two are going to fill every minute of their time together and I will get back on the canal with the kayak.'

Dad was not only a keen kayaker but president of a seniors' kayak club and a past champion in several competitions.

'I still remember us kayaking around Willow Bay and me wanting so much to go out through the channel. What was I? About twelve or thirteen?'

'Good grief, I'd forgotten how quickly you turned my hair grey that day. You'd got way ahead of me and were lining up to take yourself right out into the Southern Ocean. I'd already told you no and yet there you were, doing your own thing with no fear of the unknown.'

Dad had caught up with her before she'd reached the channel and told her in no uncertain terms to turn around before he took her kayak away for a month. At the time she'd been fuming, but later he'd explained how treacherous the channel was and she'd felt bad for scaring him.

'Am I remembering correctly that the danger in the channel is from submerged rocks along the right side?'

Her mother's voice called something in the background and Dad answered that he'd be right there. 'Time to go, but yes, that's exactly where the worst hazards are. Anyone mooring a boat in Willow Bay would know that, but kayaking is a bit different because we simply take them to any waterway by vehicle and it takes research to know the dangers. Shall we do a zoomie call later with everyone here?'

'Sure, Dad. I'd love to do a zoomie call. Give Mum a hug for me.'

She grinned at her Dad's term as they disconnected.

But then she looked at the marine map again and focused on the area they'd been kayaking that day so long ago. Her finger hovered close to the screen of the laptop, tracing the direction she'd been intent on taking. Dad was right. Had she kept going, she might have foundered on the rocks sitting just beneath the surface. But was he right and everyone who used Willow Bay to moor their boat knew about them?

One of the traits which made Joanna good at her job was attention to detail. Real attention – more than just a properly formatted report or getting the correct names of the latest trends in colours. She liked to understand every aspect of a product or a brand or line before recommending it to the high-end clients she represented. The quality of the fabric mattered. The cut and lines – would it suit a range of body types? There were considerations about current trends in Australia and where a dress or jacket or pants would fit in. And with which retailer. Clients trusted her judgement when spending huge amounts of money on the next season's best thing. It was intense and satisfying all at once and she was very good at her job.

Joanna's career was possible only because of her past.

Her passion for design and experiences creating her own clothes and swimwear and testing them until perfect. The hours she'd worked through the night, even as a teen, to finish a project. Often these were in Aunt Beryl's house and later, in the campus apartment she and Roslyn shared in Melbourne.

It should have been different.

The door to the sewing room was open. Aunt Beryl didn't seem to have made many changes to it since she'd last been in there. Three dressmaker's mannequins and of those, one was naked, another had the beginnings of a caftan such as Aunt Beryl often wore, and the third... was Joanna's unfinished work. It was beneath a lightweight sheet but she knew what it was.

A semi-formal dress in gorgeous sky-blue material.

'Oh, I'd forgotten you.' Joanna couldn't help but go to the mannequin and remove the sheet. Her fingers touched the fabric and a host of long-buried emotions vied for attention. The dress was one she'd designed. Not even with Roslyn. They'd normally shared their designs and worked on them together and almost always, it was a perfect union. But this one was for a purpose. A new dream. One which she'd had no intention of sharing with Roslyn because, by then, her best friend was also her rival.

This dress was for her perfect date... dinner and dancing and walking hand in hand beneath a starry sky. The colour matched her eyes and suited her complexion. Back then, her hair had been long and she'd planned to have it swept up in an elegant chignon or else loose in large, soft waves. There were even shoes already bought, not that she had any idea where they were now.

The dreams of young love.

Joanna moved the mannequin away from the wall and inspected the dress properly, her fingers exploring a row of fabric buttons up the back in place of a zip. The bodice was fitted with a princess-style neckline and spaghetti straps. She put her hands around the waist. This would fit her even today. All that was left to do was hem the skirt and make some adjustments. Finishing it would be a nice distraction from the shipwreck and then she could donate it to someone who might be in need of a special dress for a special occasion. Or she could keep it.

She returned the mannequin to its spot and opened the door to a tall cupboard on the other side of the room. There were two the same and Aunt Beryl had let Joanna use this one to store anything between visits. Inside were several shelves and drawers as well as a narrow hanging space.

Mostly it was carefully folded patterns, odd remnants, pins, and a multitude of mixed bits and pieces. But there were two sketchbooks which she lifted out and in the hanging space were a couple of prototype bikinis, which she left alone.

In the kitchen, Joanna put the sketchbooks on the table while she made fresh coffee. There was a message on her phone from Dad with a photo attached – Mum and Aunt Beryl hugging in the arrivals terminal. She sent back a love heart. Her aunt would be in Queensland for a week and Joanna had the feeling some of that time might be looking at housing options. Knowing Aunt Beryl, she'd want to keep her independence but possibly not have such big grounds to care for, and to be closer to her sister.

She'd want something like my house. We could swap.

She shook her head at the strange thought. Joanna's life was firmly on the Gold Coast.

Coffee made, she sat at the table and turned the pages of the first sketchbook, alternately laughing at some of her early designs and admiring others. These drawings were from high school where she'd done two years of textile designing as part of the lead-in to her degree in fashion. There were half a dozen decent ideas in there, not that she needed ideas when she was no longer wanting to start her own brand. But she had her hobby at home and perhaps could incorporate some of these. She opened the second book.

This was from her first year of studying in Melbourne. She almost closed it again as she came across notes written by Roslyn with some of the designs they'd collaborated on. But she'd never move on if she let little past hurts slow her down, so Joanna kept turning the pages.

Almost at the back there were a couple of photographs held onto a page by paperclips.

Her parents had given her a camera – a decent one – the last Christmas she ever spent in Rivers End. She then lost it a few weeks later.

These photos were taken with it.

The first was of Roslyn and Joanna together, arms around each other's shoulders and ice creams held aloft. Their smiles were huge and joyful and genuine and Joanna remembered the moment it was taken. And who took it, using her camera.

She slid the second photo from the paperclip and her breath caught in her throat. Why had she kept this? Actually, either photo?

Her memories didn't do justice to the young man in the photograph.

A smile which once lit her heart. The bluest of eyes which always felt as if they saw straight into her soul. Lean in build yet muscular enough for his arms to hold her until she was breathless...

Joanna gulped and returned the photo to its place.

Both images were taken on the same day. At the same place on the beach. He'd taken the one of the two girls and Joanna had taken his.

'I was happy then,' she whispered.

Of course she was. Nobody could see into the future, least of all a nineteen-year-old too wrapped up in love to see the danger standing beside her.

The planned beach bonfire at Rivers End didn't happen thanks to hot weather creating a fire risk, so our friends meet at Willow Bay instead. There's about ten of us and everyone brings some kind of food, although in the case of the boys it is packets of store-bought popcorn and sweets. And the same boys have Eskies with soft drinks and beneath them, beer.

All of us are friends from school or shared interests over the years. All, that is, other than the young man from yesterday. The one with gorgeous eyes. I know he moved to Rivers End recently and is working as a physiotherapist at Green Bay Hospital. He's Salina's cousin and she mentioned something about him staying at their house. He's standing a little apart from the rest of the group and gazing at the water, fingers in the pockets of his shorts.

And he looks lonely.

I'm not great at starting conversations but everyone else is busy chatting and he's on his own so I scoop up a couple of cans of soft drink and join him.

'Hi again. We met yesterday. Sort of.' Great, I'm already out of words and those hadn't come out well. I shove both cans in his direction. 'Like one?'

For a moment he looks at the cans and then at me and a slow smile lifts his lips and does something weird to my legs. 'It's Joanna? I'm Lucas.' He holds out his hand to shake but my hands are full and he notices and laughs and so do I. He takes the one from my right hand and then squeezes my fingers for a second. 'Thanks for the drink.'

'I think there's beer if you prefer?'

'This is fine. I said I'd drive anyone who wants alcohol.'

'That's nice of you.'

'Where do you live?'

We begin to stroll toward the water's edge, each opening our drinks.

'Walking distance to the town. To Rivers End. Roslyn lives in the same street which is how we became friends. Are you really a physiotherapist?'

'I really am.'

I sneak a glance at him. He looks barely older than me, yet had done however many years' training to reach this point. Lucas catches my eyes on him and grins. 'I'm twenty-four, I was one of those so-called gifted students who got to start university early.'

'Oh, sorry, I...'

'Hey, I get asked all the time. And there's still a lot ahead before I can have my own practice and ideally, that's what I want. I love helping people recover from injuries or improve their health and every day when I wake up, I can't quite believe I'm living my dream.'

We stop on the wet sand where warm foam covers our toes from shallow waves whooshing in. Behind us is a lot of laughter and talk and someone turns on some music, but here, with the gentle lapping of the water, we might have been alone. Strangers finding common ground.

Lucas faces me. 'I probably sound a bit weird. Living my dream when it's just physiotherapy. Hardly the same as becoming a rock star or astronaut.'

I think that's funny, because dreams matter. 'I imagine rock stars and astronauts would need physiotherapy after their adventures. Seems like a clever career move to me.'

Dropping his head back, Lucas lets out a laugh and then I start. Any ice is completely broken and there's a lightness in my heart I've never experienced. When he reaches out his hand, I take it and then we wander along the tideline as though it is the most natural thing in the world.

Our walk on the beach is cut short by the group deciding to swim and insisting we join in. Lucas mutters something about not being used to the ocean, but in minutes, all of us are splashing around, a few of the boys dunking each other into the water.

'Typical.' Roslyn stands in waist-deep water, hands on her hips. 'Some of these guys have no clue and no future.'

'Roslyn!'

'Joanna!'

'No, seriously, they're just having fun.'

'I'm all for fun but I'd prefer to have it with someone a bit more mature than they all act. You and I work so hard for our future and these boys...' she gestures at two who are lifting a third into the air, 'are like twelve-year-olds.'

She has a point.

But Lucas is different. And older. Maybe it was simply a case of growing up a bit. After wading a long way into the sea, he'd swum out to the pontoon and is sitting on the edge. There's another man with him and they're talking.

Roslyn glances at them. 'See, that's more like it. Us girls are way ahead of our years so let's go and hang out with men. Not boys.'

She dives beneath a small wave before I can say a word. I'm half-inclined to go back to the picnic blankets and help myself to whatever leftovers there are because I'd only nibbled on a couple of pieces of fruit while the group was eating. But Roslyn is almost at the pontoon and there's a complete stranger there. I promise my stomach some food later.

By the time I catch up, Roslyn is chatting away to both men as if they are old buddies. She has a way with people and is outgoing and friendly but it takes me a while to get comfortable in new situations. Roslyn says it's because of my dad... my biological one. He wasn't good at keeping jobs and paying rent and there were so many arguments and we had to move to lots of places in the area before he found a new family to love. It got better after he left but I guess I am slow to trust, and confrontation makes me freeze. Her dad left as well, but she turned out the opposite.

Lucas leans down and offers his arm and I let him help me scramble onto the flat surface.

'There you are,' Roslyn says. 'This is Trent. Remember him waving to us from the yacht? Trent, this is Joanna who is going to be one half of a new fashion empire. And she is just as brilliant as the other half, which is me, of course.'

I want to crawl under the pontoon at the sudden compliment and attention. Lucas looks surprised and possibly impressed by the announcement, and the other man, Trent, stares at me. Solemnly. As though it is already true and not the early days of a dream. I manage a quick smile. 'Hello, Trent.'

He's older than us all, maybe late twenties, not that I can trust my judgement after getting Lucas's age so wrong. His hair is brown and reaches his shoulders and he is very tanned and has several tattoos across his arms and chest. Rivers End isn't exactly filled with guys who look like Trent, let alone ones who have their own yacht so young.

Roslyn must have read my mind and points toward the boat. 'That one's yours?'

'That little darlin' is my home and my transport.'

'Your home?'

I peer at the yacht. It isn't particularly large or new and is made of timber. There's only one other yacht which moors here which is older like that. Quite a bit older but sleek and so beautiful. It's owned by the local jeweller.

'Spend my days on the sea in my *Spee-Dee-One*. I follow the surf competition circuit part of the year and make a fair income from riding the waves.'

'Are you a professional surfer?' Lucas asks.

'I make enough to pay my way.'

There is a casualness about Trent which is kind of interesting. I've never met anyone who surfs for a living and sails from place to place. If anything, I find the idea a bit scary because I love being safe and secure at home.

'Sounds romantic,' Roslyn says. 'Life on the open sea. New places to visit. New friends to make. Like now.'

He grins. 'Sure. Anyone want to check out the boat?'

I can't decide what to wear tonight and have been running upstairs and taking more clothes out to try all afternoon. The Christmas street party is only a couple of hours away and almost everything is done. Mum is finishing off some last-minute icing of delicious Christmas cookies and Dad is outside helping put up tables and more decorations. There's not a lot more for me to do after wrapping the last of the lucky dip gifts earlier.

Roslyn has been just as busy helping her mother cook all day.

I spend a bit of time braiding my hair all on one side, then adding a little bow on the other. Then I try on the first dress. And the next. Neither of those are right so I change tactics and slip into long pants and a top I made which has a scooped neckline and is soft and pretty. This will do. As much as I love fashion, I'm far from a fashionable person, but dressing up sometimes is nice. Particularly when there's someone to dress up for.

Lucas might not even come along to the party. He doesn't live in the street but I invited him anyway so he could meet more people. I shouldn't be getting my hopes up about him being here and yet I apply some light makeup and even a touch of perfume. Roslyn will think I've lost my mind but she's likely to turn up in shorts, thongs and a T-shirt, probably with Santa on the front of it. The silly thing is she'll still look great because she is naturally gorgeous, like a Hollywood star from the golden years. No wonder Trent asked her to go to his yacht with him the other night. She didn't, but told me later it was fun to flirt.

As much as she goes on about guys, Roslyn is like me, focused on our studies and our future business.

I gaze at myself in the mirror. What am I doing?

This is a street party for the families who live here yet I'm acting like I'm going on a date. Lucas is nice. Really nice. But I can't be distracted like this. Roslyn and I have another couple of years with our degrees and then at least another couple while we work in the industry for experience while creating enough designs to open our boutique. Both of us have worked part-time jobs since we were fifteen and saved almost all of it and my parents have already offered to help us with the start-up. This is the plan.

Not boyfriends.

My hand reaches up to take the bow from my hair but then Christmas music drifts up from the street. I look through the window where Dad and some of the other men are setting up speakers. They are all happy and the music is full-on festive and for once I want to stop thinking about business plans and designs and the future.

Just for one evening.

Roslyn actually wears a skirt and sandals but her T-shirt does have a reindeer on the front. We've made sure everyone knows to help themselves to one lucky dip each from the two boxes set out and brightly marked as 'Cool kids' or 'Boring grown-ups'. We figured that'll make the adult gifts less interesting for any youngsters and it seems to be working.

'You look pretty, JoJo,' Roslyn says. She's helped herself to one of Mum's cookies and is taking off tiny pieces of icing at a time. 'You like him, don't you. Lucas.'

I glance around but nobody is close enough to hear and the music is pretty loud anyway. 'No. I mean, yes. But as a friend.'

She takes my arm and almost drags me away from the party toward the other end of the short street. 'How long have you known me? Don't answer. I have never seen you make this much of an effort unless we've been going to a fashion event.'

What can I say to that? I shrug.

'Ha! I knew it. So all of those times in the last couple of weeks when we *accidentally* bumped into Lucas weren't accidents after all.'

'It was twice, Roslyn, and you and I often visit the beach in the evening.'

Her grin is getting annoying. 'Plus, he's been to the same parties as us on the river, and at Salina's house.'

'Which is where he lives. You know he's staying there until he finds his own place.'

'There's one for sale.'

'What are you going on about?'

'Up the road from where Daphne and John Jones live

there's a cute little cottage for sale. I saw it in the window of their real estate agency. Even has white picket fences.'

I can't help laughing. She's being ridiculous.

But then I see Lucas walking in our direction and I stop laughing. My heart does a little skip and the idea of a white picket fence isn't quite as silly anymore.

EIGHT

NOW

Joanna stared without actually seeing anything at the display window of Rivers End Real Estate.

If there'd ever been a little cottage with a white picket fence listed here then it was long sold and forgotten. She'd never come to see what it looked like and hadn't thought about it in years. But this real estate agency – which belonged to Daphne and John Jones – had barely changed and even still had the colourful pots of flowers along the brick sills beneath the windows.

She'd parked her car near the supermarket and shopped then fancied something sweet from the bakery. The apple turnover inside the paper bag in her hand would make up for missing lunch today while she'd continued her research into the shipwreck. Somehow she'd become sidetracked and spent too long reading fascinating details of past shipwrecks in the region and tales of survival and tragedy. It was compelling and reminded Joanna of school studies on the subject. She'd been on several excursions over the years to various places along the Shipwreck Coast including lighthouses and memorial lookouts.

Little of this had any bearing on the current alleged shipwreck apart from reinforcing how treacherous the waters were.

Back in the car, she subconsciously navigated to another part of town, only realising when she was almost there that she'd automatically gone home. Her first home. She was near the street where she'd grown up.

Seriously, Joanna. Where's your attention to detail now?

If there was one part of Rivers End she'd planned to avoid, it was here.

Yet, she parked around the corner and walked toward her old house. When Mum remarried, moving into their very own home which was owned, not rented, took a while to get used to. For ages, eight-year-old Joanna kept her favourite toy and book and dress packed in a small bag, ready for when they would move again. One day her new dad made her a promise. She would never have to move again until she was grown up and could make the decision for herself.

'And you kept that promise, Dad,' she whispered.

Back then, the town was half the size and land was cheap. Roslyn's mum owned the house next door after her own messy divorce and the two girls became inseparable. There were a dozen or so homes in this quiet cul-de-sac and she recognised most and remembered the families who'd lived there. Kids she'd played with. Parents who were friends of her parents. A couple of the houses had been replaced with bigger ones but still, the street had a serene, leafy feel.

Outside the last house on the right, Joanna stopped beneath a huge gum tree. Dad used to complain about it shedding bark each year and making work for him to keep the verge nice but he loved it and so did she. Her hand rested against the trunk and tears filled her eyes.

Then was a different time.

Safe. Fun. Simple. She'd had the best childhood living in this street and such an exciting future planned.

The house hadn't changed but someone had poured a lot of love into the front garden by adding roses and lavender and a lovely water feature with a pond in the base. How strange it would be to tap on the door and ask for a moment inside. She would never impose in such a way but was curious about whether the owners loved the home as much as her family once did. If they had children, did they enjoy the pretty view from her window?

Her eyes moved to the house next door, the one at the very end of the street. Growing up, it was her second home. And Roslyn probably felt the same about Joanna's house. Two girls born only weeks apart, their mums such good friends. Sleepovers and parties and family evenings with board games.

Joanna smiled. Aunt Beryl often joined them for the latter. She was brilliant at any word game. It made Joanna try harder, always wanting to beat her aunt.

Did Roslyn still live there, in the house next door?

As though on cue, its front door opened and Joanna stepped out of sight behind the trunk of the tree. She peered around and sighed in relief. It was a young mother pushing a pram with two toddlers, twins from the look of them. There was a lot of giggling from the littlies as the pram wheeled past and Joanna had to look twice because the young woman – from behind, and even her voice when speaking to her children – was so similar to Roslyn.

She couldn't be her daughter... could she?

If those were Roslyn's daughter and grandchildren then she must have followed through with her hateful promise to Joanna and married him. The final nail in the coffin of their friendship.

How could you?

Leaning against the trunk, she closed her eyes and took slow breaths. She hated feeling this way... out of control of her emotions and reactive to her environment. The memories were such a bittersweet mixture and Joanna didn't know if she could cope with the turmoil for much longer.

'Excuse me... are you feeling alright?'

A gentle voice was close by and Joanna's eyes opened. The young woman had returned and stared at her with such worry on her face that Joanna forced a smile.

'I'm fine. I'm okay, thanks.'

'It's just that I noticed you when I turned the corner and you seemed a bit upset. I'm sorry to bother you.'

'No, really, thank you for checking. That's incredibly kind.'

The young woman looked over her shoulder to the pram, which was parked on the footpath a few metres away. 'I'll get the girls to the park then.' With a hesitant smile she hurried away and in a moment was out of sight.

Any doubt that she was Roslyn's daughter were gone. She had the same nose and chin and her smile was just as pretty. Such a young mum, Roslyn must have had her only a year or two after Joanna left. It had taken all of Joanna's willpower not to ask for confirmation. That and the colour of the young woman's eyes. They were green. For some reason, that put a question into her mind. Weren't Roslyn's eyes brown? Some flicker of a memory from high-school biology told her that brown eyes and blue could never produce a green-eyed child.

She glanced back at her old house. It didn't matter. Roslyn had got what she wanted, then had the gall to put in her letter that she still remembered their friendship.

How could you, when you destroyed it?

It was time to complete the purpose of being here and go home. And this time, she'd never, ever return to Rivers End.

After packing away the shopping and failing to find out much more from her online search, Joanna had had enough for one day. Her mind was going around in circles and twice she'd begun to book an early flight home and then deleted it. She'd promised Aunt Beryl she'd look after the house until she came home and then she could leave. All she had to do was keep busy and the time would fly.

She stepped into her favourite one-piece swimsuit, from an Australian boutique brand who made a range from natural fibres. It was becoming easier to do, unlike the struggles she and Roslyn faced with synthetics. Over it she wore a short sundress which she'd made herself, and runners. She had no intention of going up and down the cliff path wearing sandals. A towel, sunscreen, and bottled water joined house keys and phone in a beach bag, and hat and sunglasses went on her head as she locked the house.

Her aim was for the jetty at Rivers End beach and if she was lucky, it wouldn't be too crowded. It was almost four in the afternoon with a warm breeze and the tide, although going out, still produced decent enough waves.

But nobody was in the water swimming or surfing. Instead, a dozen or so people scoured the tideline, eyes on the sand and shallows. Higher up on the dry sand, two men were erecting a marquee and near it, a third man was taking photographs of something on the ground. Driftwood. Except it wasn't that.

Something's happened.

This was what she'd wanted, the opportunity to see what was being washed ashore, but why was there more of it now? Almost two weeks had passed since the first planks were found and the original alarm sounded.

Her mind was racing as she neared the pieces being photographed, careful not to draw attention to herself as she walked as casually as possible. She was close enough to hear the conversation between the men who'd almost finished the marquee. Or at least, snippets of it. Both wore the distinctive orange clothing of the SES – the State Emergency Service. Its volunteers, particularly in regional areas like here, responded to events from storm damage to car accidents and searches and everything in between.

'Has to be falling apart wherever it's stuck. Reckon we'll see something soon to help identify the craft.'

The man speaking was in his early sixties and had a familiar face. Joanna dug deep. Barry someone. He was a builder and her dad used to play alongside him in the local cricket team. There was no way he'd remember Joanna and she inched closer.

'It might be an old wreck but not old enough to interest the historical groups. Times like this I wish we had access to a submersible.'

Barry laughed at that but the second man was serious. He was much younger, thirties, and now that Joanna looked more closely she noticed he had a police uniform under the orange vest. She moved away as fast as she dared as panic rushed in. Police were the last people she wanted to be near. What if it *was* his yacht? What if he was at the bottom of the ocean and it was somehow her fault?

She fled to the jetty and dropped onto the boards at the end, knees hugged against her chest as she stared at the sea.

Somehow she had to get a look at whatever was now washing up. It had been years though. Decades. What if she didn't remember enough about *Spee-Dee-One* to recognise it now it was a shipwreck?

And if it was? Surely she'd had nothing to do with the yacht going down? It must have been later. Much later. He was conscious when she dived overboard. Hurt, perhaps, thanks to falling down the steps but he'd moved and that was what galvanised her into action. To escape before he came after her again.

There were footsteps on the jetty behind her and Joanna looked up.

Straight into a pair of what were still the bluest eyes she'd ever seen.

. . .

Joanna could swear she had a heart, but it wasn't beating. She couldn't feel her legs so it was just as well she was sitting. Her brain wasn't catching up with her eyes. For some reason, she thought she was nineteen again.

The man standing a few metres away wasn't twenty-four though. He was closer to fifty. His hair was cropped short and had changed from sandy-blond to almost completely grey. There were laughter lines around his lips and those blue, blue eyes. He wore an SES vest and was the man who'd been taking the photographs and how Joanna hadn't recognised him wasn't making any more sense than coming to terms that Lucas was right in front of her.

'JoJo? It really is you.'

Not ready – not able – to speak yet, she had the silliest thought. What if she denied who she was? She could pretend to be someone else. Come up with a name and tell him he was mistaken.

When no name came to mind and her heart began beating again with a painful thud, she lifted her chin.

'Oh. Lucas. Hello.'

He didn't seem to know what to say next. Or do. His feet took a step forward, then two back. Maybe he was dancing to his own tune. Before she could embarrass herself with hysterical laughter, Joanna got to her feet with a silent prayer that she wouldn't wobble. It worked and she pointed toward the marquee. Nothing like some redirection.

'Whatever is happening there?'

He gave her the longest look. There was no smile. No 'welcome back to Rivers End'. No apology. No... nothing.

'Well, nice chat. I'm going for a swim.'

That started him. 'Joanna, wait. Please.'

She pulled the dress over her head and shoved it into the bag.

'Come and see what we've found.'

Hesitating, she looked at Lucas. 'Found?'

'Parts of a boat. For the past couple of weeks there's been evidence of a wreck washing up here and today a few more pieces.'

'What kind of evidence? Pieces, you said.'

'So far it's mainly from a hull and based on our measurements and taking other factors into account, they're from a yacht which has been underwater for a number of years. Likely it's a sloop built from a mix of spotted gum and cedar, which only marginally narrows it down. Maybe built in the 1970s or 80s. There's a lot of deterioration but enough paint to show it was once dark blue.'

With a churning stomach, Joanna moved to the side of the jetty which was open to the sea, near the ladder. Blue was the predominant colour of the yacht she'd fled from. Dark blue.

'How long has it been, JoJo?'

Lucas's voice was soft and closer and when Joanna glanced over her shoulder, he was only a metre away. Her composure was slipping. She needed to escape.

'No idea. Anyway, see you.'

She wasn't waiting another second and dived off the edge. The water was more turbulent than she expected and she had to kick hard to put some distance between herself and the jetty. Further toward the bottom it was less of a struggle and when she finally surfaced and turned, Lucas was already at the beach end of the jetty, heading toward the marquee.

What would he have said if she'd told him she'd met his daughter and grandchildren? He hadn't mentioned Roslyn. There'd been no wedding ring on his finger and yes, she had looked. It meant nothing. And nothing would erase the past.

Joanna sank beneath the surface.

NINE

When she finally was ready to leave the beach as evening approached, there was still a buzz but mostly now around the marquee. There were some spotlights set up and half a dozen people worked around a trestle table. If only she dared to get close enough to see what was being lifted onto the table, photographed and itemised, then moved to a growing stack on a tarpaulin.

The police officer had gone. So had Lucas.

Even so, Joanna kept her distance.

She'd swum until exhaustion set in. Until she'd stopped going over every second of the brief encounter with Lucas. Until she could breathe and think again. Then, she'd dragged herself up the ladder onto the jetty and sat on her towel, leaning against the rails until the shaking in her legs stopped. Ocean swimming wasn't something she did a lot of these days. Mum and Dad had a pool next door and when she did venture to Broadbeach, there wasn't the challenge which the Southern Ocean presented, particularly when the water was whipped up like today.

It was odd how strong the currents were this afternoon as

the tide went out. The day itself was average with no real heat or humidity to forewarn of a storm ahead. She made a note on her phone to check the weather for the past few weeks and whether there'd been any unusual tides.

She wasn't prepared to tackle the track up the cliff at dusk and instead, took the path beside the river, pausing in the natural tunnel beneath the cliff where the sound from cars crossing the bridge echoed. Further past the bridge, the river wound around a number of larger properties then eventually to the Otway Ranges. Well, it really was the other way around, because the river ended here at the beach. Whoever named the town hadn't been particularly creative. Rivers End.

Joanna's sense of humour was creeping back as she walked along Temple Road. What if the town had been named after Henry Temple, as the river and bridge was.

Temple Town.

Temple River's Final End.

Henry's Hamlet.

She burst into laughter and then quickly glanced around. Thank goodness nobody was close enough to hear her outburst.

Walking home this way took three times longer than going up the cliff from the beach and she had her phone's flashlight on for the last few minutes. Aunt Beryl's narrow road had no street lights and the tall gums on either side made it darker even during the day, let alone as the sun set. Joanna wasn't one to fear the streets but she found herself hurrying after strange rustling in the undergrowth. She closed and locked the door behind herself with a bit more force than she intended.

There was nothing out there, so why were the hairs on her arms raised?

She shook it off. The events from the last couple of hours were messing with her head. That and the lack of a proper meal since her early breakfast. While the apple turnover was a delicious treat, it barely touched the sides considering she'd done a run and a lot of swimming today.

After a shower, she turned the oven on to heat and cut up a mix of vegetables – pumpkin, sweet potatoes, red onion and carrot. Those went onto a tray with a can of chickpeas and she drizzled olive oil over everything then some rosemary and garlic. While those cooked, Joanna made a tahini dressing. She loved trying out recipes she'd found on social media and several times a week would make a one-tray meal with different ingredients.

All that was missing was company so it was good she was happy with her own.

Usually.

Even with her parents now living next door, her life outside of work was quiet and often centred around designing and sewing and nobody could claim those were social activities.

Except they used to be. When she and Roslyn would work for hours together on a design.

Roslyn was bubbling over with ideas, talking excitedly as she drew page after page of variations on an evening dress. It wasn't her usual kind of thing but they'd spent the week visiting fashion houses with their classmates in the first semester of their course and she was inspired by the colours and styles.

Joanna looked over her shoulder for a while, always impressed by her friend's ability to create something from nothing. She loved evening gowns and even more, she had a passion for wedding dresses. One day she would make her own.

Each new sketch Roslyn drew was a better incarnation of her vision than the one before and that was part of her process. She'd always start with a very basic idea and refine it on paper, even it meant dozens of tries.

Opening her sketch pad, Joanna took her time to draw long lines and then add some detail. Sometimes she'd spend days thinking about a design, mulling it over and discarding what wouldn't work. When she finally picked up a pencil, she usually had a strong sense of what the finished picture would look like.

'Are you serious?' There was awe in Roslyn's voice as she noticed Joanna's design. 'How do you do that? It's perfect.'

'It isn't though. See the hemline? It isn't quite right. But there was one you did before – with the scoopy neck.'

'Scoopy? Is that a new word?' But Roslyn understood and found the sketch in question. 'This one? Yes, change your hem.'

Joanna took a proper look at Roslyn's, then adjusted her drawing and turned to her friend with a smile. 'It fits perfectly!' The dress was gorgeous.

'Of course it does. Because we fit perfectly and nothing will ever change that or stop us reaching our goals. Exceeding them!' Roslyn stood and with her hands stretched above her head, she spun around. 'We'll go to the stars, JoJo, and nobody will step in our way.'

The oven timer went off and Joanna started.

For a second she'd been right there with Roslyn. At their best. Their closest. Able to work together and more than that, create something amazing.

But what Roslyn had said that night wasn't true. They'd both believed it at the time but all it took was a blue-eyed young man to destroy a lifetime of dreams.

A glass of red wine helped calm Joanna's mind. She turned the oven right down and phoned home while she stood outside on the balcony taking small sips. Not feeling like putting on a happy face with a video call, hearing the voices of the only people in the world she truly loved was almost as good.

'Can you hear all of us, love?' Mum called from a distance, from the sound of it.

'Of course she can. Can't you?'

'Yes, Dad. And Mum. Loud and clear.'

'I'm here as well, Joanna. Do you have enough to eat?'

Joanna grinned. 'Hi, Auntie. I had a nice apple turnover for lunch from Sylvia at the bakery, who even remembered me.'

'She remembers everyone. But that isn't lunch. I should have left some meals in the fridge for you.'

'Auntie, no. I appreciate being able to stay here but I'm forty-four years old and can feed myself. In fact, I have a lovely meal almost finished cooking in the oven and went shopping today so I don't use up everything you have.'

There was an odd sound at the other end. A snort, perhaps.

'It's Dad again. We checked your mail and there was none. But there was a light left on upstairs so I ducked in and turned it off.'

'Thanks and sorry about that. Have you been kayaking today?'

The conversation moved to the events of the day in Queensland, with all three of them on the other end chipping in information. It was mostly about a shopping trip with Mum to buy some new shoes for Aunt Beryl and when they finally hung up, Joanna was smiling. Everyone there was fine and it was time she pushed her memories and emotions to one side and got to the bottom of this shipwreck mystery.

According to several separate online reports, there'd been a minor earthquake off the coast and a series of storms around three weeks ago in the region, with the first being particularly damaging and causing a king tide.

Joanna had Post-it notes all over the kitchen table from her research and was beginning to put a theory together after finding a brief mention of the seismic activity not far off the coast. It was minor and caused no damage and most people on land would have slept through the tremor, but had it somehow been responsible for the parts of the boat washing up?

A map of the area was on her screen showing tidal fluctuations over the previous month. She'd scribbled notes cross-referencing the dates that mentioned pieces being found on the beach.

The first record of flotsam – which was the one causing alarm over it being from a yacht in distress – was three days after the earth tremor and one day after the biggest of the storm fronts.

If a yacht had sunk years ago and been caught on a rock or in a ditch of sorts, it might never have moved and its slowly rotting parts not reached shore, certainly not so many in one go. But a tremor dislodging it followed almost immediately by a massive storm messing with tides and currents might have created the perfect mix of events.

'But what would I know?' Joanna muttered. 'Since when am I an expert on this stuff?'

Since never, but there'd be plenty of people who were if she could work out where to look.

Changing tactics, Joanna loaded Google Earth. The internet connection wasn't very fast so she went in search of Aunt Beryl's special blend of herbal tea and put on the kettle. In the cupboard was a teapot in a pretty flower pattern plus a set of four teacups and saucers and Joanna picked one up. These had been a gift to Aunt Beryl to thank her for the use of the sewing room, and Joanna and Roslyn had spent ages selecting the perfect set from a little shop in Melbourne. Aunt Beryl's delight had been genuine. She had a nice collection of tea sets and this one was different from any other, yet fitted perfectly with the house and her personality. She'd hugged them both and set about baking them chocolate chip muffins as though they were both still kids.

Joanna couldn't smile at the bittersweet memory. This gift was given when they'd come home from their first semester and only a few months later, Joanna's world had fallen apart and she'd packed her belongings and moved to Queensland.

She replaced the teacup with a heavy sigh.

The past was behind her and being here was short-term. Of course there'd be times she'd run into memories... or people. If she could travel the world and deal with designers who all thought she should buy everything they made, learn the art of keeping them happy while disappointing them with the smaller orders for the Australian market, and manage a team of opinionated buyers when Ted wasn't around, then she could most certainly cope with a few days of disconcerting moments.

Rather than finish making tea, she poured a second glass of wine.

Google Earth had loaded and she zoomed around the planet for a few minutes before narrowing the view to the Shipwreck Coast.

Then further, closer, more detailed.

Willow Bay.

Her hand hovered over the mouse. This was where it all began and where just about all of her hopes and dreams ended... or led to them ending.

The day she'd left Rivers End closed a door.

The speculation about the identity of this unfortunate wreck opened that door a crack and the minute Joanna assured herself it was not Trent's, she'd put a big lock on it.

But if Trent's yacht was in the bottom of the ocean somewhere then she had to work out where. And why. And if he'd been on it when it sank.

Of everything, that was the most important to discover.

TEN

As soon as she'd had breakfast of toast and coffee, Joanna drove the couple of kilometres to Willow Bay. Even at eight in the morning the air was warm and becoming muggy. There were no storms forecast but growing up here, she'd often seen them appear with little notice. The humidity, winds and tides were a better indicator. Was this the kind of weather which might push more of the shipwreck to shore?

Playing on Joanna's mind was part of the letter from Roslyn, saying she was sure she recognised the pieces of yacht. To the best of her knowledge, Roslyn had never been on *Spee-Dee-One* or close enough to take real notice of much about it, and Lucas mentioning the colour sounded like new information from yesterday's haul. Her ex-friend had kept other things secret though, so what else was hidden?

She had the carpark to herself and when Joanna stepped onto the sand, she thought the beach was empty. But there was another woman dragging a small rowboat toward the water and as she did so, an oar dropped off. Joanna jogged over and collected it, catching up at the tideline.

'Hi there, you might need this,' she said, offering the handle end of the oar.

'Oh, that's where it went. I'd have been going around in circles, thanks.'

The woman was in her late thirties, with blond hair in a pony-tail and a warm smile on a beautiful face. She was slender and wore shorts and a halter-top and boat shoes. Joanna thought she was one of the couple walking the golden retriever the other night.

'Which one is yours?' Joanna asked.

'That one right in the middle. *Jasmine Sea.*'

It was an older style of timber yacht, sleek and lovely.

I remember it.

'Has that always been her name? Wasn't she owned by Mr Campbell?'

'Her name was changed a few years ago.' With a grin, the other woman extended her hand to shake. 'I'm Christie Blake. George would hate to be called mister, but this was his boat and sold to my husband.'

'Oops, sorry. I'm Joanna. I grew up in Rivers End and used to swim here a lot as a teenager.' She gazed out at the yacht in question. 'So *Jasmine Sea* belongs to your husband now?'

'Nope. She's all mine.'

'Do you sail often?'

'Not nearly enough but I'm going out now for a couple of hours. Would you like to join me?'

Joanna's reservations returned. 'I shouldn't impose. You don't know me.'

'But I am a fantastic judge of character. Actually, I'm not, but I do make friends fast and tend to keep them, so you are most welcome to come out on the open sea for a bit, assuming you like sailing?'

'I love it. I kayak a lot but yachts are the best.'

Except for one in particular.

The opportunity to look at the coastline and where the sunk boat might be was too good to pass up. And the other woman's friendly smile encouraged her to take a chance on something new.

'Shall I row?'

Breathtaking wasn't a word Joanna used often but being out on the open sea with the spinnaker full and the yacht skimming through the sparkling water was precisely that. And at last, there was real sea spray on her lips.

Christie was a confident sailor and took care navigating through the channel from Willow Bay. Joanna decided to watch rather than ask questions about submerged rocks, at least for now. The yacht was travelling in the direction of Rivers End and within minutes, the tiny beach below Aunt Beryl's house was in view. And her house.

'That's where I'm staying.' Joanna pointed.

'We're almost neighbours! Keep looking along the cliff, past all that dense bushland. Yes, you can just see our house a bit back from the edge.'

Sure enough, a long house with a deck was in a vast garden and there were glimpses of other buildings. From here, the track Joanna often took from Aunt Beryl's to Rivers End beach was visible so she must have been within calling distance to Christie many times.

'Martin has his studio to the left and I grow heaps of stuff and use herbs and botanicals in my beauty salon. So, you're staying with Beryl?'

'Um, yes. Though she's taken the opportunity of me house-sitting to spend time visiting my mother on the Gold Coast. I haven't been back here for a long time. A lot has changed.' Joanna was unsure how much to say but there was something about Christie which put her at ease. 'There's a lot of new houses and businesses.'

'One being mine, but yes, even in the few years I've lived here there's been rapid growth in the area. Lots of new holiday homes whose owners have boats and jet skis. Council are considering plans for a proper marina in Willow Bay and while that will make it safer, particularly if they build a boat ramp, it absolutely has taken away the feeling of harmony there.'

'I understand. There were no more than a dozen yachts, including this beauty, when I last lived here.'

They fell into a silence as *Jasmine Sea* sped past Rivers End then on almost as far as Green Bay. Christie got busy with the sails, then steered the yacht in a wide turn. The wind was picking up and the sea was less sparkly as clouds began forming overhead. Back near Rivers End, Christie made some more adjustments as they slowed. The marquee was still up and there were people along the tideline again, but too far away to see why.

Christie followed Joanna's line of vision.

'I imagine more has washed up from the shipwreck. You've heard about it?'

'A bit.'

'It's a terrible thing, a yacht going down.'

There was a sadness in Christie's voice which tugged at Joanna. Hadn't Aunt Beryl said something about a near-tragedy with *Jasmine Sea*? Was Christie onboard at the time?

'Do you have any theories about where it might have sunk?'

Christie seemed to gather herself. 'Oh, I always have theories, just ask my husband and father-in-law. I love a mystery and once something gets my attention, I find it hard to drop the subject until I solve the puzzle.'

I've made a mistake talking to you.

What if the other woman decided there was more to the pieces of boat than a simple, if tragic, shipwreck?

But Christie was oblivious to Joanna's worry, focused on the yacht clipping along again at a fair pace. 'There's a lot of speculation about it all but realistically, it has to have sunk within a couple of kilometres of shore because any further and the sea bed is too deep for anything to ever wash up. But that's still a lot of square miles, so it comes back to how far the wreckage is likely to travel and although this one has been submerged for years, I'd be looking somewhere between here and Driftwood Cove.'

'But that's quite a few kilometres away.'

'True. More likely between here and Willow Bay, but then why did nobody notice a whole boat disappear? There are such things as flares.' She laughed shortly but her face was dead serious. 'And no boat was reported missing in this area around that time, so unless it was stolen or the sailor was completely oblivious to navigation, something doesn't add up.'

Or the sailor was dead on board.

Joanna never got seasick but she suddenly wanted to vomit over the side. She curled her nails into her palms and forced down the bile.

By comparison to her speed in the open sea, *Jasmine Sea* crawled through the channel toward her mooring point. To the left, rocks were clearly visible just beneath the surface.

'Would rocks like those sink a yacht?'

Christie glanced over. 'For sure. But they'd likely catch it and I know the coastguards took a look around here the other week. Someone dived to check the floor but there was no sign of a wreck. And it's comparatively shallow here, and many boats have radar like this one does and I've never seen even a shadow through this channel.'

Joanna gazed at the rocks. Perhaps *Spee-Dee-One* had hit them enough to hole her but kept going and took long enough to sink to be well clear of the channel.

'Hey, don't look so worried. Apparently some marine tides

specialist is coming to town along with some fancy gear so I'd expect a result at some point soon. Most likely the yacht was sunk for insurance fraud and they'll get what's coming to them.'

Christie's words spun around in Joanna's head long after they returned to shore and went their separate ways. They'd swapped phone numbers and talked about catching up for a coffee and Christie invited her to visit her beauty salon for a free facial or whatever she'd like.

As much as she was drawn to the other woman, Joanna knew it was a bad idea to pursue the friendship. She wouldn't be here long enough.

Being out on the water was an unexpected treat, as well as giving her a lot of good insight into how local residents viewed the wreckage. If Christie owned a beauty salon, she'd hear every piece of gossip and speculation, plus she was an accomplished sailor with a good head. Before they'd said goodbye on the beach, they'd spent a minute or two looking at the sky. The clouds scuttled along, white wisps quickly overtaken by a dark, sinister thunderhead. Humidity had been rising steadily all morning and the water was now swirling around the boats in the bay. Christie had said she expected a storm to pass along out at sea but probably not make landfall and Joanna agreed.

But as she arrived home, a few drops of rain suggested otherwise.

The sea air made her hungry and as she put a salad together for lunch, the light patter on the roof became a bass drum. Any ideas about sitting outside to eat went by the wayside and she closed a few windows to avoid rain coming in, then settled in the living room to watch the storm.

There'd been a storm all those years ago after she'd got back to land. Had the yacht foundered on the other side of the cliffs and sunk, perhaps in the early hours? Even if there was a flare, most people would have been asleep. The nearest lighthouse was a fair distance but if anyone would be likely to spot a flare, it would be there.

Christie's comment about a deliberate sinking couldn't be true. Trent had lived on the boat and it was part of his lifestyle. Insurance money wouldn't be enough to replace an old yacht if he'd wanted to upgrade, surely.

Trying to remember some details was difficult.

Even dates mixed together.

Joanna had fled Rivers End only a few days after the horror of that night. She was traumatised and it had been years until she'd recognised that and taken steps to heal. For too long she'd believed she'd overreacted to what happened and now she just didn't know. Had he really intended her harm?

Before she could spiral into the dark thoughts, Joanna returned to the kitchen. She needed the exact date she'd been on that yacht in order to research the weather and tides from old records.

The diary was still on the table. Joanna knew all except the first couple of weeks was empty because she'd never picked it up again, never wanted to revisit that time. Why she'd even kept it was a mystery, but thank goodness she had. Pushing the remainder of her lunch to one side, she opened the diary. In the front was the usual stuff which she'd meticulously copied each year from the previous diary. Name and contact details and next-of-kin. A few quotes which inspired her. Goals for the year – which she flicked past along with the names and phone numbers of friends. And then the first entry.

1 *January* 2000

Welcome to the best year of my life!

My new year's resolutions are already written in the front and

I'm keeping every one of them. Today, tonight really, I'm meeting Lucas for our first real date. So there's no time to keep writing now but I'm sure there'll be heaps to add tomorrow. I like him so much.

A clap of thunder pulled Joanna from the page. Her heart thudded but it wasn't from the storm. How naive she'd been. How hopeful. And how wrong.

ELEVEN

1 JANUARY 2000

Lucas is already at Temple Bridge when I arrive and I'm a few minutes early. He looks so handsome in slacks and a white shirt which has its top two buttons undone. When he sees me and smiles, my heart does that flip-flop thing and my lips curl up in response.

'You look so pretty, JoJo.'

Lucas kisses my cheek and the scent of his warm body makes me want to stand this close forever. But he steps back and looks me up and down and I'm glad I took the time to put on some makeup and wear a skirt I just finished making today. It is ankle length and purple with white flowers and matches my white blouse.

'What would you like to do this evening?'

I'd like to kiss him but I know that's not what he means.

'Anything, really.'

'Are you up for a bit of a walk? I'd love to see more of the river and thought if you wouldn't mind showing me around a bit, then we could get a meal after.'

'Have you been up as far as Ryan Road? It's a couple of kilo-metres if we take the road but we could follow the path along the river which is a bit longer.' I'm plotting it in my mind but pointing in the general direction. 'Then we could go across to the church and school and sports grounds where there's lots of really nice houses and gardens, and walk down as far as Palmerston House. Unless that sounds too much?'

He takes my hand. 'It sounds perfect.'

It feels perfect.

There's a shortcut to the path and I lead us across the grass. My heart is singing as we stroll and chat and sometimes walk in silence. The feel of his fingers holding mine is such a beautiful connection to this young man I'm getting closer to every day. This is our first real date but we've been to the same parties around Christmas time and caught up along the beach now and then. Sometimes we've talked about nothing at all yet always we smile and laugh and gently tease each other. He is so kind and smart and has a wicked sense of humour and he looks at me as though I'm the only person in the room. When he asked me to go on a date I didn't even wait a second to say yes.

'I had no idea there were so many houses along here,' he says.

We're passing small acreages with big homes, some with their own little piers. A couple of the families are very wealthy but not always very friendly, not even letting their children attend the local school or have fun with the rest of us.

I'm so lucky with my own little family of Mum and Dad and Aunt Beryl. We might not be rich but we love each other so much. My parents are moving to Queensland in a couple of weeks where Dad accepted a promotion and I don't quite know how I'll cope without them close by. The upheaval is unsettling which I guess is probably to do with childhood memories of having to move all the time. I've been trying not to think about it too much.

We walk all the way to where the ground begins to rise and the path disappears.

'I usually cut across these meadows. The land is owned by someone but there's never been a house here.'

'But there's a house across there, through the trees.' Lucas nods toward the large property next to this one.

'That's where the Carsons live. They own Rivers End Inn.'

We cross the meadow and come out on Ryan Road. 'You seem to know everything about this town. I grew up on the other side of Melbourne and only visited Salina and her parents once, with my parents. Tell me the history?' he asks. 'I should know about the place I'm going to live.'

'Unless you have hours, I'll give you the abridged version.'

'Abridged is fine for now, we have all the time in the world ahead,' he says. With a quick smile he glances at me. 'Don't you agree?'

I don't know what to say. What is he hinting? Does he mean that he sees a future with me? Or is it more generic and he imagines living in Rivers End for a long time with me as a friend? I prefer to think the first option is correct and as we walk along the quiet road, I tell him how Rivers End was originally a timber town, bustling with the local mills owned by two families – the Ryans and the Temples. Henry Temple built Palmerston House and then Eoin Ryan beat him at poker and won the house and all its land.

'Was that even legal?'

'Apparently. Henry's wife left him and he died soon after in tragic circumstances. Rumour has it he hid many treasures in a cave or something but nobody has ever found them.'

Lucas is suitably impressed, asking more questions which make me think hard about what I really do know. Some things are easy, like how each family had different landmarks named after them. Others I don't know or remember. I tell him that and he says he loves my honesty.

We wander for ages around the town and when we are hungry we eventually settle on takeaway Chinese which Lucas pays for. I offer to pay half and he puts his arm around me and says his father taught him to be a gentleman. It might be the new century but it also feels special that he is treating this like an old-fashioned date. Taking our dinner to the river, we find a spot where we can sit with our feet in the water while we eat.

The meal is delicious – or perhaps it's the company and the beautiful warm evening which would make any food special – and we talk about all kinds of things.

Lucas tells me more about his job in Green Bay. For the next year he'll still be training but is also working in the hospital with patients who are recovering from injuries. 'I love seeing the confidence return in people. One day I'll have my own clinic and offer services like that privately as well as for sports injuries, but you know what? Working with the elderly is a real passion because too many people think that their joint stiffness or reduced mobility are part of ageing, and don't realise there are often ways to strengthen their muscles and help them stay active for longer. Being able to care for them is really my end goal.'

Lucas is so wonderful and caring and I know he'll succeed and make a difference in people's lives.

'Your turn. I want to hear about your plans. Roslyn made that big declaration before Christmas about the both of you, yet I've heard almost nothing of the details. Shall we walk?' He stands and offers his hand and we pack up the rubbish and take it with us.

There's a bin near the bridge and we go past to deposit the bag, then make our way through the natural tunnel beneath the cliff and beside the river.

'Roslyn really shouldn't have made me sound so important. I'm not brilliant or anything but I do work hard. She and I are going to create a brand of clothing. Eventually, that is. But it'll be natural fibres wherever possible, with a seaside feel and not hugely expensive. We want to cater for women of all sizes with comfortable and fashionable pieces. And maybe even add a formal-wear line as well.'

'I love the sound of it. Is that why you're both doing a degree in fashion?'

'We are. Two more years in Melbourne.'

'And after that?'

Lucas stops us both. We are still under the cliff and nobody is nearby. He puts both hands on my waist and is gazing at me as if my answer is really important. I'm a bit distracted by the heat coming off his hands.

'JoJo?'

'Sorry. After that we probably find jobs in the industry to get more real-world experience for a year or two.'

'In Melbourne?'

I hope not, because even with Mum and Dad moving away, Rivers End is where I want to spend my life. It is my safe harbour. For work experience there's a couple of places in Warrnambool which aren't too far to commute to. I should say this all to Lucas but what if it changes things?

So I shrug. 'I'm not certain yet. The industry is hard to get into and I'm really determined to succeed, wherever I end up.'

Something crosses his face. I can't tell if it is disappointment or understanding but then his hands move to my back and he slowly and gently pulls me close. He smiles at me. 'Well, wherever you end up, I'm happy that right now, you're here.'

My skin is on fire where he's touching me and when his lips meet mine, my heart bursts into flames.

Lucas walks with me to the end of our street and I watch as he disappears into the dark. I don't want to break the spell by my parents seeing him and wanting details, no matter how sweet they'd be about it.

I touch my lips and notice I'm smiling. I think I'll be happy forever.

'How was the date?'

Roslyn appears from nowhere and I jump, then laugh at myself. Then I see she's been crying and put my arms around her.

'Why are you upset?'

She leans against me for a minute but says nothing and then moves away, rubbing her eyes. For one second I wonder if she saw me with Lucas and our quick kiss goodnight but even if she did, she'd be more likely to tease me than cry.

'Were you waiting for me?' I ask.

'No. Not really. I went for a walk because Mum was a bit upset... anyway I saw you and Lucas and waited until he'd gone. I didn't want to embarrass you.'

'Is your mum okay?'

Rather than answer, Roslyn glances at her house and brushes her eyes again. Then she draws in a quick breath and looks at me. Beneath the streetlight, her expression is suddenly hard, which isn't like her at all but before I can say anything, she slips her arm through mine.

'Tell me all about your date, JoJo. Let's sit under the gum tree for a bit.'

We do and she cheers up a lot while I tell her about our walk around the town and dinner by the river. I don't say anything about the kisses though because words might spoil the magic. But even though she smiles a lot, that weird look is still there as if she's really angry and trying to hide it.

'So Lucas told you about his hopes and dreams. Did you tell him about yours?'

'A bit. About us having two more years studying then working for a while.'

'And that you have your eyes on a cadetship at the fashion house in Warrnambool?'

'Actually, no. After all, I might end up in Melbourne for a while.'

Roslyn leans forward, peering intently at me. 'What exactly did you say?'

I try to recite it as I remember, including the bit about my desire to succeed and how hard cadetships can be to get. 'He looked a bit disappointed. I think, anyway. Hard to tell. But Rossi, I've never felt like this. I've never felt so alive!'

But she doesn't even smile.

'You're so lucky, Joanna. Your life is so good.'

'I am lucky but I'm really afraid about Mum and Dad moving so far away. Even though we're in Melbourne a lot now, I can't imagine coming home and they've gone.' I guess it is playing on my mind more than I realised. 'Dad promised I'd never have to move again until I was grown up and now I am and it doesn't feel great.'

'At least you have a decent stepfather. I didn't even have that. Everything comes easy to you.' She gets to her feet. 'Family, fashion, friends. Now a cute boyfriend. And the world will be at your feet because you're clever and talented and once you decide on a course of action you rarely deviate until you get what you want. Inspiring, really.' She turns away quickly with a muttered, 'I'm going to bed.'

She's running toward her house and I'm sure she's crying again and I don't know what I've done to upset her because she's never cross with me and she's never said anything like that before. There's no point going after her in case this is all over a row with her mum, but tomorrow I'll collect her for a swim and we can work it out.

Getting up to walk home, my eyes go to where Lucas and I had stood at the corner. The way he'd gazed at my face as if he was memorising it had almost made me burst out how I feel. That his kiss earlier set my heart alight and all I long for is to be in his arms. It wasn't the first time a boy kissed me but it was the best kiss ever. I touch my lips with a finger. He cares. He really cares.

Roslyn isn't home the next day. Nobody is. I spend the day helping my parents pack, thoughts of Lucas still dancing through my head. We didn't make plans for another date and I wish we had so I have it to look forward to. Maybe I should tell my parents he might drop by so it isn't a complete surprise. Except I like having this little secret, so keep it to myself.

In between happy thoughts about Lucas I have moments of sadness about my parents. It is so weird, the endless boxes and packing tape as a lifetime of memories gets locked away. They worry about leaving me behind and now it is getting so real, I am nervous and almost cry a couple of times. I'm staying at the house until I return to Melbourne in February and just before I go, will move in with Aunt Beryl. Nothing will be the same without them, and I catch Mum crying and give her a hug and decide I need to be strong and supportive for them because Rivers End has been their home forever too, and I know they'll miss it.

Before it gets too dark, I head for the beach, hoping to find Lucas. But there's no sign of him or Roslyn or anyone I really know, so I go for a walk and then home.

For the rest of the week I hardly see either Roslyn or Lucas and while I know he would be hard at work and then probably tired or doing family stuff at Salina's, I am worrying about my best friend. We were meant to meet at Aunt Beryl's to finish some of our designs but instead, I go alone. And that's fine. My aunt helps me work on a pattern I've drawn for a special dress. She's so good at this but her passion in life is teaching, which shines through today. She's patient and encourages me to test different ideas.

Once I'm happy, she pulls some gorgeous fabric from her

special drawer, I begin to cut and she leaves me to go and work in her garden.

Before I know it, night has crept up on me and there's the makings of a spectacular dress on a mannequin. It is so lovely I can hardly believe it is mine. And in my heart, I know it is the dress I will wear one day... for a special dinner with Lucas. There's a new French restaurant opening in Warrnambool and he could wear a suit and would look so handsome. Or a home-cooked meal for two followed by dancing to romantic music. Yes, I could twirl and the dress would swirl around me. I can't wait to show it to Roslyn.

The next morning we finally catch up at the supermarket of all places. She's rushing around, throwing things into a trolley like she doesn't care what she's buying and once again I sense something is very wrong.

'I'm tied up with some stuff, Joanna. Doing things for Mum. Mostly.'

'Can I help?'

She shakes her head then throws her arms around me and mutters something about always being my best friend. Well, I know that she will be. Then she says sorry.

'Sorry?'

Roslyn takes a deep breath. 'Shall we meet at the jetty Friday night?'

'About seven?'

'Sure. I have to go now.'

Afterwards I wonder why she was sorry. Maybe for not being around much. Nobody is. I've not seen Lucas since our date except from over the road from each other early one morning. He didn't see me though, and was too far away to hear me call. Why hasn't he stopped by the house after work one day? Everyone is busy.

When Friday evening arrives I cannot wait to see the end of this week and get to the beach right on seven.

Lucas stands at the far end of the jetty and so does Roslyn. This is great. Both my favourite people in one place.

I jog across the sand and Roslyn notices me. We lock eyes and I'm grinning but her face is blank. Lucas is facing out to sea and doesn't see me.

But then Roslyn steps closer to him.

Really close.

Her arms go around his neck and I stop dead as she raises herself on her toes and kisses him.

TWELVE

NOW

The diary was closed. A cup of coffee sat cold on the table. Joanna stared into the distance, her fingers curled into fists and her knuckles white.

Twenty-five years of forgetting the past was ripped open in minutes.

That Friday evening so long ago might well have happened today, so raw was the pain.

How happy her nineteen-year-old self had been, running across the warm sand.

How naive.

Surely after days of not seeing Lucas following his kiss beneath the cliff – which had to have meant *something* – and Roslyn's weird behaviour all week, Joanna should have expected the worst. Instead, she'd stupidly believed both were as busy in their lives as she was when, all along, they'd been hooking up.

She pushed her chair back and stood, the movement so abrupt it fell. The sound of it hitting the ground stopped her and she turned and lifted it upright. Hands on its back, she let the tears come, silently weeping for the shattered young woman she'd once been. So innocent and in love and so trusting.

It wasn't fair, what Lucas did. He'd acted as though he really liked her and kissed her when all along he was interested in someone else. It was a despicable move. But Roslyn had destroyed the friendship of a lifetime and all for a boy she'd known a few weeks. It must have been worth it at least, if they'd gone on to have at least one child and now had twin grand-daughters.

'They might have been mine.'

Saying it aloud threatened to bring fresh tears and Joanna wasn't having any of it. Crying wasn't her thing. Her career was built on inner strength and keeping a calm and sensible head in the often cut-throat world of fashion. Nobody in her work or friends circle of the past twenty years or so had seen her in a moment of weakness. She even regulated how much alcohol she drank around others to avoid letting her guard down. Some peers called her cold. And she'd heard that she was selfish because she'd dedicated her life to being good at her job instead of being a wife and mother. So hateful to judge someone else's choices, but Joanna had developed a thick skin.

The storm had only come as far as the cliffs before retreating back to the horizon, leaving only puddles as evidence it had been so close. Out on the balcony, Joanna breathed in the air made fresh by the rain, letting it fill her lungs and push away the regrets and sadness reading the diary had brought back. She'd stopped too soon though. The whole purpose of reading it was to find the exact date she'd last been on that yacht and she was in no state of mind to dive back in.

There was a flash of movement on the lawn beneath the balcony and Joanna leaned over to take a better look, wetting her hands on the railing and barely avoiding soaking her top. A fox, perhaps? Certainly a four-legged animal with a thick tail had dashed from the bushes on one side, across to the other. It didn't re-emerge and Joanna went inside to dry her hands.

It wasn't until she returned to the kitchen that she heard someone calling from outside. A child. She slipped her shoes on and opened the door near the carport.

Nobody was there.

'Help! Someone help!'

The panic in the voice galvanised Joanna, sending her running around the house in the direction of the garden. She stopped in the middle of the lawn, gazing around. Was she hearing things?

Everything was wet. The trees dripped heavy drops of water and the bushes were burdened from the downpour. And from beneath one of the bushes, a pair of feet – bare and smaller than hers – gripped at the grass with their toes. The bush itself was shaking and with a jolt, Joanna remembered that there was a deep ditch on the other side.

'I'm here! Let me slide you out.'

She was on her knees, reaching for the child's ankles but they moved and a body wriggled out far enough to show the face of a boy of around ten years of age.

'I can't get a grip on her collar. She's stuck.'

'Who is?'

'Perry. My dog.'

The little boy looked ready to cry and was not only wet from head to foot but covered in mud.

Joanna inched through the bush, sliding beneath the branches, soaked in seconds. Sure enough, there was a ditch about a metre deep which was narrow and in the bottom, staring at her with wide eyes, sat a reddish-brown dog. 'Hello there, Perry.'

The boy crawled back and his arms dangled into the ditch, not long enough to reach the dog. 'I don't think she's hurt but she's stuck somehow.'

'The sides are too steep and slippery. Will she let me lift her up? She doesn't bite?'

'She loves everyone.'

But she's scared and I'm a stranger.

'What's your name?' Joanna glanced at the boy.

'Bobbie. Where's Miss Beryl?'

'Oh, you know her? She's visiting my mum in Queensland. I'm Joanna, Beryl is my aunt. If I stay here and watch Perry, can you run to the house and fetch a big towel? There's a few in the cupboard just as you go in.'

He was gone before she could give further instructions about choosing from the second lowest shelf where the old ones were kept.

The dog whined and tried to climb up.

'He'll be right back, Perry. I just think if I can wrap you in a towel it might save a fear bite or scratches and you might feel a bit safer.' She scratched under the dog's chin. 'I saw you go running across the garden but thought you were a fox.'

She lay there on her stomach, talking softly to the dog, until a bunched-up towel suddenly appeared nearby.

'Is this one okay?'

Apart from it being one of Aunt Beryl's favourites...

'Yes. Now, can you encourage Perry to try and stand so I can loop this around her?' Joanna folded the towel lengthwise several times until it was a narrow and long band.

Bobbie dropped his arms down again but was smart and did it a bit further along the ditch so Perry was on her feet in an instant, trying to lick his hands. 'Good girl, stay still now.'

It took a bit more wiggling forward but Joanna managed to manipulate the towel under Perry's torso. 'Okay, as I lift, can you take her collar as soon as you can reach? Just hold it firmly to help support her.'

Despite a few whimpers and her legs flailing around, Perry didn't protest and in seconds, Bobbie had hold of her collar and she was out of the ditch. Joanna slid backwards. 'Let go of her while we get out from under here, matey. I've got her.' There was no way she was releasing the dog from her grasp after this ordeal but the minute she was free of the bush and managed to sit, Bobbie threw his arms around them both.

'Thank you, thank you! You saved her!'

'We both did.'

Joanna hugged him back, careful not to squash Perry between them. This wasn't what she'd expected today. And as wet and muddy as she was, Joanna felt good. Really good.

Bobbie agreed that a bath was in order for the mud-covered Perry, and while Joanna filled the tub in the second bathroom, he cleaned himself up as best he could. He didn't want to leave his dog to have a shower in the other room but scrubbed his face and neck and arms and legs with a washer.

Perry was the sweetest of dogs. Clearly of mixed parentage, she was about the size of a fox. With her colouring, no wonder Joanna thought she was one and it bothered her that the dog might have been at risk had she ventured onto a farm in the area. While she loved foxes, and all animals, not everyone was so accepting.

'Does she normally run off?'

'Never, but she got a scare with the thunder. We were walking on the beach and she normally just plays in the sand and on the rocks but there was a huge clap and she ran up the cliff.'

Joanna turned to look at him, her hands still soaping the dog. 'You were down on the beach in this weather?'

He grinned suddenly. 'I like storms.' But then his face dropped. 'I never thought it might scare her.'

'Come and give me a hand. Actually, first would you get another towel but maybe from the lower shelf? Two, in fact.'

She'd replace the good towel used earlier and it could be relegated to the bottom shelf. Saving little Perry mattered more and Aunt Beryl would feel the same way.

Perry was thoroughly washed then towel-dried without complaint.

'She's my own dog. Well, I guess she belongs to everyone but she hangs around with me the most.'

'Where do you live?'

'Just a few houses away. The first one as you come along the road. I live with Dad and my big brothers.'

Joanna tried to visualise the house in question but drew a blank. Most of the properties along here were set back from the narrow road and lined with native bushland. But her main concern was why a kid was at what could be a treacherous beach on his own. In bad weather. Not wanting to upset him after his already scary afternoon, she thought about how to phrase her question. If he lived with older brothers, why weren't they supervising him, assuming his father worked? Hopefully he wasn't alone at home each day after school.

'Do you go to the beach alone very often?'

'Sure. Well, mostly with Cal and Mattie, my brothers. And Dad. But they were playing a computer game. Cal and Mattie. I didn't exactly say I was going out...' His voice wavered as the words trailed off.

Perry was as dry as they could get her and after a final shake, she took off to explore the house. Deciding to clean up later, Joanna went in search of a makeshift lead, settling on a length of offcut fabric. She found the dog and made a loop for a handle, then tied the other end to her collar.

'Come on, let's get you both home.'

'I can help clean up.'

'Well, I appreciate the offer but sooner or later your brothers will notice you're both missing.'

He screwed up his face. 'Yeah. Guess so.'

Joanna got her keys and phone and locked up on the way out. The sky was clearing and the earlier wind had dropped, leaving the afternoon pleasant. They walked along the narrow road, Perry zigzagging a little ahead at the end of her pretend lead.

'Have you always lived here, Bobbie?'

'Nah. We live with Mum half the time since she and Dad are divorced. She's in Green Bay.'

'That's not too far.'

'Yeah. Mattie's nineteen and drives so it's easy to do extra visits if we want.'

It sounded like a good arrangement and Bobbie's explanation about going out on his own reminded her of plenty of times she'd gone to the beach without her mum knowing. Always with Roslyn rather than a dog, though.

'Do you want to come say hi?'

Bobbie stopped at the letterbox beside a driveway.

'I'm pretty grotty and wouldn't mind a shower. Unless you'd like me to explain why Perry had a bath?'

'Nah. I'll explain but they probably won't notice if they're still gaming.'

'Is your dad working?'

'Yeah. But not in his job. He's in SES and is helping with the boat parts which keep washing up.'

For the first time Joanna noticed Bobbie's bright blue eyes.

'Go home, then, and see if you can dry Perry off a bit more.'

'See ya. And thanks for saving my dog.'

With a wave, the boy ran down the driveway, Perry racing beside him as if they were out having the best fun together.

He isn't Lucas's son, he can't be. Roslyn doesn't live in Green Bay.

Joanna wandered toward home.

How many blue-eyed kids are there? Millions.

But the number of blue-eyed kids whose father was a

member of SES in this small town? What if Lucas had more than one family? For all Joanna knew, he and Roslyn might have split up after their daughter was born. He could have multiple marriages behind him. A dozen children to support.

She giggled at her stupid thoughts then sighed.

It was her own fault she had no intel on Lucas. Or Roslyn. Insisting that her parents and Aunt Beryl never speak of Roslyn had kept her in the dark and for most of her life, it was exactly what she'd wanted. But now?

Joanna glanced back at where she'd left Bobbie and Perry.

Seeing Roslyn and Lucas's daughter and grandchildren had set something in motion, deep inside Joanna. A yearning of sorts. Not for losing her friend and boyfriend, but for the life she might have found had she not shut off her heart afterwards. One with her own children. Her own family, as she'd dreamed of having when her home was in Rivers End.

All in the past, Joanna. Looking back doesn't help anyone.

She returned to Aunt Beryl's house and locked herself inside.

THIRTEEN

It was a night and almost a full day before Joanna decided she'd had enough of her own company and ventured out again.

She'd immersed herself in research and now had a basic understanding of how undercurrents and tides and different weather conditions affected local shipwrecks. At least, the big, old ones. There were several in the immediate area, mostly closer to Driftwood Cove and then beyond where there was a longer stretch of sunken vessels. Diving into this subject was more than a desire to learn and understand. It was a distraction from her thoughts and more, her feelings. The diary was still on the table but hadn't been opened again.

The weather was gorgeous. Not overly hot with clear skies and a light breeze. She considered going for a swim but didn't want to risk running into Lucas again if the SES was still on Rivers End beach.

You are such a coward.

Despite the negative thought, she grinned as she slung a bag over her shoulder and checked herself in the hall mirror. She'd decided to have dinner out and that alone was cheering her up because she always enjoyed eating alone in a restaurant. People-watching was fun. Her eyes smiled back at her and she applied lipstick then ran fingers through her short hair, peering closer. No greys. Or else they were less noticeable with her natural ash-blond colour. Lucas was going grey, but it suited him. A silver fox.

'Joanna!' She rebuked herself but at least she wasn't getting all mopey at the thought of her once-boyfriend.

She locked up and headed in the direction of the road which connected Rivers End to the bigger towns in the south-west of the state. Passing Bobbie's driveway, she couldn't help looking along it but all was quiet, with no sign of the sweet boy or his doggie friend.

The walk down the hill was punctuated with her moving onto the verge every couple of minutes, rather than rarely having to step off the bitumen as it had been when she'd last lived here. So many road users now, and going in both directions. One car went past up the hill then abruptly pulled over. Joanna glanced back. It was a large black ute with black tinting and as she watched, it U-turned and again, pulled over on the edge, this time on her side. It was far enough away she couldn't see the driver but when it began to slowly drive down the hill, two wheels on the shoulder, a shiver ran down her spine.

There was no reason to think anything other than that the driver was lost, or had forgotten something at home, or even thought they knew her... If the latter was the case then it might be Roslyn, although it was hard to imagine her driving such a vehicle.

Joanna quickened her pace and moved as far over as possible. Palmerston House was just ahead and the verge widened considerably as the ground evened out. She hugged the fence line, willing the car to pass or turn around again but when she looked over her shoulder, her heart sank. It was closer, and driving just as slowly.

Taking her phone out as she hurried, Joanna turned the

camera to selfie mode and held it just above her shoulder as steady as she could in an attempt to get the number plate.

At that point, the car accelerated and sped by and she was able to get another photograph before it turned the corner ahead. The minute it was out of sight Joanna stopped and gave herself a moment to catch her breath and slow the thumping of her heart. This was the second time in a few days she'd felt a sense of danger and the actions of the driver had only fuelled it.

Once she was sure the car had gone, she checked the photos she'd taken. Neither was any good, just blurs of black car.

On the Gold Coast or in Paris or New York City she might be extra vigilant, alert for strangers getting too close. But Rivers End was a safe place and there was no reason why anyone would be watching her. Who even knew she was visiting?

Her parents, of course, and Aunt Beryl. And anyone her aunt might have told.

Lucas, although he wouldn't know where she was staying. Joanna couldn't remember ever taking him to her aunt's home.

The lady from the bistro – Tessa.

Bobbie.

Christie Blake. She knew Aunt Beryl and the house but was relatively new to town and had no history with Joanna.

Of those, the only ones who knew she was staying at the house were her parents, Aunt Beryl, ten-year-old Bobbie, and Christie. Of course, Bobbie may have told his brothers and father which then added some unknowns. Christie owned the beauty salon, so had she talked about the woman she'd taken sailing?

For all I know, she might be besties with Roslyn.

Chances were Roslyn knew she was here. If Lucas mentioned them meeting at the beach, or even if the young woman had told her mother she'd seen someone under the gum tree... small-town secrets were never secret for long and Roslyn had been adamant Joanna needed to visit.

As unnerving as it was, none of her musings explained why the car had appeared to have deliberately turned and followed her, or why she'd had the sensation of being watched the other day. It was an overactive imagination or heightened emotions playing with her mind, and jumping at shadows was unproductive. Too much time alone with only stories of shipwrecks to keep her company. One shipwreck in particular.

Rivers End Food & Wine Co might have been a jewel in any major city in the world. It was slick and inviting all at the same time, with a stunning bar and beautiful decor. The baby grand piano was a lovely touch and played with quiet passion by a young man in a colourful waistcoat. The staff, who were similarly dressed, were attentive and friendly and seemed to know just about everyone in the place.

Joanna was at a small window table which was a bit lower than normal, with tub chairs rather than standard ones. It made for a comfortable and almost luxurious experience, along with the extensive wine list and a menu which made her mouth water. She sipped from a glass of local Chardonnay while she waited for her meal, gazing around the intimate space. The bar had three sides, including two with stools and one more informal where several people stood and chatted. Toward the back of the room, the tables were larger and a couple of groups took up most of the space. Everywhere else were tables similar to hers in varying sizes. It was almost full in here already yet barely seven at night.

'Here are the first of your little plates.' A young man with a name badge on his waistcoat saying *Leo* carefully placed three small offerings on the table. 'This is your first visit?'

'It is. But what gave you that impression?'

'You didn't order the rice paper rolls with peanut sauce... although I didn't take into account you might be allergic to peanuts.'

'I'm not.' She couldn't help smiling. 'Are they a local secret?'

'Definitely. Shall I bring you a complimentary dish to try?'

'Please do. This is a fabulous place.'

Leo beamed. 'Thank you. My sister and I thrive on compliments so please keep them coming. The rest of your plates won't be long.'

Joanna loved seeing young people succeed. If a brother and sister had brought this wine bar into fruition and kept it filled, then they'd done a lot right. The food might have come out of a magazine and when she ate – starting with the lightest tempura-battered vegetables imaginable and an Asian-inspired dipping sauce – her taste buds sang.

The atmosphere encouraged her to stay long after the meal was a delicious memory. She moved to a stool at the bar and watched the bartenders create cocktails on par with those she'd sampled in New York. With nobody here to impress or more importantly, to guard herself from, Joanna asked Leo for a cocktail and left it up to him. He enquired about anything she disliked, rather than what she liked, then grinned and collected ingredients. He was as comfortable behind the bar as bringing meals to his customers and he was popular with everyone she'd seen.

'Try this one. It isn't heavy on the alcohol but leans into the flavour combination.' Leo placed a martini-style glass in front of Joanna. 'It is a work in progress so I'd like your feedback and because it's an experiment, it doesn't have a price tag.'

Before Joanna could tell him she was happy to pay regardless, he'd gone to look after another customer.

One sip and she was lost in a magical world of cherries and chocolate and just enough cream and a touch of rum. It was the perfect ending to a dinner which had exceeded her expectations. Her parents would love this place. She took out her phone and made a note to tell them about it when they spoke next. Mum adored finding little family-owned shops of all kinds, with a particular love of cafés, and would tell everyone she knew once she discovered a new favourite.

'There's nothing left, so I'm guessing you enjoyed it?' Leo was back and picked up her empty glass.

'Divine.'

'Nice praise. There's a distillery up in the mountains and it just happens they're close to a chocolatier. Perfect marriage of flavours, and the dark chocolate rum is new.'

'Well it works very well and deserves to be on the menu.'

The young man grinned, his eyes showing how much he appreciated the comment. 'Are you visiting Rivers End? Or moving here? Or... prefer to remain clandestine.'

Probably the last one.

'I'm staying at my aunt Beryl's house.'

'Up on the cliff? Miss Evans was one of my teachers and then became the principal while my younger siblings were still there. She's wonderful.'

Of course everyone knows her.

'She really is.'

'Please give her my best. And bring her in for dinner one night.'

Joanna returned her phone to her bag and smiled. 'I must go, but thank you and your team here for a lovely evening.'

After paying and saying more goodbyes, Joanna stepped out into the night, unsure why she'd again shared more than she'd intended.

Although it was heading toward ten at night, Rivers End still had people around, giving a vibe of a town bigger than it was. The addition of new eateries and upgrade of the bistro was certainly drawing people in and that had to be good for the local economy. There were far fewer empty shops than when she and Roslyn used to play their game of finding the perfect place for their fashion boutique.

There was one space they'd gone back to time and again.

Joanna wandered along one and then the other side of the main shopping strip. She stopped outside the beauty salon and peered into the darkness. Christie had done a wonderful job of creating an inviting and modern salon complete with a spa pool through glass doors at the back, several hair and beauty stations, and a couple of private rooms. There were rows of fat candles in jars along a wall and hair and beauty products for sale.

Further along, on the corner, the bookshop had new displays in each window. Joanna wished she had more time for reading. Her job only got busier with every new client she took on.

Being at their beck and call – and Ted's – was exhausting.

Will buying the company change that?

She'd never considered the impact on her life of owning such a busy and hands-on business. Ted rarely took a day off. Nor did she, for that matter.

Joanna turned the corner and walked along what had always been a quieter shopping area. Last time she was here there were two empty shops out of three. The one open was a craft shop and to her surprise, it was still there. Next to it was one of the perpetually empty spaces.

'I think nobody wants it because it is out of sight of the main street.' Roslyn had given it a lot of thought. *'And when you look inside, it has a sad feeling.'*

Joanna agreed. 'What it needs is new paint and clean windows and some love. Same as the one next to it.'

They'd go and stare at the next one. This shop was different. It had a pretty set of windows which were framed with timber and windowsills longing for flowerpots like Mrs Jones had at

Rivers End Real Estate. The door was glass and timber and set in between the windows and a bit back.

'I'd paint all the timber green or maybe sky blue,' Roslyn announced. 'And on one side we could do a display of everyday wear and on the other—'

'Evening wear!'

Roslyn rolled her eyes. 'I was going to say kid's clothes but sure.'

'And wedding dresses.'

'You really are pushing a friendship.'

They'd laughed and with their arms over each other's shoulders, made more plans.

Out of all the shops in Rivers End, this was the one they wanted for their own.

The shop which they'd thought unloved and sad was now a florist. It was vibrant and pretty and Joanna smiled. Flowers made everything better.

Beside it was the space they'd chosen as their own.

Also no longer empty.

For long minutes Joanna gazed at each window, not really understanding what she saw. Her mind couldn't quite comprehend seeing dreams come to life.

In one window was a display of ladies' clothes. Well cut and smartly designed. And in the other was a children's range. It didn't make sense. Would Roslyn actually have continued their dream... the one both of them had for so long... without her?

She stepped back and looked up at the signage.

Joalyn Designs

FOURTEEN

She shouldn't have expected anything else.

Of course Roslyn achieved her dream.

Our dream.

The ruthlessness she'd shown concerning Lucas had been a shock to Joanna but she'd always known her dearest friend was stubborn and determined. It was always Roslyn who refused to accept anything less than perfection from their designs. Roslyn who researched and then announced which degree in which university the two of them would pursue.

And Roslyn who'd chosen the name for their brand.

Now she's stolen our name as well as our dream and my boyfriend and our friendship.

Somewhere inside the funny, loving and clever Roslyn there'd been a side alien to the nineteen-year-old Joanna, but recognisable now thanks to life experience and a jaded view of the world. Roslyn was selfish and ambitious and cruel.

Joanna stalked away, not caring in which direction as long as she left the shop behind.

Her phone beeped and she stopped long enough to check the message, surprised it was from her aunt.

Call me when you get a chance. If you're still up
then so am I. Or else tomorrow.

What would be so urgent? Joanna quickly dialled as thoughts rushed through her mind about her parents. Was something wrong?

'Hello, darling. I wondered if you were still up.'

At least her aunt's voice was friendly and warm and calm.

'Are you okay? Are Mum and Dad?'

'Oh, I worried you. I'm sorry. We're all just fine and healthy, although your mother may have had one nightcap too many and needed a hand up the stairs.'

Walking again, but not as fast, Joanna was relieved and amused. 'Are you a bad influence on Mum?'

The chuckle on the other end removed any residual worry.

'Quite possibly. I persuaded her to join me at a class of t'ai chi on the beach this morning. It's something I've been doing at home and I found a casual class up here.'

'You're kidding. Mum is a night owl, let alone not one for joining any kind of class, unless it is flower arranging.'

'Nope, I tapped on her door in a suitably annoying fashion at dawn until your father sent her out. She complained the whole way to the class but then I promised her breakfast of her choice and she actually allowed herself to enjoy the whole experience. However, I feel if I wake her too early tomorrow I may pay dearly.'

Joanna crossed a road, laughing.

'Anyway, there is a reason for my call. Your parents had Ted and Hazel here for dinner tonight and after spending time with them, I do understand why Molly may have imbibed a little more than usual.'

'Oh dear.'

'And I know I'm interfering, so you'll have to forgive me, but I thought you should know. Everything was going well until

Ted announced he is selling the business in the next few months.'

'*That* soon?'

He'd mentioned a year, not months. Was it even possible for her to buy him out so quickly? There'd be so much to do to make it happen.

'Hazel started going on about how you taking a month off had added to Ted's workload and she'd given him an ultimatum about selling. Molly got into it with her, although completely in her sweet and quiet way. Told Hazel that you've dedicated more than fifteen years to making the company thrive and never taken more than a few days off for personal time, while never begrudging the long hours.'

'She said that? Aw.'

'Takes a lot to rile Molly, but Hazel is so self-centred and as much as the two are friendly, your mother knows Hazel sees you as just one of the staff, rather than Ted's right hand.'

Right hand, negotiator, team leader, head planner, and chief buyer. No wonder I'm tired.

Aunt Beryl continued. 'At that point, Ted said something which is the reason for me wanting to speak with you.'

'I'm listening.'

'Not to alarm you, but he mentioned he's been approached by one of your competitors and been made an offer.'

Joanna stopped again. 'An offer to buy?'

'Yes, darling.'

'But... darn. I'm unlikely to be able to match any offer another company will make. I guess you don't know but the night I got the letter from Roslyn, Ted asked if I'd be interested in taking over the business in a year. Does he think I'm not keen because I needed some time off?'

'I had no idea... oh, what a shock. If you need some investment money then I can help a bit, and your parents will.'

'No, I would never ask nor accept that from you or them,

but I love you so much for offering. Auntie, Ted will let me know when he's ready and I've just got to prepare for some changes either way. Buying the company would turn my world upside down, but so will working for a different employer.'

'Well I hope he talks to you soon because he'd never find a better person to continue his company. Everything you do is from the heart and honest, and he'd know it was in safe hands because you are above board in the way you deal with people.'

Aunt Beryl chatted for a bit longer but Joanna barely heard a word. She wasn't above board. Or honest. There was every chance she'd let a man go to his death inside a sinking yacht, so what kind of person did that make her?

Somehow Joanna ended up on Rivers End beach. The moon was almost full, casting enough light on the sand for her to avoid the occasional crab scuttling to its hole. A breeze had whipped up the waves which were crashing against the jetty and the rocks near the stone steps which led up to the graveyard.

Her grandparents on both sides were buried there and she hadn't even gone to pay her respects yet.

Joanna stood at the bottom of the steps, her shoes in one hand, and decided against climbing them. She was too upset and perhaps just a little tipsy from the wine and cocktail.

'I'm like Mum and need a hand up the stairs,' she said aloud and it was only partly a joke. A fall down these would be terrible and who knows when she'd be found if she was badly injured. Joanna made a note in her phone to buy flowers tomorrow and visit the graveyard.

The florist she'd seen earlier was obviously the best place to buy really nice flowers but then she'd be within sight of Roslyn's shop.

She sat on the bottom step and after placing the shoes on the ground, dropped her head into her hands. What on earth was she to do? Pretend Roslyn didn't exist? Or confront her? Neither option sat well with Joanna. She could buy the flowers then go next door and say hello as though nothing had ever happened. Even take her a bunch for old times' sake. Forget-me-knots. Or death lilies. They'd represent the death of the friendship which was meant to last forever.

Nothing lasts forever. Not even my career.

'Miss? You okay there?'

A sudden light on her and a male voice shook her out of her spiralling mood. Her head shot up and she held up a hand to stop the glare from a massive flashlight.

'I'm fine, please point that away.'

The light came off her eyes, but looped around her and across her body a bit like a prison spotlight. Grabbing her shoes, Joanna stood, trying to see who held the flashlight.

'No drugs on you? Or alcohol?'

'No. Not either. I'm just sitting here watching the ocean.'

Facing the flashlight down, the man came a little closer. He was the police officer from the other day at the marquee.

'Looked like you were upset.'

'Me? Not at all. So I'll head home now, but thanks for checking I was alright.'

'Just gonna make fresh coffee if you'd like a cup.'

Tonight is getting stranger by the minute.

About to politely refuse, Joanna suddenly noticed the man was holding a long piece of timber in his other hand. He lifted it to show her. 'More pieces from a boat we reckon sank a while back. We're doing shifts overnight, me and a few of the SES folk, and the sea is delivering a bit this evening.'

'So you're alone?'

'Until midnight.'

'Coffee sounds nice, thanks.'

They walked along the tideline for a bit until past the lagoon, then through the heavier sand in the direction of the marquee. This was bright with a couple of big lights on stands facing inwards and another outwards. There were two long tables and behind them camping chairs and a smaller table with a hot water urn, and a collection of Eskies and boxes.

'We use solar to keep everything charged. Big batteries which save on running a generator. The name is Mick. Senior Constable Mick Hammond.' He put down the flashlight and offered his hand to shake. 'Born and bred in Rivers End and proud to serve the community.'

Joanna knew the surname but couldn't quite remember why. She shook his hand. 'Joanna. I keep hearing about the ship-wreck but don't know anyone who is an expert on the subject.'

Mick was about a decade younger than her, thickset with a round face and red cheeks. He placed the piece of timber on one of the tables. 'Black coffee okay? Ran out of the long-life milk.'

'Black is fine, thanks.'

While he busied himself making coffee, Joanna took a proper look at the closest table. On here, along with the new piece, were half a dozen others of varying sizes and condition. Each were planks but some were short fragments while others were longer, with ragged ends. There was a distinct blue paint on a couple.

The second table was a bit more organised, with several piles of matching sizes and lengths as well as a few items which were not timber.

'Here you go. Not often you get a coffee from a friendly cop, eh?'

Joanna accepted the coffee. What would a coffee be like if served by an *unfriendly* cop? She didn't want to contemplate what might happen if she confessed to her part in the tragedy of the yacht... if that was what had happened.

'Have you found a lot of pieces?'

'About fifty now. Maybe more. Mostly timber from a hull, as

well as decking. Actually, lots from decking. But then there's other stuff. Weirdest would be a clear plastic box with underwear and socks, believe it or not. Not watertight, so they're too far gone to help with sizes even. We found parts of a mast, and that's being examined by experts to narrow down the age and even the manufacturer. That'll help, as so far there's little to identify the yacht but we do have some facts.'

'Oh, you do?' Joanna smiled, hoping the man would keep talking.

He did.

'What we know is the wreckage has been submerged somewhere between twenty and thirty years. There's been tests to show that. We know it's a yacht thanks to the mast. And we know it sank somewhere within ten kilometres of Rivers End because the currents and tides fit. Any further and it would either surface out at sea and then eventually sink again, or wash up in a different place.'

'But wouldn't a yacht be reported missing?'

'You'd think so. I'm continuing to search old records but so far there's been nothing come up on registered vessels. Even out-of-state ones. Now it might be a homemade job and never registered, or from another country, in which case we might never find out.'

'What else has washed up, other than the timber?'

Gesturing to the second table, Mick slurped some coffee. Joanna wanted to look more closely, but would that seem suspicious?

'Take a look. Don't touch, of course. All of it is being recorded with measurements and photographs and the like, then taken to the community hall.'

Joanna was only interested in the non-timber items.

'So there's a winch handle but nothing else to do with the winch system. Some running lights, and they're pretty smashed up. And here?' Mick pointed at a large, flattish and damaged shape. 'Rudder. And that's a decent indicator the boat was around twenty feet in length, given its size.'

So many similarities.

'You said you were born here, Mick and you've never heard stories about a yacht disappearing?'

'No, I...' His voice trailed off and his eyes were blank for a moment before he shook his head. 'Moment there I thought there was a memory of something. Talk about watching a boat as a kid but jeez, that's so long ago it could mean anything. Never liked being on the beaches when I was young so it would have been strange to go and watch one.' He snorted. 'Not like we have big marinas to encourage the rich and famous or racing boats and bring some money into the town.'

If Mick Hammond was in his mid-thirties he'd have been around ten on that awful night. Too young to be wandering around Willow Bay so late. Having a witness to what happened was about the worst thing Joanna could imagine.

Mick was using a pair of binoculars. 'Gimme a sec. Be right back.'

He tossed out the dregs of his coffee and left the cup on a table before heading to the tide line. It was easy enough to see an object in the waves as they rushed in and out and the man had to wade up to his knees to stop it disappearing back out to sea. The shape was strange and it was only when he was almost back that Joanna made out what he had. Although it was incomplete, there was no mistaking it.

If Joanna had thought nothing was worse than a witness coming forward, she'd underestimated what secrets the ocean was still to reveal.

Her stomach lurched as Mick placed his find on the first table.

'Reckon we found ourselves the remains of a guitar.'

FIFTEEN
JANUARY 2000

I should demand to know why my best friend is kissing my boyfriend. I should step up onto the jetty and confront them both. But it makes no sense, what I'm seeing. My heart is pounding so hard it hurts. I turn and run. Nobody calls me back to say it was a joke or a mistake. I can't look over my shoulder because seeing them still kissing will kill me.

At the end of Rivers End beach I slow enough to cross around the entire end of the cliff on the flat rocks exposed by the low tide. Once I'm on the little beach beneath Aunt Beryl's house I look up. But if I go there and I'm upset then there'll be questions I can't answer and I don't think I can hold in my tears much longer. So I scramble around the next lot of rocks and keep going until I reach Willow Bay.

There's nobody about and I can stop running at last.

I have a favourite spot between two trees right on the edge of the sand and I sink onto the ground between them. I draw my legs up against my chest and hug them, trying not to shake so much.

How could Roslyn do such a thing? I know she saw me, but

Lucas didn't. Would he have kissed her back if he knew I was watching? He didn't exactly stop her.

This is why they've both been avoiding me all week.

Roslyn acted weird from the minute she knew I was serious about Lucas. And I'd shared all my feelings about him with her. I never said we'd kissed, so did she think I was joking around? Is this all a terrible misunderstanding?

Wanting to believe it won't make it so. She knew I was coming to the beach at seven and she looked at me and then kissed him. Roslyn did this all on purpose.

My forehead drops against my knees and a rush of sadness and anger all comes at once and I am crying so hard I can hardly breathe. I lean back against one of the trees, my eyes closed to try and stop the tears but I don't think anything will ever be good again. I'm not sobbing aloud but my face is so wet and my neck is as well. Why am I not brave enough to go back and ask them what is going on?

Through it all there's a sense someone is close to me and for one tiny second I think it must be Lucas. He's come to find me.

'Hey... don't cry, baby. Or do. But here's a hanky.'

I open my eyes a crack. Trent's hand holds out a big white handkerchief from where he's squatting a couple of feet away.

Embarrassment doesn't even begin to explain a whole new set of feelings.

I'm not a crier. Only sometimes in the darkness of a cinema or alone with a really sad book. Not in front of people and especially not strangers. And now he's seen me cry, will Trent tell other people? My friends?

What friends?

He settles down on the sand facing me. 'Our secret, Joanna. You've gone to the trouble of finding a private spot to release some emotion and I've intruded, but there's not another soul around. Take the hanky. Keep it if you like.'

The tears have dried up and I use the handkerchief to clean my face and blow my nose. I realise I can hardly hand it back all used, so decide I'll keep it but I'll make him some new ones to replace it. And to say thank you for trying to help and keeping my privacy safe. If anyone else ever found out how weak I am… if Roslyn or Lucas ever discover they've hurt me, then how will I ever face them again?

'I just walked back from town,' Trent says. There's a couple of shopping bags beside him. 'Some of the stuff is cold so I need to get it into my fridge on the boat, so would you like to come with me?'

'With you?'

'Yeah. I'm kinda hungry so might make some burgers. Course, you can sit and cry here if you want, or on the boat, but at least you'll get fed on *Spee-Dee-One*.'

Although my eyes feel puffy I can focus enough to take a good look at Trent. His face is sincere. I just don't know him, apart from meeting him twice. Some of my friends group, the boys, went to his boat after the party here before Christmas and I know they had a good time and I heard talk of plenty of alcohol on offer. But who is he really, other than a surfer who travels alone?

'Not everyone trusts me,' he says. 'I get judged by my tatts and being transient. And maybe I'm not a good guy the way society sees it, but I'd never harm another person.'

It's as though he can read my thoughts.

My mother would call Trent a bad boy, for sure. She'd warn me that my biological dad was just like him. Roslyn would be horrified.

'I'd love a burger.'

His boat isn't big but it has a galley. I sit on the end of his bed which is the only place as he has no table or chairs, just piles of waterproof boxes like we have to go kayaking. They're mostly chained together to stop them moving too much and several are small and bright yellow and remind me of the one I've been keeping my new camera in, while others are much larger. And there's three surfboards secured against one side and a photograph of Trent surfing. I get up to take a closer look.

'My first finals placing when I was eighteen. Hawaii. I didn't win but that's a great shot.'

'Do you win a lot now? I never met a pro surfer.'

'Some. Enough to keep me fed. Do you like onions on yours?'

Until this minute my stomach has churned so much I've had no idea how I'll take even one bite but Trent is piling lettuce and tomato onto a bun and has fried onions in a pan and all of a sudden I'm hungry.

We climb up the dozen or so steps to the deck and eat there, sitting on the bow with our feet dangling over. There's icy cold cola which I drink too fast but I feel better. Not great, but better. Dusk makes the bay pretty with enough light to show ripples from the movement of the boat on the otherwise still surface of the water. Any other time I'd be relaxed and happy to sit and observe because the changing colours are inspiring. Lovely dark blues and browns and golds make an interesting palette for pants and a blouse and jacket I've been designing. But I can't be bothered paying it more than a passing glance.

'I'm good at listening. If you want to talk.'

Trent is different than I thought. He might have tattoos and long hair and live on a boat but he's easy-going and kind. But I can't talk to him or anyone about what I saw.

'You've been really nice to feed me and I should get home.' I pull my feet from the water and get to my feet. 'Here, I'll wash up, seeing as you cooked.'

He keeps hold of his plate as he stands. 'No, you're my guest so no washing up for you. Give me two minutes and I'll get you back to shore.' Taking my plate and empty bottle, Trent disappears below.

I'm a bit relieved not to have to swim back. It isn't terribly far but it is almost dark and then there's the fact I have my bag which is far from waterproof. Tonight turned out a lot different from what I'd expected walking onto the sand earlier and nothing is ever going to be the same in my life.

Nobody at home notices anything different about me over the next few days so I'm doing a good job of hiding my heartache. Dad is busy packing up the garage for their move now that the house is almost done. There's boxes everywhere marked in black pen which room they'll go into. Mum and Dad have visited their new house twice and have it all worked out. There's more land there, which makes them both happy. I just can't believe they'll be gone in a few days.

I stare out of my bedroom window.

There's almost a month until the first semester of the year starts in Melbourne but how am I going to go back to university, living in the same apartment as Roslyn, studying with her, and pretending nothing has changed? She hasn't come near me since the other night.

As I watch, she comes out of her house and turns back to do something I can't see from here. Maybe she's speaking to her mother. I still feel something is wrong between them and it started just before my life was destroyed. What if they had a falling-out and for some reason Roslyn wanted to hurt me over it? Her mother was never thrilled about her daughter being away so much in Melbourne, so did I somehow become the bad guy? Well it isn't on me. Roslyn is a young adult and able to make her own decisions, as she has so recently proved.

I can't help watching, though. From here the front door is out of sight but Roslyn reappears and almost runs before stopping under the tree outside our house. Afraid she might look up, I step back enough that she shouldn't be able to see me but I can see her.

Why did you do this to me? To us?

My heart hurts and when she leans against the tree, obviously crying, all I want is to go to her. But she straightens and wipes her eyes with a tissue and lifts her head. With not even a glance in my direction, Roslyn strides away, out of the street.

It has been a week since I saw her kiss Lucas. Neither of them has contacted me at all. For that matter, all of our mutual friends have gone quiet. This time of year we'd normally have meet-ups all the time either on the beach or the shops and be in and out of each other's houses. And sure, I've not gone to visit anyone but it's like a bubble of silence fell out of the sky when it comes to my social life.

What if I just turn up at Salina's place? Lucas won't be there... I don't think. It is early afternoon on a Friday so he'll be at work in Green Bay. But I can talk to her. We always got on well at school and maybe she'll know what is happening. It isn't as if I've seen him with Roslyn since last week so is it possible it was just a spur-of-the-moment thing and both regret it but are too ashamed to see me? This is the most positive I've felt in days. There could be hope if it was all a silly mistake.

I brush my hair and change into nicer pants and top and let Mum know I'll be back in a while.

Salina isn't home and her mother suggests I might find her in Willow Bay for the big picnic. What big picnic? How can I have been left out of the invitations? For a minute I try to talk myself out of gatecrashing. It doesn't work, because I can hardly be gatecrashing a regular get-together with my friend group. Instead of retreating into the sadness which weighs me down every hour I'm awake, I go to the supermarket and buy a big packet of biscuits and a large bottle of cola and then walk to Willow Bay.

I follow the road and when I go past the dirt carpark there's a couple of cars. One of them is Lucas's and my chest tightens. It is all I can do to keep walking toward the beach. But I am determined that I'm going to get him away from the others and find out what really happened, and why he kissed me if it wasn't real.

There's guitar music playing at the far end of the little beach and in the shade of the trees, my friends are lounging around on the sand. I can't see Lucas or Roslyn and stop for a minute to gaze out at the water. A few people are swimming but the afternoon sun glares off the sea, making it impossible to tell who they are. Salina sees me and waves and gradually everyone turns as I get closer and the music stops. They aren't acting like I'm unwelcome and one of the guys comes and takes the bag of goodies with a grin. Trent is right under the trees, almost where I sat when he found me crying. He winks at me.

Unsure what to do, I finally sit at the edge of the group.

'Hey, Joanna,' Salina calls in greeting. 'When did you get back?'

'Back from where?'

'Queensland.'

'I haven't been anywhere.'

Salina frowns. 'Oh. We all thought you'd decided to move to Queensland with your parents. Roslyn told us that.'

'I did not.'

Roslyn and Lucas appear from somewhere, both dripping wet. She grabs a towel and wraps it around herself. He is gazing at me and I can't read his expression. It isn't unfriendly but not guilty either. I feel like he's trying to work something out.

'Yes you *did*, Roslyn,' Salina says. 'Last Saturday, I heard you say that.'

Lucas turns his attention to Roslyn and now he looks confused.

She leans up and kisses him and everyone makes stupid whoop-whoop noises.

Except me.

My heart is like a stone and I can't even swallow. If my legs weren't so frozen in place I'd get up and run and never come back.

'Time for a song, eh?' Trent lifts a guitar from where it was leaning against a tree and begins to strum, his eyes on me like he's offering a lifeline.

SIXTEEN

NOW

Overnight the rain returned and this time settled in, although not accompanied by a storm.

Woken at three a.m. by the tapping on the roof, Joanna pulled her blanket up and told her brain to go back to sleep. She might as well have commanded the rain to cease as visions of Trent strumming his guitar turned to scenes of what had followed. Not the same night but later. A different side of him revealed as his livelihood, maybe his freedom, came under threat. A side which forced her to protect herself in a way which haunted her.

She must have drifted into dreams because it was morning next time her eyes opened, this time to daylight made dull by heavy clouds and continual rain. The idea of finding a book and retreating to bed for the day with some tea and toast was appealing but Joanna's nature was to work and be active and with a mutter about too many late nights, she got into a shower. The residual bits of memory lingered but the more she moved about, making coffee and boiling some eggs, the less painful they became. It all happened so long ago and she'd kept the worst of it locked up mentally until that darned letter from Roslyn.

Last night she'd walked home soon after Mick found the guitar, or what remained of it. The water damage was extreme, corroding the strings and eating away at the timber. While he'd begun taking photos and making notes, Joanna quietly left the marquee.

It was warm enough outside as she ate breakfast on the balcony. The rain hadn't reached the table and chairs and in the far distance, the sky was beginning to clear.

Had more pieces of the yacht washed up since last night? More and more it was pointing toward being Trent's boat, and the time would come when somebody worked it out.

And they'll start looking at who knew Trent.

Before the panic could rise, Joanna moved to the kitchen. She made another hot drink and opened her laptop.

Last night, as she'd stood beneath the marquee, Senior Constable Hammond had said something which stuck in her mind.

'I thought there was a memory of something. Talk about watching a boat as a kid but jeez, that's so long ago it could mean anything. Never liked being on the beaches when I was young so it would have been strange to go and watch one.'

He'd been surprised at whatever had surfaced in his memories but shaken it off just as fast. It surely wasn't anything to do with that night. After all, why would a kid be out so late to watch a boat? Watch it do what, precisely?

Joanna opened a browser and typed in his name, including his rank.

There were a couple of newspaper articles which she read – both involving him arresting people. Another which mentioned him as a member of SES and having been part of a recent rescue operation following a cave collapse. He had a personal Facebook page which had very little content but was more than ten years old. One post mentioned having to clean up his image so he'd probably deleted anything not in keeping with his position in the community rather than simply making it a private account.

As she kept searching there was less about him but more about the Hammond family, and that was when Joanna remembered the name.

The Hammonds had had a dreadful reputation as criminals in the area. They'd been in Rivers End for generations, keeping to themselves out on a farmhouse at the foot of the mountains, and had been known to threaten anyone who stepped foot on their land uninvited. Joanna's parents had warned her to stay clear of them and never go near their property but it was only as a teen she heard more about the decades of theft and connections to old, unsolved crimes.

'And young Mick goes and becomes a copper,' she said. 'Wonder if you get invited to family barbecues.'

She scrolled through a few more pages, making notes but not forming any conclusions. There was no reason to connect the Hammonds to the shipwreck. None of the family ever hung around with the people she knew. It was interesting but not worth wasting more time on and she closed the browser and opened her work email account.

There was an email from Ted with no subject line, sent early this morning. If he'd really wanted her to see this quickly, Ted would have copied it to her personal address and her gut told her it was less to do with respecting her annual leave than buying himself some time, while being able to prove he had reached out.

The email was typical Ted, waffling about his latest round of golf and then having a lovely evening last night and how nice it was to see Beryl again. Right at the end he mentioned his surprise at being offered a substantial sum for the company by its closest competitor. If she was interested in making her own offer his door was always open. And to enjoy the rest of her break.

'Sure. Not only do I have the past to deal with, but my future too. Thanks, boss.'

Not even really certain why she bothered, Joanna logged into her online banking portal. Since she'd moved to Queensland close to twenty-five years ago, she'd kept two accounts. One for day-to-day expenses and to receive her salary. The other for proper savings. Initially it was for every spare dollar she could squirrel away. After a few years and gaining employment in the fashion industry, it began to grow so quickly that she'd purchased her house. And later, working for Ted with a salary above anything she'd ever expected and generous bonuses for some of the big deals she landed, she'd begun a portfolio of stocks and shares.

It still surprised her that she'd gone from having to skimp and save from part-time jobs as she'd studied, to having more disposable income than she knew what to do with.

But even if she cashed in her portfolio and drew everything from her investment account, it probably wouldn't come close to what another company would pay Ted. She'd need to remortgage her house and take a loan and if it was enough and she failed... then what? Her life's savings gone. Her dreams come to nothing.

Again.

Joanna closed the laptop with a deep sigh. What she and Roslyn dreamed about and planned wasn't in the same financial league as this yet it had felt almost impossible at nineteen. Even so, faith in themselves kept the dream alive.

One of them had fulfilled the dream. And it wasn't her.

Joanna was in her car, parked across the road from Joalyn Designs.

She'd stopped twice, driven around the block twice, then told herself to quit stalling. After twenty minutes watching the shop she still couldn't bring herself to leave the car.

There was no sign of Roslyn, but people wandered in and out of the shop as she watched, some leaving with branded carry bags and others probably just browsing. Was the shop always so busy? It wasn't the same as a franchise in a shopping mall but for a small-town boutique, around the corner from the main shopping strip, it was getting good foot traffic.

Her fingers tightened on the steering wheel. She had so many questions, but asking them would only expose her failure to let go of the past. How long has the shop been open? What clothes do people like most? Were our ideas transferrable to real-life products?

For that matter... did you keep my patterns for your own benefit? Like you did with my boyfriend.

Joanna pushed the door open and climbed out.

The sole purpose of her visit and the only question to ask was what Roslyn knew about the shipwreck and why she thought it was Trent's yacht.

Grabbing her handbag, she locked the car and dug deep for courage, then crossed the road. She deviated to the florist and selected flowers to take to the graveyard later, two beautiful bunches of roses. Rather than leave them in the car, she clutched them against her chest and stood between the shops for a moment, every fibre urging her to walk away. Even now, as a mature woman – a successful businesswoman – confrontation reminded her of being a little girl caught between two angry parents.

But then a lady came out and held the door open with a smile. 'You've got your hands full!'

'Oh, thanks.'

And just like that, Joanna was inside the shop. Her eyes shot to the left, where two daydreaming teenagers once planned to put a counter and sure enough, a computer discreetly sat on one end of an elegant and slightly curved timber and glass bench. Goosebumps rose on her arms. This was wonderful.

She was alone in the shop and wandered, looking at the racks of clothes and display mannequins. Quality pants and tops and shorts and skirts. Dresses with elegant, timeless cuts in linen and cotton and hemp. The shop wasn't large but everything was so well laid out that there was room for a pram or wheelchair or walker to move around unencumbered. Music played quietly and the colour scheme was subtle and the carpet soft.

'Exactly as we dreamed,' she whispered.

The lightness in her heart vanished, replaced with crushing grief, and tears filled her eyes before she could bite her lip and stop them. She dropped her face close to the roses and inhaled their fragrance, desperate to redirect the surging emotions and keep them under control.

'JoJo?'

No, not yet. Not now.

Joanna turned in the direction of the voice. A woman stood in the doorway leading to what was probably a kitchen. She was thin, with curly grey hair held back from her face by a colourful bandana and she wore wide-legged pants and a short-sleeve blouse both in undyed cotton. This wasn't Roslyn – surely not – but an older woman with deep lines on her face, yet when she smiled and stepped forward, her brown eyes were the same warm and intelligent ones which Joanna had never forgotten.

When Joanna didn't respond, Roslyn took a visible breath. 'What lovely flowers. I didn't expect you to—'

'I didn't. These are for my grandparents' graves.'

Her voice came out flat, abrupt, and Roslyn's eyes narrowed but her smile remained. 'Beryl visits them weekly and sometimes I do as well. I remember your mother's parents as kind people but never met your father's folks.'

The idea of Aunt Beryl and Roslyn merrily going places together made Joanna's stomach turn. What else did they do? Have high tea? How could her auntie be friendly with someone who'd hurt her own niece so deeply?

'Would you like some tea? I just made a pot of a nice herb blend.'

From my aunt?

'I only came to ask you something.'

Roslyn crossed the distance between them. She really was thin... almost like some of the more extreme models Joanna came across at fashion shows.

'We should have dinner tonight. Catch up properly.'

'No. I, um, I don't have time. Sorry.'

'Another day then?' Roslyn headed for the counter. 'I'll give you my address and number and you should come over.' She scribbled on a card. 'Any evening. Or all of tomorrow because I have someone here once a week and work at home.'

'Really, I'm very busy. But I have to ask you about the letter you sent. The subject of it.'

Still behind the counter, Roslyn held out the card, waiting.

It was only good manners which made Joanna walk across and take it, shoving it into a pocket without a glance. She wasn't going to visit Roslyn and pretend they were friends and the card would go into the bin at home.

'What do you know about these boat pieces which keep washing up? Why would you think they have anything to do with me?'

After pulling a stool closer, Roslyn sat, all the while keeping one hand on the counter.

'One day there were ten yachts in Willow Bay and the next there were nine. We both know which one was no longer there, Joanna. Which one was never seen again.'

Joanna's blood ran cold.

'But what does any of this have to do with me?'

The rolling of Roslyn's eyes was so familiar that in spite of her heightened emotions, Joanna almost laughed. Some things hadn't changed.

Customers wandered in, two older ladies who called a cheery hello to Roslyn.

'I'll be right with you, lovelies.'

There was no chance the discussion could continue with other people around. Joanna would have to come back. Or she could phone Roslyn rather than face her again.

'Let me go and help them and then we'll have that tea, okay?' Roslyn gazed at Joanna. 'You look so well, JoJo.'

The minute she was with her customers, Joanna slipped through the door and ran over the road to the car.

SEVENTEEN

After visiting her paternal grandparents and splitting one bunch of roses between two graves, Joanna moved a few rows away. Her father's parents died long before he married her mother and she knew little about them. And her biological father's parents were buried in an entirely different country. But she'd grown up having her mother's parents living in Rivers End. Nanna was just like Mum, quiet and always kind unless she saw an injustice and then she'd speak her mind. Grandpa loved to tell jokes and play pranks, even as he'd aged, and he taught Joanna how to climb a tree without falling. When his heart suddenly gave out, Nanna only waited a few days to join him. It was devastating for the family but a testament to the devotion of a lifetime.

'I always wanted a love like yours, Nanna.' Joanna sat on the grass between Nanna and Grandpa's final resting places, the rest of the roses spread out in front of her. Earlier in the day the sun had sent the rainclouds on their way and everything was dry from the warmth. 'The two of you finished each other's sentences and brought each other little gifts all the time.'

Grandpa would bring a flower for Nanna every time he

went for a walk around the neighbourhood, usually plucked from those peeking through garden fences or else from their own lovely display. She'd kiss him and put the stem into one of more than a dozen assorted vases she had just for the purpose. And she'd make him the same cooked breakfast he'd loved and eaten during their entire married lives.

'Mum and Dad as well. They are just as devoted. More, even, since they've retired and spend almost every hour together.'

Joanna had long since given up on having her own true love. Two long-term relationships over the last two decades had ended before marriage and several shorter ones didn't make it past a month or two. They'd all been nice men, good people. The issue was always the same. At some point in the relationship, each of them questioned Joanna's commitment to her career. Never their own – not one would entertain reducing their hours to care for any future children but wanted her to stop travelling internationally and move to part-time, once a family was started.

'The silly thing is I would have done exactly that, so I could be the mum I always dreamed about. They just didn't trust me to make my own decisions and weren't the kind of fathers I'd want for my children.'

Talking to her grandparents about this all was good. She'd never said any of this aloud, not even to her mum or dad. Despite the rocky early start, once her mother remarried, life had been wonderful in a calm and happy home. Joanna had long since made peace with staying single, rather than compromise her feelings about a permanent union.

Would Lucas have been the one?

Her romantic memories of the short time they knew each other longed to say yes. In reality, life wasn't so simple.

She stayed for a while, periodically placing the roses on each grave while telling them about her house on the canal and the career she'd poured herself into. She asked what she should do. Try to buy the company or take this as an opportunity to change direction?

Her stomach growled. She'd skipped lunch, too nervous about seeing Roslyn to risk eating. Now it was only a couple of hours until dinner.

There was nothing more to say. No more memories to share. Promising she'd be back to say goodbye before leaving Rivers End, Joanna groaned a little as she straightened. Before going to the car, she wandered around the graveyard. It sprawled across a couple of acres between the carpark, road, and a sheer cliff-face. Bushes lined the edge and a low fence warned of the danger of going beyond, where the drop was sudden. This was the town's original graveyard and favoured by anyone not belonging to either of the two churches, which had their own smaller ones.

Henry Temple was buried here. And Eoin Ryan who had taken Palmerston House from Henry in a poker game.

On her way to the carpark one headstone caught her eye. Planted along the base of the headstone were bright yellow pansies and an old memory made her smile. Roslyn's mum was able to grow almost any vegetable but despaired of keeping flowers alive, all apart from rows of pansies along the garden path she sowed each spring. Yellow were her favourite.

The smile dropped as she read the headstone.

It belonged to Roslyn's mum. And it was dated less than one year after Joanna left Rivers End.

Joanna knelt beside the grave, her fingers touching a delicate pansy. How could this be? Such a young woman... what had happened?

Why didn't anyone tell me?

What would she have done if she'd known? Flown down to the funeral to support Roslyn? Would she have done? Back then her heart was still reeling and she had laid down the law about not wanting to know a thing about Rivers End, and especially not any news of her former best friend. Her parents and Aunt Beryl had honoured her wishes.

You made your own bed, Joanna.

A tear trickled down her check and she got up, wiping it away with a hand.

'Joanna? Are you okay?'

She hadn't noticed Christie a few plots away, tending to one on her knees.

'I didn't know... my next-door neighbour growing up is buried here and I never heard she'd passed away.'

'Oh, I am sorry. Were you close?'

'Her daughter was my best friend.'

Christie's forehead furrowed. 'But she didn't tell you her mother died?'

'By then we'd... lost touch.' Joanna joined Christie, who tossed her gardening tools into a bucket and stood, wiping her hands on her shorts. 'Someone special to you?'

'My gran. Dorothy Ryan. She was the oldest child of the last Ryan family to live in Palmerston House. I lived with her after my parents died, until I was old enough to leave, which I did the minute I could. She wasn't a kind woman.' Christie smiled as she said that, but it was wistful. 'I was raised surrounded by wealth, when all I wanted was love.'

'That's so terribly sad. I'm kind of the opposite. I grew up with love but now I'm surrounded by wealth. Perhaps not the wealth of the mega-rich but a home worth a bit and a high-paying job. I'm so lucky my parents and aunt are still in my life, but a long time ago I lost everything I'd dreamed of.' She couldn't stop talking. 'My best friend gone from my life. Our shared plans for the future destroyed. The young man I really liked... oh goodness, this isn't something I meant to say aloud. Not ever.'

Joanna covered her mouth with both her hands, mortified she would open up this way to a virtual stranger.

Christie hurried around the plot and threw her arms around Joanna, holding her tightly. 'I never share other people's secrets. And I'm touched you've told me something so important.'

After a moment, Joanna returned the hug before stepping back, unsure what to do or say.

'You are a strong woman, Joanna. So am I, although it took me a long time to reach a place where I could see it. We have to walk through fire to find our passions and true selves, so it doesn't matter if I had wealth then but love now, or you had the reverse... we share resilience and intelligence and compassion.' Christie touched Joanna's arm, her eyes sincere. 'You wouldn't believe the stuff I tolerated from my ex until I finally worked out I deserved more, or Gran for that matter. How many times I stumbled. Joanna? Believe in yourself. Your passion is still there and it is not too late. Never too late.'

Every word resonated and it was all Joanna could do not to weep or blurt out her deepest feelings to this intuitive woman. But somehow she kept her eyes dry and put her arms around Christie, this time with a whispered, 'Thank you.'

Talking about herself – the real Joanna – was something she'd never intended to do, other than with a therapist. And she'd spent enough time with them over the years as she'd struggled to navigate through a life different from the one she'd planned. But Christie had found her at a vulnerable moment and been so genuine and kind. How easy it would be to grow this fledgling friendship into something strong and enduring.

Except I'm leaving again once I sort out this mess.

Joanna sat on soft sand, her back against a rock at the base of the cliff below Aunt Beryl's house. Drawn by the need for the calming influence of the sea and desperate for solace, she'd trekked down to the tiny beach, pleased the tide was out. For a while she'd paddled, letting the warm water tickle her legs and smiling at small fish racing back and forth with the gentle waves, breathing deeply of the salty air until her body was again relaxed and her mind clear.

She'd come to Rivers End for the sole purpose of assuring herself Trent's yacht had safely sailed away from Rivers End. Trouble was, the longer she stayed and the more digging around she did, the more clouded her purpose became.

All the research she'd done only raised more questions, but the evidence was piling up that the pieces washing ashore belonged to Trent's boat. The guitar made it difficult to ignore the connection between the pieces and the yacht. What really puzzled Joanna was why Roslyn was convinced of it. When she'd written the letter, there was still a general belief in the community of a boat in distress rather than an old wreck, yet something prompted her to breach twenty-five years of silence. Today, in the shop, there'd been no chance to delve into it. What had Roslyn said?

'One day there were ten yachts in Willow Bay and the next there were nine. We both know which one was no longer there, Joanna. Which one was never seen again.'

Joanna closed her eyes and leaned back to rest her head on the rock. The sun was delicious on her face. The idea of going to Roslyn's home made her queasy and there'd been too much of that lately. She had to deal with this and go back to Queensland, to her busy and stressful but far less complicated life.

An excited yip from a dog disturbed her thoughts and as she straightened and opened her eyes, Perry and Bobbie raced toward her. The dog reached her first, flopping at her side and demanding tummy rubs.

'Hello, you two.'

'Hi Joanna! I can't believe you're here.'

Bobbie carried a beach towel and wore a huge smile.

'I used to spend a lot of time here when I was a kid.'

'Really? But weren't you scared, being alone on this beach?'

'Why would I be scared?'

Looking at Joanna as though she was clueless, he whispered, 'The pirates.'

'Sorry... did you say pirates?'

He nodded solemnly.

It was all Joanna could do to not burst into laughter.

'How old do you think I am?'

'Older than my little athletics coach who always tells me to pretend I'm racing away from the pirates who used to sail along the coast. I mean, she knows about them so you might have actually seen them.'

'I'm fairly confident I missed out on that excitement. But I did see a lot of whales come by over the years. Have you seen any?'

He nodded vigorously.

'There's a good spot at the edge of Aunt Beryl's garden which gives a terrific view when they are here. She has a couple of sets of binoculars which makes it even better and you know what else? A telescope. As soon as it is whale-watching season, she sets it up on the balcony.'

Bobbie's eyes were huge. 'I'd love to look through that telescope.'

'Well, what if I leave a note on her fridge about it and she can let you know once they come back?'

'Yes please!' Bobbie wrapped his arms around Joanna's neck for a moment. 'You are the best!'

This was the second time he'd hugged her and she couldn't believe how happy it made her. She wasn't an aunt or sister. Kids were great but she had so few in her life other than those of a couple of friends.

'Bobbie, you look like you're strangling Joanna.'

The familiar voice sounded amused and when Bobbie stepped away, Lucas was approaching, smiling.

'Whoops, sorry, Joanna. Dad, this is the lady I told you about and can I swim now?'

'Stay this side of the breakers and I'll be there in a minute or two.'

And just like that, my afternoon is ruined.

Joanna climbed to her feet and shook the sand off her legs.

'Don't go. We won't intrude any more on your sun bath.'

She looked directly at Lucas, the glare of the sun in her eyes enough to make her blink. 'Did you really say sun bath?'

'Ever since I heard you say it, it slipped into my vocabulary. Never forget you telling me in great detail how if a person is sunbathing, then they are enjoying a sun bath.' He shrugged a cooler bag off his shoulder. 'Thank you for rescuing Perry and getting Bobbie home the other day. I had no idea until just now it was you.' He gazed at the water where Bobbie and Perry were splashing around. 'He was vague on the details.'

'Did he tell you they were down here in a storm?'

'He did. We've had a long chat about safety and responsibility, me and the three boys. There's a plan in place now to check in with each other more and the days I'm working, Mattie and Cal will take turns spending time with him.'

You really are Bobbie's dad. Father of three boys. And a girl?

'I need to go swim with him but please stay. We've got water and some fruit if you'd like to share?'

'Come on, Dad!'

Lucas stared at Joanna, his eyes telling her something but whatever it was, she didn't want to know. He'd chosen Roslyn even though he'd kissed Joanna. He'd never explained his change of feelings. There wasn't a thing he could say today which would alter the past or her feelings about what happened.

'I have to go.' She grabbed her sandals and stomped past him.

'And you do it again.'

'What?' Joanna paused and looked back. 'What do I do again?'

'Leave, JoJo. You don't have conversations. You just leave, every single time.'

Lucas wasn't making sense but he'd obviously tired of talking to her, pulling off his T-shirt before jogging to meet his son in the ocean

EIGHTEEN

All the way up the track, Lucas's words went round and round in Joanna's head. She couldn't stop them rotating, nor did she understand what he meant.

And you do it again.

He'd said it almost sadly. With resignation.

Leave, JoJo. You don't have conversations. You just leave, every single time.

Except she wasn't the one who left their blossoming relationship.

Every single time.

She shook her head to cancel the internal monologue.

You just leave. Leave.

At the top she looked down. The late afternoon sun glistened off the deep blue sea. Bobbie was with Lucas way out past the breakers, a confident swimmer. Both confident swimmers.

'But you never were. The ocean used to intimidate you.'

Lucas would swim as far as the pontoon but that was the extent of his interest in the sea. He told Joanna on their first date that he'd only swum it that first time so they could keep talking and that was when she'd told him about having a sun bath. Well, he was as happy in the Southern Ocean now as anyone she'd ever seen.

But what did he mean about her leaving without having a conversation?

When he'd followed her to the end of the jetty the other day, he'd wanted to talk. She'd barely given him the time of day other than when he mentioned the shipwreck, and then when he'd tried to engage with her, she'd dived in the sea.

Probably counts as not having a conversation and leaving.

Hardly a pattern.

Perry was racing up and down the tideline barking in sheer delight, occasionally running in as far as the first wave then bouncing out again. How wonderful to be as free and happy as a dog who was adored.

Standing here wasn't helping her state of mind.

Joanna went inside and showered, letting the warm water stream over her head longer than usual and trying to force her muddled emotions down the drain. The problems weren't going to go away on their own. She knew herself well enough to understand her need for action. To take control of a situation. So far she'd let this all control her.

From the moment she'd read the letter from Roslyn, her emotions had taken over. She thought about how she'd crumpled the letter, thrown it across the room, and burst into tears. None of those actions were typical.

Taking annual leave on short notice was also completely out of character. No wonder Ted was considering an outside offer rather than working with Joanna on a plan to transition the business to her over a timeframe which was good for them both. She'd messed up and probably thrown away a once-in-a-lifetime opportunity.

She turned off the taps and reached for a towel. This reminded her she needed to replace the one she'd used to dry a very muddy dog and her mood lightened. It had taken her more than an hour to clean the bathroom that day but she'd sung as she'd worked, not minding at all because her heart was still happy from the time with Bobbie and Perry.

Lucas's son.

Dressed and in the kitchen, Joanna picked up her phone to dial her aunt. For the first time ever, she needed to know what had happened over the years. About the town. Roslyn. And Lucas.

Partway through dialling, she stopped.

If she spoke to her aunt or her parents right now, she might not manage her feelings about Roslyn's mother. They'd done everything she'd asked by not speaking about Rivers End in any way. What a dreadful position she'd put them in, particularly her mother, who was such good friends with their neighbour. No, that was a conversation for another day and one where she would apologise for being so unfair.

She found the card Roslyn had given her and rang the number before she could stop herself.

Roslyn's house was on a small acreage a few minutes' drive outside Rivers End and with no immediate neighbours. Her road was just off the main route to the Otway Ranges and surrounded by a mix of open paddocks and bushland.

Joanna followed a circular driveway and parked to one side with the car facing the road.

I might need a quick escape.

It was a bit after six in the evening. Not the time Joanna had wanted to come here, so close to dinner – which might include a husband – but Roslyn had said it suited her. It didn't suit Joanna because she was over-hungry and not ready to see her ex-friend twice in one day.

You have to focus on why you're here. Keep it quick. Businesslike.

Her mouth was dry and her fingers almost dropped the keys as she locked the car. She'd rehearsed her questions, which now included some about Roslyn's mother. First though, she had to find out about the shipwreck.

The house was pretty, with jasmine and climbing roses enjoying late sunshine along the railings of a long front porch. Sitting at the top of half a dozen timber steps was a calico cat who stretched and then greeted Joanna with a meow, its tail held straight up. She offered her fingers to sniff and the cat stepped beneath them then looked up as if to ask for a scratch, so Joanna obliged. She adored cats and had one for a while but when she began travelling so often, her parents took him and there he lived a long and happy life.

'It *is* you. Come on in and she can join us.' Roslyn pushed open the screen door. 'This is Patchwork. Patch, Patchy, Patchikins.'

'Perfect name.'

'Agree. I'm going back to the kitchen so have a look around if you want.'

Roslyn had changed into a cream maxi dress with a V-neck and half sleeves. Her feet were bare and she had a plain red hairband in place of the earlier bandana.

Joanna almost asked if she sold the dress in the shop because with its pockets and a cute scalloped hemline she could see herself in it. And Mum. But she wasn't here to buy clothes or admire Roslyn's craftsmanship or fashion sense – all things she'd always had. Nor did she intend to get comfortable in this house. She left her sandals inside the door and followed the cat, which was disappearing down a long hallway.

The kitchen was as inviting as Aunt Beryl's but more modern, with double wall ovens and an induction stove built into a long counter. Roslyn was perched on a stool, chopping up salad items. A delicious aroma wafting from one of the ovens reminded Joanna how hungry she was.

'Help yourself to a drink, JoJo. There's filtered water, juice, wine, beer. Then come and sit with me while I finish this.'

To refuse would look churlish. And her throat needed something so she could speak without croaking like a frog. Joanna poured a tall glass of water. 'Would you like one? Or anything?'

'Actually, would you refill mine?' Roslyn pushed an almost empty glass closer. 'Thirsty work, cooking.'

Sitting down opposite Roslyn was surreal.

They'd been apart for longer than they'd been friends yet Joanna knew Roslyn's face as well as her own... now she'd overcome the surprise of how differently they'd aged. Close up, Roslyn's forearms and wrists were so thin that it was worrying, yet her hands were strong as they deftly sliced tomatoes. She must still sew.

'We'll eat outside so you can see my lovely garden better.'

'Eat? Oh, no, I didn't come for dinner.'

'Not going to eat this all on my own.'

'On your own?'

Roslyn raised both her eyebrows. 'Do you see anyone else here? Long time since I had a husband and my daughter is grown with her own family. And Patch isn't a fan of salad, though she might try the quiche.'

You never remarried after Lucas?

Unsure how she felt about that, let alone about their marriage, Joanna returned to the subject at hand. 'I only came to continue our discussion from earlier today.'

'Which we can do over a meal. Can you still make a vinaigrette?' Roslyn stood, pausing a moment to look at Joanna. 'I need to check the oven.'

'I make them all the time. Where are the ingredients?'

.   .   .

Patchwork, the calico cat, curled up on a chair at the end of the table while they ate. There was space for a dozen people here on a cobbled courtyard overlooking a beautiful garden filled with flowers. Toward the back were rows of vegetable beds and a compost heap beside a glasshouse.

'Used to grow orchids in the glasshouse and even won a few local competitions with them.'

Joanna had no idea how to respond, or even how to begin with the questions burning in her mind, so she put quiche in her mouth instead. It was the perfect texture, with mushrooms and feta and red onion and herbs and went so well with the salad and its tangy dressing.

'My chooks laid the eggs I used for the quiche.'

'Where are they?'

'Locked in for the night, thanks to a fox who'd like them for dinner. Around the side of the house there is a huge pen and chicken-house for them, and when I'm pottering in the garden they get full run of the place.'

'It is lovely here. A lovely way of life.' Joanna gazed around at the serenity.

'But? Come on, you could never imagine me living this way.' Roslyn was grinning. 'You always said I'd live in a penthouse somewhere for fashion season and in a luxury beach house for the rest of the year.'

'True. While this isn't a beach house, for all I know you have a penthouse as well.'

Roslyn snorted and Joanna couldn't hold back a smile.

'No penthouse for me. Enough to do here and for the business.' Roslyn collected some salad on her fork. 'How big is your garden?'

Did Aunt Beryl not tell you where I live?

Yet they went to the graveyard together. Shared pots of tea. Hung out.

'My garden? Hmm... there's a nice outdoor entertaining

area which is about the same size as this but covered. Next to it is a spa pool and sun loungers. Between those, they take up all but about three metres which is covered in artificial turf and faces onto a canal.'

'A canal? On the Gold Coast?'

'No, Venice.'

How she kept a straight face was beyond her, but seeing the different expressions on Roslyn's face was worth the effort. Incredulous, then admiring, then realisation.

'Ha. Ha. There's no way you'd live overseas.'

'Those gondolas are pretty romantic. Singing. Wine. Moonlight.'

Roslyn threw a piece of tomato at Joanna, who had excellent reflexes and caught it and threw it back. It landed in the middle of Roslyn's forehead and after a second of shock, they both burst into gales of laughter. Poor Patch woke up with a start and growled at them before stalking off.

This wasn't supposed to happen. Roslyn wasn't her friend. Joanna grabbed a napkin and offered it with a quick, 'Sorry.'

'I guess I did start it.' Roslyn used several napkins to remove all traces of tomato from her face. 'Remember how we used to splash each other in the sea until one of us would surrender?'

'Or more likely dive and then pull the other one by the ankles.'

'How on earth did we survive?'

Again, the laughter.

Why did we lose each other? Why did you turn your back on me?

Joanna stared at Roslyn. She'd expected them to be like strangers. Wary of each other. Even hostile. Not like this.

'What do you know about this so-called shipwreck?'

Roslyn's mouth was full and she made a weird hand gesture to show she was chewing. Patch returned to her seat at the end of the table, turning her back as she settled again.

'Have you been to the community hall?' Roslyn reached her glass of water and took a sip. 'You can go and look at everything washed up but usually best first thing in the morning, as they only have limited volunteers.'

'I only found out that's where the pieces are late last night after speaking to Mick Hammond at the marquee.'

'Oh, he'd have enjoyed some company. Go and take a look tomorrow and make your own mind up. Whatever happened to Trent's boat, it didn't get very far from Willow Bay and my theory is it hit a rock in the channel and he was too drunk or stoned to notice and when it sank, it got caught on something and stuck there for all this time.'

'Stoned?'

Appetite gone, Joanna rested her fork on her plate and took a gulp of water.

'My sweet innocent JoJo. Did you really never see that side of him? Regardless, one way or another it sank and that is where it should have ended but now... sooner or later the remains of the wreck will be identified and then there'll be an inquiry and the police may have questions.'

For me. Questions for me. Accusations... He wasn't stoned that night, but possibly dazed, concussed, even, from me pushing him down the steps. If his death was my fault I'll go to jail. Lose everything.

'Are you okay? Joanna, you've turned completely white. I'll get you some brandy.'

'No. No, really, I'm fine and I'm driving, so no alcohol.' She had to keep it together. Nobody else in the world knew what really happened that night, so this was pure speculation from Roslyn. But if she thought it, then so would others. 'Has anyone else suggested this is *Spee-Dee-One*?'

With a shake of her head, Roslyn stood and began clearing the table. 'I only remember because I was worried about you hanging out with Trent so much. He wasn't your type and as I said before, you really were such an innocent girl.'

No, Lucas was my type. And you stole him from me.

Innocent she had been back then. Gullible. But not now. She'd let her guard down briefly but Joanna wasn't about to let Roslyn appeal to their old friendship and get away with what she'd done.

NINETEEN

JANUARY 2000

Mum and Dad left this morning.

I thought I'd be fine but I'm so lost. We'd talked things through again about how I would live here until the beginning of the next semester then move into Aunt Beryl's. The house is for sale and it means I can let a real estate agent bring people through. They said if I ever want to move to Queensland then there will be a bedroom waiting. For the first time ever, it actually sounds appealing.

Watching them leave made me want to run after them. I'm not ready to be alone.

I never thought they would be the ones to leave home.

Before, I imagined this time as an adventure. Before Roslyn did what she did. I'd have had my best friend next door. I could come and go as I pleased without worrying about my parents saying I was out too late. Eat when it suited me. Maybe even have a romantic dinner for two here.

None of that is going to happen now and I don't even want to leave the house.

My bedroom and the kitchen are pretty much all that is

habitable now. My bed will be dismantled and, with my dressing table, taken to Aunt Beryl's by a friend of Dad's who has a trailer, along with the stools from the kitchen, the boxes I'll pack, and any bits and pieces left behind. The same friend is taking our fridge and washing machine to one of the charities once I move out. So everything is planned and now I just have to get through the next few weeks.

I wander through each room with a lifetime of memories everywhere I look. Mum had cried again when she'd done a last check of the house and then Dad held her in his arms and reminded her of the adventures ahead for them. But even his eyes glistened.

Mum left two meals in the fridge but I can't imagine ever feeling hungry again. I'll be eating alone from now on. Doing everything alone.

Before I make myself any more depressed, I change into swimwear and shorts and throw together a bag for the beach. If I spend the day swimming then I'll be tired enough to fall asleep tonight. All I hope is that nobody from my friends group is around or, even worse, Roslyn and Lucas. If they are, I might get the bus to Driftwood Cove instead.

But I'm in luck and although there are plenty of people at Willow Bay, it is mainly families. I'm able to find a spot at the far end of the beach where there's some tree coverage and a bit of distance from the holidaymakers.

The water is lovely and I swim out a long way from the beach then turn and tread water for a while, letting the weight of my sadness drop into the sea. I like the sound of my thoughts sometimes.

Trent is on his boat and he sees me and waves. I wave back and swim in his direction. The other day at that awful picnic he was so kind, encouraging me to sit with him and come up with songs for him to play. After a while, Roslyn looked bored and left, going off hand in hand with Lucas. I must have got quiet again because Trent stopped playing and suggested a swim. When we got back, the others were packing up but Salina gave me a hug and said she was glad to see me and apologised for the misunderstanding. It still makes no sense that Roslyn told everyone I'd gone to Queensland, even though she denied it.

'Care to come aboard?' Trent called. 'Got some bottles of cola in the fridge.'

How can I resist? I swim around to the stern and climb aboard and Trent tosses me a towel. 'Take a seat and I'll be back.'

I wrap myself in the towel and find a spot under a shade sail Trent has erected. The day is warming faster than I expected and I'll burn to a crisp if I stay out in it much longer. Already my skin is pink.

Trent runs up the steps and hands me an open cola before sitting nearby, but in the sun.

'Do you burn even though you're so tanned?' I ask.

He holds an arm out and inspects it. 'Never really noticed. I spend more time in the sun than out of it. Maybe the tatts help. Dunno.'

There are a lot of tatts on his arms.

'Do they have special meanings? The tattoos?'

'Some. Like this one of a sea serpent. It was after my first ever adult surfing win and someone reckoned I'd reminded them of a sea serpent the way I did a series of cutbacks. It sounded cool. Others are just places I've been. Do you have any?'

'Tattoos?'

I must have sounded shocked because Trent began to laugh.

'No, and sorry if I made them sound bad or something, but my parents would die if I got any.'

His laughter stopped and he got serious. 'You're not a little kid anymore, Joanna.'

'Tell me about it. Apparently I'm old enough to leave alone in our house for the rest of the summer break – and I do mean alone. Nearly all the furniture is gone. I won't see Mum and Dad again until at least the end of the year...' A sob catches in my throat.

'What does that song say about big girls not crying? I reckon the best way to learn about life is by being alone. Relying on yourself. I promise you'll be fine. No tears, okay?'

He is right. I can do this. I lift my bottle and tap his. 'No tears. Cheers.'

To pass the time in the evenings I start sorting out my bedroom in anticipation of moving to Aunt Beryl's house.

I pack up a lot of clothes I've outgrown or don't really care for and will see if one of the church shops would like them. They fill up several boxes which I carry downstairs and leave on the floor in the hallway.

Back upstairs I try to get serious about what to keep from my childhood and teens. There's stuffed toys in good condition, some which have meaning more than others. School projects as well as a few boxes filled with things Mum insisted on keeping. Reports, artwork, photographs from school camp and the like. I sort into 'keep', 'throw', and 'maybe' and then leave it for another day. But along the way I unearth something I was given in my last year of high school. It is a thick magazine-style book which includes a heap of information about career paths and what courses different universities offer.

I take it to the kitchen and flick through it as I eat a meal of Mum's I'd heated in the oven. This book is where Roslyn and I found our perfect degree to pursue. We'd weighed up at least a dozen universities offering design courses and aimed for one. Getting into our first choice was a sign to us. We were going to make it big.

Now I'm not sure. Actually, I can't see the way forward and this is an alien feeling because since the beginning of high school, Roslyn and I have been *Joalyn*.

Dinner finished, I keep looking through the book. There's a design course in Queensland I quite like the sound of. Similar to mine and there's a sister degree in business recommended. I have never thought about that because the course I'm doing includes the basics in running a business, but what if I focused on that side as well? A double degree. The university is in Brisbane so I could commute from where my parents have gone although it is a fair drive, or else try to get a place on campus. Either would work and if I got a move on I could apply and see if I can transfer from my current course.

More than anything, I can't bear thinking about going back to Melbourne.

How could I share the apartment with Roslyn now?

Breakfast at Aunt Beryl's is always a treat. She loves cooking and has her own chickens laying the freshest eggs imaginable, with tomatoes from her garden and bread she baked before I arrived. She lives alone apart from a couple of cats and her chooks and teaches at the local high school and is about the happiest person I know.

'While you're on your own I want you to come here as often as you want.' Aunt Beryl piles two plates with omelette and toast. 'My kitchen is always open and there's nothing to stop you bringing some of your things over early and beginning to settle in.'

'Do you mind if I do some sewing today?'

'Mind? I love you sewing here. Is Roslyn joining you? I can make some of those ginger snaps she likes.'

Rather than answer I stuff egg into my mouth. Nobody

knows what's happened. Not even about me going out with Lucas although I have mentioned him in passing as Salina's cousin who recently moved to the area and is a physiotherapist. My other friends might have wondered if we were going out because we hung out so much at every get-together but the only person who knew we went on a date, and that I had feelings for him, was Roslyn.

'Darling? Is everything alright with you two? I haven't seen Roslyn for a couple of weeks.'

'She's been busy, Auntie. Lots going on at home.'

Although my aunt gives me a long look, she eventually nods and bites into her toast. I long to tell her everything. To share my hurt and confusion and let her comfort me. But I feel so silly for letting myself believe in a young man I barely know so I change the subject. I'm getting good at that.

'Dad called last night to say they're both alright but very tired. They got there before the moving truck and everything is now in the house to start unpacking today. Mum made up their bed and they got takeaway and then were going to get some sleep after we talked.'

'Aw. Big job. I only moved from Rivers End township to here and that was a massive exercise. I know this is such an opportunity for your dad but wish they weren't so far away.' She looks so sad. 'Molly and I have always lived within ten minutes of each other. At least I still have you, dear child.'

When I go into the sewing room a bit later, all I can think about is how much Aunt Beryl is looking forward to me moving in and I feel guilty about even considering leaving Rivers End. My fingers won't co-operate because I'm thinking too much and not concentrating but eventually I've cut and hemmed three handkerchiefs and put a fancy "T" in the corner of each. I iron and fold them and slide them into a white envelope to take to Trent later. I'm about to leave when I notice the mannequin with the partly finished blue dress. The one for the special date which will never happen. Before I can get my scissors and slice the fabric into a million pieces, I grab the envelope and go to let my aunt know I'm heading off.

Trent's dinghy is high up on the sand so he isn't on the yacht. I've come straight from Aunt Beryl's, around the rocks, and sit in my usual spot between the trees to wait. If he doesn't arrive soon I've got swimwear under my dress so will have a swim.

The wind is a bit blustery and there's only a few people here, preparing to go diving. They are in a group of six plus a man who seems to be in charge, helping with wetsuits and checking masks and tanks. Willow Bay is good for snorkelling and diving, even for beginners, if away from where the boats are moored, because it has a lot of sea life and is pretty calm most of the time.

In pairs, the people go into the shallows, checking their flippers and putting mouthpieces in before disappearing beneath the waves. The man is last to go and is almost at the tideline when Trent runs down from the carpark and calls to him.

I stand up, ready to go to him but he catches up with the other man.

It's too far to hear a word, but Trent looks upset. He waves his arms around and the other man keeps shaking his head and eventually turns and follows the other divers. Trent goes in as far as his knees, his voice raised, but then the man is out of sight.

The last thing I want is for Trent to think I saw all of that and maybe embarrass him so I wind back toward the carpark through the trees and make it look like I've just arrived. He's stalking across the sand toward his dinghy.

'Hi Trent!' I call and wave and smile.

He glances at me and I almost falter because his face is dark red and he's scowling. But I want to give him the handkerchiefs so jog to catch up, reaching him as he turns the dinghy over.

'What's wrong, Joanna?' Even his voice is cross.

'Oh, sorry, nothing is. This is for you.' I pull the white envelope from a pocket and shove it in his direction.

Trent stops what he's doing and glares at me. 'No way. Not with a teenager and never with you.'

'Huh? Never what? I made you some hankies to replace the one I took that time.'

'Hankies?' His whole demeanour relaxes and he takes the envelope and opens it. 'I'd forgotten about that. You made these?' He opens one. 'Even with my initial... thanks. Can't remember the last time anyone gave me something. Not this nice.'

'What did you think was in the envelope?'

'Don't worry about it. Had a bad day, that's all. Coming to the yacht for a bit?'

I'm unsure. What if he gets mad again but at me?

'Joanna, look, being a surfer I get a lot of young girls wanting to... you know.'

Oh my goodness, did he think I was after *sex*? My face heats up and I barely know where to look. I can't even imagine what he would think was in the envelope because would a teenage girl offer money? Clearly I am way too naive and sheltered.

He grins. 'As I said, teenagers are off limits and you will always be. You're like a little sister. So are you going to run for the hills or come and learn some more guitar?'

We spend plenty of time together over the next few days, long hot afternoons in the sun and sea. I'm getting better at playing guitar. Trent doesn't get upset again and I'm grateful to have a friend, however unlikely. It makes my evenings in the house a bit less lonely, knowing I have at least one person in the world, other than family, who isn't out to hurt me.

I've just finished washing up after dinner when there's a knock on the front door. The last person I expect or want to see is Roslyn, yet there she is.

She doesn't wait to be asked, just walks right in and begins to go from room to room.

'Wow, this looks so different without the furniture. Really empty. I'll miss your parents and coming here all the time.'

'Why *are* you here, Roslyn?' I catch up with her in the kitchen where she is flicking through the book about university courses. I take it away from her and hold it against my chest like armour.

'Trent.'

'What about him?'

'Be careful of him, okay? He might not be what you think.'

About to say that she's mistaken, I remember him arguing on the beach with the diver and how angry he was, even with me for a minute. And his weird reaction to the envelope.

'I know you get on with him but soon enough he'll sail away and be gone forever. He said at the start this is just a layover for him.'

'And you're worried about me?'

A little spark of hope lights up inside me. She's barely spoken to me in weeks and never nicely but even the way she's looking at me is like the old Roslyn. The best friend who I miss so terribly.

'Of course I am, JoJo.' Her voice is soft. 'I don't want you leaving with Trent. Or going anywhere, really.'

She puts her left hand on the counter and for the first time I notice a ring on the third finger. My heart just about stops and she looks where I'm looking and a horrible smirk crosses her face.

'Lucas is so sweet,' she says.

'You need to go.'

'I only just arrived.'

'Now, please.' I march to the front door and hold it open until she finally goes outside.

'Don't trust Trent, Joanna. Just don't.'

I close the door on her face and after a moment hear her footsteps walking away. Then, regardless of whether big girls cry or not, I sink onto the floor and weep.

TWENTY
NOW

Roslyn refused to answer any more questions until she'd washed up and made a pot of herbal tea.

'Are you certain you don't prefer wine?'

I'd love a whole bottle.

'As I mentioned, I'm driving, so no. Thanks.'

'There's a guest room made up all the time and you are welcome to stay the night.'

'I won't be here too much longer.'

If Roslyn cared one way or another it didn't show on her face, yet this couldn't be easy for her. Knowing she'd destroyed a friendship and a future business partnership had to weigh on her... didn't it? She'd cared enough to write the letter.

They moved into the living room, a comfortable space with a soft sofa and armchairs, lovely artwork on the walls, and flowers in a rustic assortment of vases. Patch climbed onto the back of the armchair where Roslyn sat, occasionally tapping her neck with a paw. This was a long way from how Joanna had imagined Roslyn's lifestyle. More gentle. Harmonious. She even kept chickens.

'I'm so sorry about your mother.'

Roslyn stopped pouring tea to glance up in surprise.

'I was at the graveyard and saw her headstone.'

'Oh. Well, thank you. It was a very long time ago.' She finished pouring and offered a cup to Joanna. 'I never knew if your family told you or not.'

'Thank you.' The tea smelled sweet although unsugared, and a little bit like ginger. 'When I moved to Queensland I made my parents and Aunt Beryl promise to keep any news from here to themselves and they did that. For Mum to bring me a letter from you because my aunt thought it important, well that was a first.'

'I hope you weren't cross with them because I did have to persuade your aunt it was something you needed to know about. Beryl told me more than once you'd cut ties with Rivers End and although I didn't understand why, I guessed you wanted a clean start.'

'You didn't understand why... Oh, Roslyn.'

'Anyway you came to talk about the shipwreck so let's do that. I might be completely wrong and whatever is washing up is from some completely different boat but doesn't it all seem a bit too coincidental? People who know about boats have placed its time submerged to fit with when Trent left. He went without a goodbye. Certainly not to me or our friend group and he'd hung around us all enough to make it odd he wouldn't say he was leaving. Did he tell you?'

Joanna shook her head.

'When did you last see him? Was it the day he left?'

'Goodness, is this an interrogation?' Joanna sipped the tea. 'I like this blend. There's ginger and turmeric and something sweet but not too sweet.'

'Why are you changing the subject?' Roslyn put her cup on a side table and leaned forward. 'I've always wondered about that night. It was clear something bad happened but you refused to say anything. And then you were gone a few days later and our entire future lives went with you.' Her eyes glistened. 'I was just having a bit of fun. With a boy. I needed a distraction.'

If there was one thing which always got through her defences, it was seeing another woman in tears. Even as one trickled down Roslyn's cheek, a surge of emotion battled with the logic of staying angry about the past. Anger kept her strong. Protected her.

'For goodness' sake, Roslyn, no crying! Have you got any tissues?'

Using her hand to wipe the tear, Roslyn leaned back again. 'I know I messed up. I know that now but back then I was in so much pain I just... I turned into a monster for a while. Did what I wanted. Took what I wanted.'

'Lucas.'

There. It was out in the open.

Silence fell and dragged.

Both women looked anywhere but at each other. Then Patchwork jumped down and stretched.

'My mum was so ill—'

'My heart was shattered... Sorry, what?' Joanna lifted her gaze, shocked at the sorrow on Roslyn's face. 'Was she ill back then? Is that why you seemed so upset sometimes?'

'Were you watching my every move? But yes, probably. She knew before Christmas but kept it secret until New Year's Day so as not to spoil things. She had cancer and it had spread and there was nothing anyone could do. There was chemo and stuff but it was a long shot which didn't pay off. She went into a hospice a few months after you left and only made it through one more Christmas.' Her lips wouldn't stop quivering and she bit them and then gazed at Joanna through wide, distraught eyes.

In a second Joanna was at her side, perching on the arm of the chair and pulling Roslyn against her. She rubbed her back while sobs rocked Roslyn's shoulders, barely able to keep her own eyes dry.

Patchwork leapt onto Roslyn's lap and inserted herself into the cuddle which made them both laugh. Joanna went in search of a box of tissues and when she returned with it, Roslyn was holding the cat in her arms, both their eyes closed.

You look so defeated. So drawn.

'Found them. I like the bathroom. Always wanted a claw foot bath.' Joanna placed the tissues within easy reach and returned to her seat. 'Have you lived here long?'

After dabbing at her face with a handful of tissues, Roslyn straightened and the cat settled on her lap, purring loudly. 'It seems a long time but only a few years. When Sally married I gave her the house. My mum's house. Best start for a young couple, being able to own a home and not have to pay a huge mortgage or rent.'

'I think I met her.'

Roslyn nodded. 'I think you did. She told me there was a woman who seemed a bit upset leaning against the old gum outside your house. I didn't think much of it until you came to the shop but then I figured you'd gone to look at the home you grew up in.'

'It was unbelievably strange being back. And then she came out of your house with twins. *Grandma.*' Joanna said this with a grin.

'Nanna, thank you very much. Those adorable cherubs are Emily and Kathryn and they are the loves of my life. She married as young as I did but *her* husband is a keeper. I shall bore you to pieces showing you photographs of them one day as well as Sally's wedding photos and then there's the engagement party and plenty of Christmas and birthday moments. We'll have dinner all together soon so you can meet them.'

Except I won't be here long enough.

A little tug of something made Joanna pause. It was regret

of a kind. And it made no sense because this was Roslyn's world, not hers. Roslyn and Lucas's world.

'Seeing as I'm asking nosy questions... how long since your divorce?' Joanna tried her tea but it was too cold and all of a sudden the idea of a glass of wine sounded wonderful.

'I've never divorced. Caleb died in a car accident after only five years of marriage. I can't say it was devastating other than for Sally, because he wasn't the person I thought. Seems I was too much like Mum and chose the wrong partner.'

'Caleb?'

The air was thicker than normal. Harder to breathe.

'We met just after Mum passed. Married three months later. Why do you look so surprised?'

'You didn't marry Lucas?'

'Of course not. He only ever had eyes for you.'

A stone dropped into Joanna's stomach.

The wine in Joanna's glass was ruby red. She preferred dry white wines but back at Aunt Beryl's house had only managed to find reds. A whole rack of them. She sent a message to her aunt asking if she minded her opening another bottle. Her phone rang.

'Might as well drink them, darling. Better than transporting them to Queensland.'

'Can I put you on speaker while I pour a glass?'

'As long as I can put you on speaker to include Molly and Malcolm.'

'Good idea.'

While Joanna opened the bottle then poured a glass, almost to capacity, Aunt Beryl explained herself.

'I've made a decision and I hope you'll be happy because we all are.'

'We certainly are!' Mum's voice called.

'The time has come for me to properly retire. Be close to my family again and take it a bit easier than I have over the past couple of years. So, I'm going to put my house on the market and I plan to move up here.'

Thank goodness the call wasn't video because Joanna couldn't make her face look happy right now. It was absolutely the best thing and long overdue but this lovely beach house with so many memories... how sad to lose it.

You can't appear every twenty-five years and expect nothing to change!

'Still there, darling?'

'Sorry, just had a mouthful of wine. That is wonderful, Auntie.'

'Just think how much fun we'll all have,' Dad added. 'Four makes a better number for our board games and when Molly and Beryl are off doing sisterly things, you and I will get more time kayaking.'

'Do you have any ideas of where you'll buy?' Joanna asked.

'Molly's real estate agent friend is going to send through a list of houses currently on the market as well as keep an eye out for upcoming sales. All in the same area. But it will take a while to sell my home and once that's done, I can stay in a hotel or—'

She was drowned out by all three of them saying no such thing would happen and she could stay in one or the other house for as long as needed.

'Actually, I'll be travelling from the end of January through to March or April so my place is a good option, if you've sold by then. And there's more space than I'll ever need so if you prefer, just move in with me permanently.'

Mum asked something which was a bit muffled.

'I didn't quite hear you.'

Dad answered for Mum. 'She asked about Ted. Because if you buy his company, you might not be travelling as much.'

Joanna sank onto a stool and briefly closed her eyes. So many complications.

'Ted emailed me about the offer from a competitor and sort of suggested I make my own when I'm back. There's a lot for me to think about.'

They all chatted for a few more minutes, then with a chorus of 'love you' and 'talk to you soon', the call ended. Joanna stared at her wine glass. The entire day had tested her on many levels and this last piece of news, while not totally unexpected, added another layer of pressure.

She picked up the bottle and glass and went outside to the balcony, checking for spiders before settling onto a chair. She kept the lights off and allowed the warm, salty air to envelop her as she sipped more of the full-bodied wine.

The time at Roslyn's house was dreamlike. Never had she expected to feel anything other than anger or resentment toward the woman, yet they'd parted with a hug, albeit brief. Rekindling the friendship wasn't possible, even though Roslyn had justified her actions as a result of her mother's terrible illness. It still didn't excuse her behaviour entirely, nor explain Lucas's part in it all. What on earth led him to cut ties with Joanna and move on to a new romance?

'He only ever had eyes for you.'

Roslyn had been sincere when she'd said that. Not the least disappointed. She'd started to talk about what happened after Joanna suddenly left town but that was one thing too many. Joanna made an excuse of expecting a call from her parents and left but deep down, she was desperate to know more. To ask a million questions.

As she'd driven past Lucas's driveway she was overcome with a ridiculous need to find him and demand an explanation. Well, he didn't owe her one. Nobody did. This was all in the distant past when they were young and made rash decisions. Besides, she was hardly going to intrude in his life when his children were with him. His sons... because he wasn't Sally's father.

The tide was coming in, heavy waves crashing against the rocks below the edge of the garden. Mingling with the sea air was the powerful scent of roses and gardenias which were planted near the balcony. A rustling in the tree was the possum visiting, probably seeing if Joanna had any goodies on offer.

How can Aunt Beryl leave here?

The wine was making her melancholy.

Lucas hadn't been interested in Roslyn. He'd only had eyes for Joanna. But he'd gone along with whatever hurtful game Roslyn had been playing.

Ted was about to sell the company from under her after suggesting he'd like her to be the one to take over in time.

There was every reason to believe Trent's yacht had sunk and that she might have been involved in it. Her career might soon be over no matter what Ted did.

And this beach house she loved so dearly was about to be sold.

Joanna was frozen inside. There was too much for her to filter and deposit into carefully crafted boxes in her head. If she thought about any one of these things too hard or looked too closely at the ramifications then she might fall into an abyss and never return.

She refilled her wine glass and stared into the night.

TWENTY-ONE

Rivers End Community Hall was two blocks away from the main shopping strip and on the same land as several sports clubs. It wasn't far from the primary school and a church.

Joanna had walked from home, hoping the exercise and morning sun on her face might shake the dark thoughts which remained from last night. She'd slept fitfully, dreaming about being underwater and swimming away from people she loved from now and the past. When she'd woken, her face was wet from tears and she lay in bed until her heart slowed to a normal beat. Stress was getting to her.

There was a door, open, which led to a small foyer with posters on the walls and a noticeboard. A couple of doors led to restrooms and the office of whoever was currently head of the committee running the hall. Then closed but unlocked double doors to the main public area. She let herself in, unnoticed by the handful of people working at one end of a long row of trestle tables.

In here she'd learned to play chess and table tennis and attended plays and even been in some. Little had changed, not even the slightly musty smell. The old timber floor still creaked alarmingly in certain spots. A raised stage at one end with its curtains closed. The slight echoing as people talked.

A couple of large, wheeled whiteboards were the subject of interest of the people in the room. They gathered around them, one person in between the boards and holding court.

Each of the tables was covered in thick brown paper and upon them lay a host of items.

Long timber strips. Metal parts Joanna didn't recognise. Pieces of a mast. A plastic box. There was so much more variety and volume than she'd imagined.

She wanted to get a closer look at the tables and the whiteboards. Even from the distance it was clear one board was a work in progress as a yacht was reconstructed – presumably from the discoveries on the beach.

The small meeting broke up and people began to leave. Joanna wandered along one wall which had glassed displays of old artwork and creations from kids over the years, along with a couple of timber boards listing the people who'd been particularly valuable to the different associations who used the hall. Her parents were both listed as well as Aunt Beryl and it gave her a little surge of pride. She took some photographs because these had been installed since her parents left Rivers End.

'No photos in here, please, ma'am.'

Joanna swung around. A gentleman in his seventies approached. He wore a tweed jacket and slacks despite the warm morning and had been the person speaking at the whiteboards. A scowl deepened lines around his mouth and forehead. He looked rather ferocious and Joanna wondered if he'd ever been a school principal.

'Oh, good morning. I just wanted to send a photo of the honour board to my parents and aunt, who are all mentioned on it.' She gestured back at the board in question. 'Would you rather I delete the images?'

The gentleman had a pair of spectacles on his head and he

pulled them down to his nose to take a better look at her. 'I thought you were a journalist here about the sunken vessel. We are trying to control the media's interest in it. Please, go ahead and send the photos to your family. I'm Emmett Fairlie.' He held out a hand to shake.

'Nice to meet you, Mr Fairlie. I'm Joanna Johnson.' She took his hand.

'Ah. Malcolm and Molly's daughter. What a long time this has been.'

'I imagine it has.' Joanna smiled. She didn't remember him at all. 'I saw you speaking to some other people near the whiteboards.'

'You must have heard about our recent excitement? Come and take a look.'

Mr Fairlie led the way and Joanna didn't hesitate to follow.

'What a pity you weren't here a little earlier. We have quite a talented group of local residents contributing to this mystery, mostly driven by our historical society and our boating association. George Campbell, for example. He was quite the sailor in his day and kept his yacht in Willow Bay for decades. She's still there, renamed, and owned by his godson's wife.'

Jasmine Sea.

The man tapped on one board. 'As you can see, we have a general list of what has washed up. Of course, everything is properly recorded and itemised digitally but it is useful to keep a running list anyone can add to.'

There were several headings such as 'hull', 'deck', 'below deck', 'fixtures', and 'personal items'.

The latter was of most interest to Joanna but also had the shortest list.

Acoustic guitar

Wetsuit pieces

'On this board we're attempting to use the various parts to

create an image of the vessel. Quite tricky when the ocean is seeing fit to deliver the clues on her terms.'

Joanna was warming to the man. 'How much more do you need before this mystery is solved?'

'Far too many more, I fear. Weather and tide conditions are gradually returning to normal, so whatever broke free after the sea tremor is likely already on these tables. Mind you, there'll be another storm front developing later in the week so anything still lurking around the coastline might make an appearance if Neptune is willing to give up his treasure.'

They began to slowly walk along the line of tables.

'I read about the early concerns that all of this belonged to a boat in distress.'

'Our coastguard and local boat owners spent considerable time and effort looking, but thank goodness there was no boat lost. Not recently. Once a couple of people, including George, took a look at the amount of decay on the interior timber, the search was called off and the investigation pivoted.' Mr Fairlie pushed his spectacles up onto his head again. 'All a bit peculiar. Somebody has to know whose boat it is. Current thinking is someone deliberately sank it for an insurance claim and our police officer has sent off enquiries to the major insurers with a rough time estimate. Most likely nobody will ever find the truth.'

Tension drained from Joanna's shoulders. This was the best news she could have hoped for.

'How much longer will you and your group continue on this project?'

'Another few days and then, if nothing more washes up, it'll be packed up and stored somewhere, just in case evidence is required in the future. I don't wish to be rude, but I have an appointment in town shortly.'

'Of course. And thank you for showing this to me.'

'You are welcome. Please pass my regards to Molly and Malcolm.'

They walked out together, Mr Fairlie locking the double doors and then the front door in their wake. While he got into his car, Joanna headed to the church next door. One of her neighbours was buried in the graveyard and she found their headstone easily, remembering it from the first funeral she'd ever attended as a child. On her way back out, she looked over at the community hall.

There were no cars parked near it but she was certain a man just walked behind the building.

Joanna waited and sure enough, someone emerged from the back. He was older than her, muscular, in a singlet and frayed shorts with work boots. A cap pulled down over his eyes made it hard to see his face. He went to the front door and rattled the door hard. When it didn't give, he stalked away, cutting across the carpark in the direction of the sports field between it and the primary school.

If he'd been part of the group talking inside then she didn't remember him but there were dozens of reasons why he might be there. Except, most people didn't walk right around a building and then rattle the main door. She should have taken a photo.

Stop jumping at shadows.

There was no point creating problems where they didn't exist. It was time to enjoy a coffee and pastry from the bakery.

A tap on the door caught Joanna by surprise as she was about to take washing outside to hang. It was so soft she thought she'd misheard but then it came again.

Opening it to Roslyn was even more surprising and it must have shown on her face.

'Sorry, I should have called first.'

Roslyn carried a large cardboard box which she seemed to be struggling with.

'Do you want at hand with that?'

'Actually, yes. It's heavier than I expected and I probably shouldn't be carrying it, but you know what it's like when you're accustomed to doing everything yourself.'

Joanna took the box which was indeed quite heavy. 'What on earth is in here? And why shouldn't you be carrying it? Are you injured?' She stepped away from the front door. 'Come in and I'll put this on the kitchen table.'

Unsure how she felt about the sudden intrusion, Joanna took the box into the kitchen and forced her face into a smile as Roslyn appeared through the doorway behind her. 'Tea? Coffee?'

'Just some water if you don't mind. Can I sit for a minute?'

'Of course.'

The sense that something wasn't quite right with Roslyn was back but Joanna couldn't put her finger on what it was, or how to broach the subject. She filled two glasses and sat opposite Roslyn.

'You didn't walk all the way here?'

'Sadly no, my days of flitting all over the place, beach-hopping and going from lagoon to mountain on foot, are behind me. The car is at the end of the driveway.'

'And the box?'

Roslyn finished the water and leaned her arms on the table. 'I'm worried I upset you last night. More than I already have. This morning I woke up after a strange dream and for a few seconds my brain told me I'd imagined your visit.'

And in my dreams I was swimming away from you. From everyone.

'As you can see, I am here. After I got home last night I spoke to Mum and Dad and Aunt Beryl. She's going to move to Queensland.'

'Oh.' Roslyn sat back with a frown. 'Oh, that is sad. I really shall miss her.'

How close are you both?

'Well, she misses my mother a lot so it isn't a big surprise. I just can't imagine the beach house without her.'

'I know. But...' Roslyn brightened. 'You can live here.'

'Er, no. I have a career which takes up a lot of my time so sadly to say, Auntie will put the place on the market soon. At least I can help her for a week or two once she's back to do what needs taking care of in preparation for a real estate agent.' Even saying it was depressing.

'But will your career ever look as good as this house?'

'I'd forgotten how annoying you are when you're set on something.' This time, Joanna's smile was genuine. 'My career is what pays the bills and I happen to own a nice house already.'

'Not like this one!' Roslyn got to her feet. 'Let's start here in this kitchen. Does your nice house include a double oven of this vintage? You know they're trendy now?' She headed off in the direction of the living room. 'And how about this classic fireplace?'

Barely able to stop herself laughing, Joanna followed.

Roslyn was in the middle of the room, pointing at the large fireplace with its marble mantelpiece and limestone surrounds.

'I don't think Aunt Beryl uses it. She has central heating and air conditioning these days. But I will admit that the view from the balcony is impossible to match.' To prove the point, Joanna slid the door open and stepped out. 'I can see the canal from my outdoor living area, kitchen, one bedroom, and of all things, the laundry. But here, the horizon is an ever-changing thing depending on time of day and weather, and I see boats of all kinds and have, in the past, whale-watched.'

'Bobbie told me he's going to ask Beryl if he can search for whales through her telescope.' Roslyn rested her hands on the rail and looked at Joanna, her eyes intense. 'If you lived here, then he won't be disappointed.'

'Really? A guilt-trip about a child I've met twice?'

Who gives the best hugs in the world.

With a shrug, Roslyn went inside. 'All's fair, as they say.'

No, none of this was fair. Not why she'd left Rivers End in the first place and definitely not how many connections she was making after such a short time back here. Whatever she did was going to hurt and returning to her normal life offered the least resistance.

Roslyn was back in the kitchen, opening the box.

'You've missed so much, Joanna. Weddings, funerals, births, birthday parties, Christmas events.' Roslyn lifted out a photo album. 'You'll love these. I even have one in here filled with photos from the shop from the very first coat of paint on the wall through to the opening day.'

'Please don't...' Joanna's voice faltered as her chest tightened.

'I can't wait to show you—'

'The washing needs hanging.'

Joanna fled to the laundry where she collected the full basket of wet washing and then she was outside and hurrying down the path to the washing line.

TWENTY-TWO

Joanna's hands shook, the pegs falling from her fingers as she tried to hang the washing. She persevered, concentrating on the simple task. The sheets at least stayed in place if she laid them evenly over the line but the pillowcases refused to cooperate, both dropping to the ground.

She scooped them up and shook the grass off then tossed the pillowcases back into the basket to rewash.

'I've done it again, haven't I? Upset you.'

Roslyn walked down the path and began picking up pegs from under the line.

'Just leave them.'

'Got them all.' Roslyn added them to the peg basket and turned her eyes to Joanna. 'You look ready to cry.'

'No, I don't.'

The lump in her throat wasn't going anywhere, no matter how hard she swallowed.

'What if I leave everything in the box and you can look later. When you're not busy. I should have called first rather than show up.'

'I don't mean to sound rude, Roslyn, but why do you want to share the last twenty-five years of your life with me?'

'Why wouldn't I now you're here? Since you've come home again at last. It broke my heart you leaving so suddenly and then Beryl wouldn't give me your new address or pass on anything to you.' Roslyn was wringing her hands, her voice pitching up. 'I had to go back to university alone. Find a new roommate. Go through a bad marriage and widowhood and being a single mum alone. I built the business by myself. My best friend just vanished from the life we planned.'

Walk away, Joanna. Carry the box to her car. Say goodbye.

Joanna lifted the basket, not daring to speak as outrage burned through her body.

'I was the only person dealing with Mum's treatments and watched her die almost alone. Dad never cared, not even about me and what I was losing.'

The whimper which followed Roslyn's words cut deeply yet Joanna stayed silent.

Neither moved.

This was the end of everything. There could be no way forward.

The breeze strengthened, moving the hoist in a circular direction until there was a sheet between them and then it stopped. Roslyn's feet were the only part visible and Joanna burst into laughter.

'Charming. Even the sheet separates us and you think it funny.'

Putting her hand up, Joanna rotated the hoist until she could see Roslyn again. 'It was either that or yell at you.'

'I guess you made the better choice.'

'I'd forgotten how much you make me laugh.'

Roslyn screwed up her face. 'Back-handed compliment?'

'Real compliment.'

'Then you don't hate me?'

For the longest moment the silence returned. As it dragged, Roslyn's eyes glistened with unshed tears. Joanna couldn't bear the tension and the thought of confrontation was churning her stomach but maybe the air had to be cleared. Even if it hurt them both, was it any worse than what had already occurred?

'When you kissed Lucas in front of me on the jetty, I didn't hate you. I never have, but Roslyn, I left because I couldn't stay. Not only had I lost my boyfriend, but my best friend. I felt our future was completely gone. How can you not know this?'

'Boyfriend?'

'Seriously, I feel like I'm in an alternate reality. You knew I had strong feelings for Lucas. You *knew* we'd gone as far as to have a proper date.'

The colour drained from Roslyn's face and when she swayed, Joanna dropped the basket and went to her, putting an arm around her waist.

'Are you okay to walk back in?'

'Sure. Just got a bit light-headed.'

They took their time going back up the slope to the house, going at Roslyn's pace. Back inside, she sank onto an armchair in the living room with a small laugh.

'Goodness, how weird. I have low blood pressure and it felt like I might faint for a second.'

Joanna brought her water and watched her drink. The colour was coming back into her face. 'Have you eaten lunch?'

'I wasn't hungry today. Bit silly of me.'

'Do you need a doctor?'

'Absolutely not! I just got myself a bit distressed so I'll sit for a minute, if that's okay? Then I'll head home.'

'Do you have to be home? I mean, is there anything stopping you from staying a while? Does Patchwork need feeding?' There was no chance Joanna was letting Roslyn leave until she was clearly fit to drive. 'I'm getting hungry so what if I throw together some nibblies and we can sit on the balcony and drink tea and talk. Even look at your photos.'

As much as Joanna was afraid to delve into the past, she was more afraid that something was really wrong with Roslyn. Keeping her here for a while would allow her to observe.

'But I'm intruding.'

'Yes, you are. I'll make an exception this one time.' Joanna tried to keep the smile hidden but failed. 'Would you rather sit here or come and talk to me while I make some food?'

For the first time since Aunt Beryl left for Queensland, the kitchen truly felt warm and happy and comforting. Roslyn sat at the table, chatting about everything from the recent weather to the joys and woes of being a trader in a small town. Joanna sliced cheeses and bread, added crackers and olives and sun-dried tomatoes, shredded beetroot and carrot, relish, pickled onions, and fresh cherries and blackberries.

'Outside? Or do you prefer to stay where you are?'

'Definitely the balcony. What can I bring?'

Joanna gave her a long look. Roslyn was back to her usual self, including her colour, and had reported no further light-headedness.

'What would you like to drink? A pot of tea? I have water, obviously. Orange juice. Some kombucha,' Joanna said.

'Wine?'

'Nope. You're driving. And you got dizzy earlier.'

'Okay, okay. Juice. I'll get it.'

They settled at the table and for a while ate and enjoyed the view over the sea. The washing line was just visible on the far side of the garden and the sheets already looked dry. With the warmth and full sun on them, it hadn't taken long but now she'd need to find pillowcases from the linen cupboard.

'I need to make a note, sorry.' Joanna opened her phone. 'I

owe Aunt Beryl a new towel after using a nice one to dry Perry the other day.' She tapped a note to herself and put the phone down, but not before seeing a message pop up from Ted.

'You can give her your towels. I imagine you keep a whole closet of quality towels and sheets in Queensland and that way she won't have to transport hers, plus you can then just use what she leaves here.'

'Are you going to keep on about me moving here?'

'I am.' Roslyn made an open-faced sandwich from the sourdough bread topped with a mix of ingredients from the platter. She then cut it into four pieces. 'And I know you believe I had a part in you going... but, I don't want to lose you again.'

Why are you oblivious to what you did?

It took a minute to work out how to say what had to be said. Filtering the emotional stuff and keeping to the facts. Once Roslyn was chomping on her second piece of sandwich, Joanna took a deep breath.

'You did have a part in my decision to leave Rivers End. A huge part. Do you remember us talking in the street that night? The night I had the date with Lucas?'

Roslyn swallowed and sipped some juice before putting down the rest of the piece and giving Joanna her full attention. 'Not really.'

'It's as clear as your face is now to me. It was late and you came out of the darkness the minute Lucas left. I hugged you because you'd been crying but you wanted to sit under the tree and talk about my date.'

'And did you?'

'Of course I did. And you asked if I'd told Lucas my hopes and dreams and I said yes, but mostly about having two more years at university and then a cadetship.'

'Well, there you go. He obviously realised you'd have your hands full for ages and wouldn't be able to commit to a long-term relationship for several years. You have to remember he's older than us, which doesn't matter now but maybe back then he was wanting to settle down sooner. Or something.'

'Why wouldn't he have told me that?'

'Why don't you ask him? Actually, why even bother with all this now?'

'Because... because he kissed me, Roslyn. A real kiss and more than once, and he cared about me.'

Too focused on her plate to look up, Roslyn shrugged. 'I never knew he kissed you, JoJo. Lucas is a good man. Really decent and kind but he probably didn't know what he wanted back then.'

'Hang on, you just said he was probably looking for a long-term relationship. And you also said he only had eyes for me.' Keeping her voice calm was taking a lot of self-control but Joanna had plenty of experience dealing with difficult clients and there was no point escalating things again. 'So why you? Why did he change his mind about me and turn to you? Yet he didn't marry you.'

Roslyn's discomfort was showing. She played with her food and her feet were tapping the floorboards. 'Like I said, maybe he didn't know what he wanted. Maybe he thought you were too serious. Or not enough. But for me it was just a bit of fun, Joanna. A summer fling to take my mind off other things.'

Except I was falling in love with him.

Was it possible Lucas really hadn't felt the same way? Shocked at how quickly he'd got so close to the first woman who welcomed him to the group of friends he'd been pushed into by his cousin? Had she mistaken his interest when all along he was just being polite?

Roslyn touched her arm and she looked up.

'In hindsight, I was a terrible friend, JoJo. Mum was always upset and I didn't know what to do. She made me promise to keep her illness a secret. Partly because she didn't want to worry your mum right in the middle of moving, but mostly because she was such a private person and was concerned about my father trying to muscle his way back into our family.'

Joanna took her hand and squeezed. 'If I'd known—'

'I couldn't say a word. I promised not to. And it messed with my head, not just then but for years. I couldn't control anything around me so I began to control what I ate.' She stretched out one of her arms, touching it with her other hand. 'So much lost muscle and I still have the effects of years of starving myself. It was only when Sally was about three and she pushed an almost-full plate away like I used to, well, like I still do sometimes, that I woke up to myself. There was no way I was passing on my problems to her so I went into therapy. Thank goodness I did because when Caleb passed away, it was another stressful time but by then I had healthier ways to manage it.'

'I'm proud of you. Taking control like that.'

Finally, a smile. 'Thanks. I'm proud of me as well. Even raised a good kid. Like to see some photos now?'

They sat on the floor in the living room, photo albums scattered around them and a pot of tea on the lowest of the coffee tables.

'Sally's wedding was so beautiful. Really simple. And her husband is the best son-in-law.' Roslyn picked up one of the albums. 'He's an electrician and volunteer firefighter and such a good dad.'

Joanna refilled their cups with fragrant lemon and ginger tea. This harmony, the easiness between them, was a gift. She had so many questions about Roslyn's behaviour back then, including the ring on her finger the last time they'd spoken which she'd implied was from Lucas, but how could she keep pushing the point?

Roslyn was happy in the moment. There was a light in her eyes Joanna had forgotten and it hurt how much they'd missed of each other's lives.

'Tell me about the shop.'

'Oh. Really?' Roslyn closed the album and smiled. 'I kept it as true to our joint plans as possible. Did you like it?'

'It's beautiful. Somehow the atmosphere is both luxurious and accessible and I have no idea how. I got the sense that no matter the demographic of the customer, they'd feel at home and that is a real skill.'

'People say that all the time. I mean, in other words. I couldn't believe it when the shop was for lease again. All those times we'd stare through the windows and come up with ideas.'

'Better than the fast food place you wanted.'

'Which is now converted into the wine bar.'

'I've been there. And that is another place with fantastic atmosphere.'

'And food,' Roslyn said. 'The town must have changed so much for you.'

For ages they sat talking and looking at photographs. Joanna showed pictures of her house and some of her parents, which was enough to make Roslyn tear up again and then they both laughed at how often Joanna had looked for tissues for her recently.

'I really should make some hankies for myself.'

'It would save some trees.' Joanna might have joked but the comment had swept her back to the day she'd given Trent the envelope of hankies and he'd reacted like she was offering contraband.

'Now I should get going. Patch will be expecting a meal and I might go past Sally's house to return this album to her. She was very sweet loaning it to me but also rather concerned I might lose it. Hold on to the rest, and there's more stuff in the box as well. Some you might prefer to look at with a glass of wine in hand.'

They wandered to the end of the driveway together. There was some light left but soon the sun would set and the air was cooling. Roslyn stowed the album and her handbag on the back seat then held her arms out and Joanna went in for a hug.

'Thank you, JoJo. Thank you for everything. Come and see me at the shop soon.'

'I will. Drive carefully.'

Joanna watched Roslyn drive away. A dog barked in the distance, sounding like Perry. The road was quiet and once Roslyn was gone, the sound of the sea and the breeze in the trees vied for dominance.

But there was a sharp crack. Close by.

'Hello?'

She scanned the bushland around her. Nothing moved. It was most likely a daytime creature settling for the night or an early rising nocturnal.

The hairs on her arms were standing straight up.

Joanna returned to the house via the clothes line, whipping the sheets off and getting inside as fast as she could. It might be a silly response to a normal sound, but she'd already felt she was being watched more than once. She went around the house locking everything up but leaving the balcony sliding door open. It was too far for anyone to easily climb and the screen door had a lock, which she turned.

After tidying up the living room she returned to the kitchen with an armful of photo albums. Taking Roslyn's advice, she poured a glass of wine before reopening the cardboard box.

There was another photo album, the pocket-book kind with plastic sleeves large enough for one picture. The year 2000 and the word 'memories' was engraved on the front and Joanna almost returned it to the box. But she'd already come this far, so opened it to the first page.

It was taken at Willow Bay and was focused on the boats. On *Spee-Dee-One*.

TWENTY-THREE
JANUARY 2000

Wandering around late at night alone probably isn't the smartest thing to do, but here I am doing it.

After I'd stopped crying and feeling sorry for myself over Lucas, I got mad. Whatever Roslyn is playing at has to stop. She needs to explain herself. So I take nothing but my house keys and go next door. I stand outside her home, hoping to catch sight of her through a window because I don't want to knock and disturb her mother. But the only light on is the one over the porch.

And that's why I'm at Rivers End beach.

I need to find them. Lucas and Roslyn. My almost-boyfriend and my ex-best friend. If she's going to come to my home and tell me to be careful of Trent, who has been kind to me all this time, then I'm going to warn Lucas about her. Hopefully I'll have worked out exactly what I'm warning him about before I find them.

This burning anger is so much better than being sad. It's as though I can take action and be in charge of my life instead of being passive.

A full moon is radiant over the Southern Ocean and for a while I stand near the lagoon just watching the waves. I close my eyes and their sound is soothing. How easy it would be to lie here on the sand and sleep to the endless rhythm. My body is so tense though. I may never sleep properly again.

I walk in the direction of Willow Bay, stopping at the base of the cliff and deciding not to risk going around it over the rocks at night. Nobody at all is on the beach so I go all the way back, double-checking the jetty, then continuing to the cave.

That would be the perfect place for them to be.

Away from prying eyes. Alone.

I shudder at the thought of what I might see but how can anything get any worse? My only goal for tonight is to find out why Lucas dumped me without a word and why Roslyn chose him over our lifelong friendship. I stand just outside the entrance and strain my ears but can't hear a sound from inside, so I take a couple of steps in.

The cave isn't big but comes in handy as a place to escape the sun or rain. I don't want to think about what else might go on in here but am well aware it is a rendezvous for couples. At least there are no couples in here right now. Just me.

Back outside, I climb partway up the stone steps and sit. It must be midnight or later so no wonder the beach is deserted. But there's running lights of a boat approaching the jetty, which is strange because not many boats tie up there. Sometimes a passing yacht might stop for a couple of hours while the occupants shop in Rivers End, but mostly it is only dinghies belonging to hobby fishermen.

Although a fair distance away, I recognise *Spee-Dee-One*.

'Well, what on earth are you doing here?' I murmur and stand to better see.

There's no shops open this late. No people to collect for a sail.

Except there *are* people.

I sit again.

By the time the yacht is alongside the jetty, rocking in the swell, two men have crossed the sand from the river and are waiting. How I wish I could get closer because I'm sure one of the men was the one from the other day. The diving instructor.

This is bizarre. Trent and the diver had had words of some kind, I remember, enough to have put him in a foul mood. Here they are meeting again, only this time, there is hand-shaking and back-slapping going on. The other man has a cap pulled down over longish hair and I don't recognise him. Trent is on the jetty with them and laughter drifts across the sand. I don't have a hope of hearing words though and some deep instinct kicks in and tells me I need to leave.

I sneak up the rest of the steps and at the top, lie on my stomach so only my head is over the side. There's no way anyone will see me but I'm not taking chances.

Something weird is going on. People don't normally move their yachts in the dead of night to another beach just to have a chat on a jetty. I try to work out who the other men are and fail. I wish I had my camera and could zoom in.

Trent is back on the boat and the other men leave the jetty.

Instead of going back toward the tunnel beside the river, they head for the steps.

My heart jumps and I scramble to my feet and run in the direction of the road. There's no cars in the carpark but I don't hang around to see where they go. I get onto the main road and cross to a path which leads through bushland to some empty fields and will get me out of sight. I have to stop running to avoid tripping over but it is a shortcut to the river and once I reach it, I double back to the bridge.

Locking myself back into the house is the biggest relief.

I'm out of breath, covered in sand as well as grass on my front. This wasn't what I'd expected leaving the house, not in any way. I strip off my clothes and throw myself under a shower, my heart still thudding not only from the run but the sudden flight response.

Whatever those men were up to, I'm sure it wasn't good.

Who is Trent, really?

Aunt Beryl is baking and her kitchen smells so good I don't ever want to leave. I've helped her with a bit of the prep but she said I should go and sew for a while.

I stand in the sewing room for ages trying to come up with ideas but it's as though all the designs and plans which normally bubble around in my head have vanished. Was I even ever creative? Roslyn used to joke she was one with the flair and for the first time ever, I think she's right. Why else would my mind be blank?

Eventually I tinker a bit more with the dress I started earlier in the month. It is too special to pull apart and Aunt Beryl would be disappointed as the fabric is expensive. I'll never wear it but there's no reason it couldn't become part of a fashion line. At least this is a positive thought and I spend an hour working on the bodice until I'm happy with it. Then I cover it with a sheet and tidy up after myself.

As I near the kitchen, I hear sobs and run in.

'Auntie? Did you hurt yourself?'

She's at the kitchen sink, her hands in soapy water and her shoulders shaking. I gently lift her hands and check them then use a tea towel to dry her fingers. Tears pour down her face and I don't know what to do. I can't recall ever seeing Aunt Beryl cry.

'Sit down and I'll make tea.'

It seems to be what people do when someone's upset and she nods and sinks onto a chair at the kitchen table, dabbing her eyes with a handkerchief while I put the kettle on. By the time I bring the pot and cups over, her eyes are dry and she gives me a smile which I'm sure is just to reassure me. We have some tea and I must look anxious because she squeezes my hand.

'Goodness knows what set me off, JoJo, but all of a sudden it hit me that I can't just pop over to your house to see Molly.'

Oh... poor Auntie. She and Mum are so close and this is the first time they've not both lived in the same town. Of course it will be hard for her, and Mum. And then if I do decide to move to Queensland, she won't have any family here.

'I know you'll miss your parents as well, darling. At least you've got your studies and will soon be back in Melbourne and busy with Roslyn. But then you'll be back between semesters and actually living with me and I can't tell you how much I'm looking forward to having you here.'

I open my mouth to admit I'm thinking about following Mum and Dad but Auntie looks happier again so I nod and the subject changes.

Walking home later with a basket filled with meals for the fridge and cake and pies, I feel so confused. This town is my home. The place my heart belongs and although I enjoy being in Melbourne for university, I also count down the days until I'm back here where the sea spray makes my lips salty and the ocean is my playground. Everything is planned for a life here as an adult. Aunt Beryl is here and so are my friends.

I stop at the empty shop Roslyn and I like the most. Over the years it has been a café and a shoe shop and a travel agency. None of them lasted all that long and the 'For Lease' sign across the window has been there long enough to have faded and chipped.

Some people say the shop is out of the way and easy to forget because it is around the corner from most of the shops but I think the right business has yet to open there.

'Except it might not be ours now,' I whisper. Chances are Roslyn will tell me she doesn't want to continue our plans, now she is busy with Lucas. Or if she does, it will be alone. That makes me too sad to consider. If only I knew what went so horribly wrong.

After a morning of wind and rain, the weather reverts to sunshine and blue skies during the afternoon. I've finished packing everything other than my day-to-day things like clothes, and enough stuff in the kitchen to make and eat meals. Aunt Beryl is repainting the room I'm moving into and won't let me help because she wants to surprise me. She thinks it will be ready this time next week, which is only a few days before I head to Melbourne. And the real estate agent has put the big 'For Sale' sign out the front and already two families have had a look through.

My life is upside down. I'm living in an empty house surrounded by my mostly packed belongings. I have no idea where I'll be in a month. Or if I will be alone. The only times I've seen Roslyn, she's been driving her mother somewhere or other. Both of us have our licences but owning a car isn't necessary – or hasn't been until now, for me anyway. I always borrowed Mum's car if I needed but hers is now at their new home, same as Dad's. Roslyn's mother gets nervous with other people driving so it is weird seeing Roslyn behind the wheel so much but I am caring less and less each day about what goes on next door.

Yet here I am staring in the direction of her house from my bedroom window, again.

It annoys me being so needy and I change into my swimwear, shorts and halter top, pulling my hair into a ponytail. My beach bag is always ready so I slip on some shoes and at the last minute collect my camera. Because I'll have it at the beach I take an airtight, waterproof container Dad gave me from our supply for the kayaks. It fits the camera perfectly and is bright yellow so easy to spot.

I head to Willow Bay because I want to sit under the trees in between some long swims. Hopefully I can take some good photos of the boats and birds and the water and the thought cheers me up immensely. Once I get the film developed I'll have the best ones duplicated and send them to Mum and Dad. But it is a bit disappointing because the tide is high and the water is churning, with waves coming halfway up the beach. Out further the boats move with the heavy swell, slowly pitching side to side and straining against their moorings.

I don't mind being out in rough weather in a boat or even a kayak but not swimming so much if I'm alone. And I can't go and get my kayak because it is another thing that's now in Queensland so I have it to use when I visit later in the year. If I can't swim today then I'll take photos.

'What great weather!'

I hadn't noticed Trent, who must have followed me up from town. He has a backpack on and carries a bottle of water.

'I hoped to swim today.'

'It'll settle. Come to the boat and have some of the custard tart I just bought. No way I'll eat it all myself but it looked too good to leave at the bakery.' He's at his dinghy and begins to pull it into the water. 'You're not scared of the waves are you?'

I sling my beach bag on my shoulder and help him push the dinghy out. Good thing I don't get seasick because the small boat gets tossed around more than I expected, but Trent is a strong rower and gets us to his yacht safely. Climbing aboard offers its own challenges but apart from most of my hair coming out of its ponytail and being somewhat wet from the spray, I'm fine.

We share custard tart and cola and I take photos. At first Trent is a bit edgy about my camera. He says not to take any photos of the boat so I turn the lens to the shore and the other boats. After patiently waiting for a seagull to land on a nearby boat, I get a perfect shot of it and then Trent tells me to pose and he takes some pictures of me. When I get the camera back there's only one shot left so I pretend I'm putting it away and when his attention is elsewhere, quickly use the last one on him.

He's right about the swell settling and I get a chance to swim around the boat for a bit. Trent stays onboard. He says he has to write a letter and when I climb back on board, he has it in an envelope ready to post.

'I'm going back to shore now. Can you get ready to leave?'

I'm drying my hair. 'Sure. I'll just use the bathroom first.' I take my beach bag which has a comb in it and hurry below.

After using the bathroom I quickly comb my hair and try to put it back in the ponytail but the hairband is wet which makes it tricky.

'Joanna? Can we please go.'

It is more a command than request and I yell that I'm coming and shove my towel and comb in the bag and run up the steps.

We walk into town together and he holds my hand for a bit, not like a boyfriend but as if something is upsetting him and I'm some kind of comfort. At the road where he needs to turn to go to the post office, he releases my hand and gives me the strangest look.

'You know, sooner or later I'll be leaving so why don't you come with me?'

'Go with you? Where?'

'Everywhere. There's not a lot holding you here and we get on so well. I like having you around.'

'But you said I'm not girlfriend material.'

He grins. 'You're not. But you are a friend. We'd have fun. Sometimes I get busy with... business. But it's the best way to see the world, so think about it?'

I tell him I will and we part ways. His life is too transient for me. Trent doesn't care about places or people or settling down. It is all about adventure and travel and surfing and whatever this business of his is. His midnight meeting the other night still makes me uneasy although I can't imagine what he would be involved with. Surely nothing illegal or wrong.

At the next corner something makes me glance back.

Trent is still standing where I left him, watching me.

TWENTY-FOUR

NOW

Joanna woke several times during the night, even getting up once to check the house was locked. She felt as though she'd dozed rather than slept, her mind going over the events of the previous day until it was a muddled mess.

With her first coffee of the day made, she took the small photo album onto the balcony and went through it again.

The photos were all taken by Roslyn's camera and at first glance were a random mix across the final summer Joanna lived in Rivers End. There were two of *Spee-Dee-One*, the other being a wider shot which included all the boats in the bay. On the back of the photo was the date, which was the day the yacht was last seen.

Joanna hadn't been on the beach during the day on that date. Only in the evening before Trent ferried her across to his yacht for dinner.

No wonder Roslyn had made the comment the other night about there being ten boats one day and nine the next. It was easy to count them in the photograph. The closer up image didn't give Joanna any new information but the name of the boat was clear. Had Roslyn had a genuine reason for the photo? An underlying concern about Trent?

Knowing what she did now about Trent, Joanna couldn't believe he'd encouraged her visits to the boat. He'd felt safe having her there and liked her company... until that night. She must have come across as so naive. So unworldly.

Not anymore. Not after years around the fashion industry.

She stopped at a photo of Lucas. He was sitting with his cousin Salina and they were having a conversation. His face was strained. Not a sign of his ready smile. If anything, he looked miserable. Despite everything, it tugged at her. Where would their lives be today had he not turned his back on their fledgling relationship? Would they have married? But then Bobbie wouldn't exist, or his brothers.

It was a futile exercise, revisiting the past.

Joanna made a second coffee and finally opened the email app on her phone. Ted had left a second message overnight and she sighed and clicked on the first.

Hi Joanna,

Sorry to interrupt your holiday but I'm under some pressure to make a decision and it won't wait until you return.

I received an offer in writing which, quite frankly, made my eyes water. Well in excess of my expectations and more than Hazel and I need to retire on. She's urged me to accept it and if it wasn't for you, I would with no hesitation.

Although I can't reveal the details of the offer, I'm a man of my word and want to give you the opportunity to buy if you can come close to it. Your parents are friends of ours and I like to think you and I have a good relationship. You've been the biggest asset to the company and I've already told this other group they'd be wise to keep you on if they are the successful purchaser. I want your job to be secure, one way or another.

If you are serious about buying the company, send me your best offer.

Hope your holiday is relaxing.

Ted.

She almost spluttered her coffee out. Relaxing was the last word she'd use. Joanna opened the second message.

Me again,

I'll need your offer by close of business tomorrow.

Ted.

'So, my job is secure, one way or another? What cheek.'

For all she knew, the negotiations he was in might well include her staying in the employment of the company for a minimum time but it wasn't because he was looking out for her. No, Ted was smart enough to know her value. Joanna had some of the best connections with the international market in the country and a solid reputation for bringing new clients to him.

She already knew she couldn't match the offer he'd said made his eyes water.

The only decision she had to make was whether to meekly accept being shunted from boss to boss with no say in her future... or to find a new career. Joanna turned off her phone. She wasn't taking any further messages today.

. . .

'I'm so happy to see you!' Roslyn almost squealed when she noticed Joanna browsing the racks.

A couple of other customers looked around to see who she meant and Joanna tried to hide her face as it reddened. She'd never been good with unexpected attention. In a minute she was in the middle of a hug.

'I did hope you'd drop in.'

'Oddly enough... I want to buy some clothes.'

Roslyn's eyebrows shot up. '*My* clothes?' She stepped back.

'Unless you're stocking other designers?'

'As if. In that case, how may I help today?'

Her voice was warm and genuinely interested and Joanna had the strangest compulsion to ask for Roslyn's full attention to buy an entire summer wardrobe. How interesting to be a customer in the shop she'd expected to co-own and be served with such grace by the person who should have been her business partner. Any resentment was gone. Joanna was in admiration and knew why this little boutique away from the main shopping strip was such a success.

People matter.

Except, she didn't matter to Ted now. She was a commodity.

I'm too old for that rubbish.

Pretending she was indeed a new customer, Joanna nodded. 'I might have a look first.'

'Please do. I'm always floating around so call out when you'd like to try something on, or if you need any assistance.'

With a beautiful smile, Roslyn wandered away to check another customer.

Joanna shopped at a lot of boutiques as well as franchises and department stores. She had a budget to do so each year and made it her business to understand what customers wanted. And what shops wanted.

She selected several pieces to try on, confident of the fit but wanting to see herself in them. The changing rooms were spacious with multiple mirrors, several hooks, good seating and importantly, decent lighting. Joanna was a firm believer in making the customer comfortable *and* able to accurately see what they were buying. No shadowy stalls or misleading mirrors for her.

After a few minutes Roslyn tapped on the door. 'Just me. How is the sizing? Are you happy with the colours or can I bring you something different?'

'Help me decide.' Joanna opened the door and stepped out. She did a dramatic whirl, loving the feel of the silky material against her bare legs. The dress she wore was similar to the one she'd admired on Roslyn the other night, but with a scooped neckline and in a dark forest green.

'Stop twirling around and let me see,' Roslyn commanded, although it was with a smile.

Joanna complied and Roslyn adjusted the neckline and stepped back.

'To get the most out of it I'd wear a bra with a bit of padding. Otherwise, I can easily alter the fit ever so slightly.'

'So can I.'

'No doubt. But I won't sell you the dress without it fitting perfectly.' There was a definite smirk on Roslyn's face. 'We offer a full service here for our valued clients and I can't have anyone thinking they can make their own alterations.'

'Hmm, in that case I might need to go to Green Bay to look for a dress—'

'Enough of that. Take this one off and let me bring another. I have one in mind.'

Amused by Roslyn's bossiness, Joanna removed the dress and waited in her lingerie, checking herself in the mirror. There was nothing wrong with her figure. She liked her bust size and wasn't in the habit of emphasising it.

'Okay, we both know you were always the one the boys

liked most but no need to flaunt it in here.' Roslyn still grinned and somehow it took the edge off the words. 'Let's see you in this. It is a little different from the other but the colour is perfect for your skin tone.' She hung a dress on a hook. 'Need help?'

'I need privacy.'

With a chuckle, Roslyn closed the door on the changing room. 'I know the dark green is good on you but this deep olive is better. No zips. Straight over the head.'

'I'm guessing I can work out how to dress myself.'

'Not if you won't optimise the first dress with a little enhancement. Or a nip and tuck of the needle and thread variety. Whoops, phone's ringing.'

When they were friends – when they were *best* friends, Roslyn used to complain about how pretty Joanna was. How boys would gravitate to her at parties and when they were living in Melbourne, flirt with her at a coffee shop or the like while ignoring her companion. Roslyn always laughed it off though, saying that looks don't last but personality did. Joanna had always thought of Roslyn as the one with confidence and such a beautiful face that there was no competition. Actually, she'd never tried to compete, but maybe Roslyn had.

This dress was lovely and Joanna couldn't believe she'd missed it. Like the other, it was ankle-length but sleeveless with thick straps over the shoulders and a straight neckline which was surprisingly flattering. The skirt was slightly pleated below the waist before finishing with a straight hemline. It was so simple yet managed to be both elegant and wear-anywhere at the same time.

'Oh, yes. So good on you.'

Joanna had left the changing room to stand in front of the much larger mirror at the end of the room.

'Dress it up with heels and diamonds for a gala dinner. Or sandals and chunky jewellery for an outdoor Christmas event.'

Roslyn looked over her shoulder, into the mirror. 'Do you like it, JoJo?'

'I love it.' She ran her hands down the fabric. 'It might have been made just for me.'

Meeting Roslyn's eyes in the mirror, Joanna saw a flash of sadness, even grief.

'Everything I make is for us both, you know. The shop. The name. All the clothes.'

Joanna had nothing to say. For the first time she was seeing the lost years from Roslyn's perspective.

'If you like this, then it is my gift to you.'

'I do like it but I'm buying it. You aren't running a charity.'

'See what else you like from your choices and I'll leave you in peace for a while.'

It took little time for Joanna to try on and approve the selection of tops and long pants she'd found and she carried them and the dress to the counter, waiting while a customer finished telling Roslyn a story about her visiting grandson.

There were no other customers once the lady left and Joanna laid her choices on the counter.

'You should increase your prices.'

'Not a chance. Not in Rivers End where half of my clients are on fixed incomes yet still budget to buy at least a piece or two every season.'

Smart. You really know your demographic.

'What about the other half?'

Roslyn rolled her eyes. 'Okay, for two weeks a year I increase my prices by thirty per cent because that's when the tourists arrive in force and my regulars are bunkering down to avoid them. And I almost sell out, even at the higher price, which then gives me a decent boost for the next few months and lets me add a nice bonus to my sewing team.'

'All of these clothes are made in Australia?'

The look Roslyn gave her was almost comical in its disbelief. 'All of these clothes are made in *Rivers End*, Joanna.'

'Like we always wanted.'

'Exactly as we always wanted. And I'd love to introduce you to more of the locals who love this boutique almost as much as I do. So how about it? Accept the dress as my gift to you and come to the community party tonight. Come and meet the people who have helped me achieve our dream.'

Although she'd finally accepted the gift of the dress, Joanna hadn't committed to the event in the evening. Roslyn had written the time and place on the back of a card and told Joanna not to worry about bringing a plate as there'd be plenty of food there. She'd mentioned it was an annual get-together held on the last Saturday of November as an early Christmas present to the town. It was sponsored by a dozen or so retailers and in its seventh year, but in a new location for the first time.

The feeling of being pulled back into the local community was double-edged.

For years she'd mourned losing the close-knit group she'd known her whole life. Leaving so abruptly, Joanna hadn't even said goodbye to most of her friends nor contacted them once she was settled in her new life. It was as though the only way to avoid falling apart was to make a clean break. Only Aunt Beryl kept her connected to the town.

And that awful night with the yacht.

She wouldn't even be here had the boat stayed submerged.

Joanna stood at the edge of the garden, gazing down at the small beach. The water called her and the sand was deserted. Surely she wouldn't be so unlucky as last time if she went for a swim? But the idea of Lucas appearing again put her off and with a deep sigh, she returned to the house.

What he'd said on the sand still played on her mind. His

intense stare and words about her leaving, again. Running away... was that what he'd said?

Breaking her earlier promise about no more messages today, she turned the phone on. Nothing more from Ted but she reread his words. Just over a day to decide her future. There was no ignoring something so significant. Not like nineteen-year-old Joanna who fled because her emotions overtook her logic. This time she had to be in charge of her life.

TWENTY-FIVE

Even had Joanna not been given the address of the community event, she'd have easily found it. Almost every shop had a poster in its window – although she hadn't noticed them until now as she passed three in a row. But she'd hardly been looking for things to do in town, other than a bit of shopping and the dinners out.

Until almost six she'd had no plans to attend, focusing on the research into the shipwreck. Now that more pieces had washed up, local press interest in the story had increased and the online newspaper was updated with speculation about the forecast for upcoming storms and the potential for more flotsam. This time tomorrow, the first storm would have come and gone, according to reports, and there'd be members of the team out in force on the beach as soon as it was safe.

And this time tomorrow, I'll have made a choice about my future.

Except... what if the storm raised the wreck completely?

She'd been so caught up with her history with Roslyn that she'd dropped the ball about the reason she was here – to see for herself that this wreckage did not come from Trent's yacht. This outcome which would reassure her he had simply sailed away as he'd planned and was living his life somewhere else, even if not a life she could endorse.

But more and more evidence was piling up to the contrary and her mindset was changing. What if she'd caused the boat to sink? There was every chance her future might actually be out of her hands. As frightening as this was to consider, Joanna would face whatever came.

But knowledge was power and where better to get more information than from the community itself? Joanna was well versed in the art of listening and if she was honest, yearned for some company.

A few streets back from the main shopping area was a new complex which took up a full corner and covered several acres. Joanna remembered it as a big paddock but now it was fronted by a huge single-level building with a sign:

Rivers End Assisted Living Community.

A family a bit ahead of her turned at a driveway past the main entrance and when she reached the same point, there was a colourful sign pointing behind the building. The driveway opened up to a large grassed area so beautifully decorated, Joanna stopped in awe.

Fairy lights were strung in a criss-cross pattern between trees and what looked like an indoor swimming pool and recreational area. There were garden beds filled with flowers and benches scattered around and all were sparkling with lights. A fountain cascaded into a pool which was lit from within. The main building and the pool building were connected by a wide covered walkway where there was enough space for a live Christmas tree, all twinkling with lights. How pretty this would look once it was completely dark. Joanna had to control a sudden urge to clap her hands.

Near the Christmas tree, several people were setting up two large tables with red tablecloths. Christmas music played through small speakers. Some people had picnic blankets on the ground while others congregated around small tables dotted around the area. People of all ages mingled and laughter filled the air.

This was so like the street parties when she was a child and teen. Families banding together to make the street pretty with paper lanterns, food at the end of the cul-de-sac for all to share while people's decorations and Christmas trees shone through their windows. It was a time for people to relax and enjoy the evening without the pressures of a family dinner or being alone. Often, extended family and friends would attend and always there was laughter and singing. Joanna had never experienced anything like those evenings since leaving the town.

'Come and join us, dear. We have a spare seat.'

A woman beckoned from a small table nearby. She sat with two other women around her age, which Joanna guessed was mid to late seventies. A Cavalier King Charles spaniel was curled up beneath the table.

Joanna glanced around. The event was getting busier by the minute and from the direction of the driveway, the familiar voice of Lucas in the distance made up her mind.

'Are you sure?'

'You looked all alone there but had such a sweet smile as you took in our lovely home. I'm Bess. This is Annette and this is Marge. We live here and have been friends forever.'

'You do exaggerate. Nobody is friends forever,' Marge said. She was thin and had quite a stern expression, with salt-and-pepper hair cut in a severe bob.

'Well we three have *always* been friends. Annette and I since primary school and then Marge came along in our twenties, so not quite forever but—'

'It feels like it.'

Marge sounded so mournful that the other women laughed.

Joanna warmed to them immediately. She sat on the spare chair and the small dog got up to say hello. 'Well, aren't you a sweetheart?' She scratched under his chin, smiling at his big, brown eyes.

'That is James Regal and he loves everyone,' Marge announced.

'Not everyone, dear,' Bess said. 'He's never liked any of the Hammonds, although he tolerates young Mick.'

Hammonds?

'He has good taste. That family are bad news, with the exception of Mick, and better to avoid.' Annette glanced at Joanna. 'We are being so rude talking about people behind their backs, though; we'd better stop. What is your name?'

'Oh, I am sorry. I'm Joanna Johnson.'

All three peered at her, leaning forward.

'Goodness me, Molly's little girl, we knew you as a child! How are your parents?'

There was another animated conversation about how each woman knew Molly and Malcolm and as interesting as it was, Joanna's attention drifted to another table, where Lucas and Bobbie had settled with two teen boys, who she assumed were Cal and Mattie. A woman was with them and there was a lot of laughing.

Of course he has someone in his life.

Why would she have thought otherwise? And why did it even matter? He'd walked away from her, even if he did accuse her of being the one to leave. Joanna didn't want a relationship with him. It was normal to have latent feelings from a past relationship and that was all it was. Yet she couldn't help watching Lucas. His ready smile. His handsome face made more attractive by age, if that was possible.

Bobbie noticed her and jumped up. It took him only seconds to race over the grass and throw his arms around her in one of those heartfelt hugs Joanna was getting accustomed to receiving. 'Joanna! I'm so, so, so, so happy you're here!' He finally let go and grinned at the ladies around the table. 'Hello, I'm Bobbie.'

'Nice to see you, Bobbie.' Annette smiled. 'I think we have met once or twice.'

His face screwed up as if trying to remember but then he grabbed Joanna's hand. 'Come and say hello. Come and meet everyone. We left Perry at home though.'

'Do you mind if I sit here a while? I'm sure there's plenty of time to meet everyone and I'm just getting to know these lovely ladies.'

'Okies. Bye, everyone.'

With his arm held straight up and his hand waving, Bobbie ran back to his family.

'He only knows one speed,' Bess said. 'Such a sweet child.'

Lucas looked up as Bobbie reached him and his eyes met Joanna's. She couldn't break the connection but he did, when the woman with the family spoke. But a moment later, she felt his eyes on her again.

'You really should meet Lucas,' Annette said.

'I met him when he first arrived in Rivers End back in 1999.' Joanna hadn't meant to say it aloud.

All three women were gazing at her, expecting some other revelation, no doubt. She shrugged. 'I was friends with his cousin, Salina. And it was a long time ago.'

'He is the best physiotherapist I've ever had. *And* easy on the eye.' Bess turned to wave in his direction.

Marge tapped her on the hand. 'Good grief, you are incorrigible.'

That didn't dampen Bess's spirits in the least as she settled back in her seat. 'Moving here was such a good idea. Not only a lovely community and such delicious food but we get wonderful care, including our very own physiotherapist.'

You always hoped to work with older people. Look at you achieving your dreams. Everything you wanted came true.

The sudden pride for him disappeared like a puff of smoke. Lucas had accomplished what he'd set out to do. Roslyn as well.

And I'm losing my career, which wasn't even the one I wanted.

After a main meal, dessert was announced and the ladies tried to race each other to the tables. Joanna excused herself. There were visitor restrooms in the main building and she hid for a while, reapplying makeup and trying to talk herself into staying longer to gather information about the wreck, if anyone was willing to talk about it.

Bess, Annette, and even Marge were all so sweet and friendly but spent more time continuing their amusing bickering than talking about other subjects. They weren't particularly interested in the shipwreck and when Joanna raised it, Marge cryptically declared they'd had enough of shipwrecks and treasure hunts. At one point, Roslyn stopped at the table and hugged all four of them before telling the older ladies to look after her best friend while she was busy with the other traders. They'd taken it quite literally, squabbling over who would get more food for Joanna until she got some herself. Deep inside, she'd felt the strangest mix of sadness and joy. Did Roslyn truly think of her as her best friend?

Another woman came in to use the restroom and it was only when she emerged to wash her hands that Joanna realised she was Lucas's friend. Date. Girlfriend?

'You're Joanna?'

'Er. Yes.'

'Thank you for rescuing Perry. Bobbie can't stop talking about you. I'm Wanda.'

'It was my pleasure. Nice to meet you.'

Wanda used paper towel to dry her hands, gazing at Joanna as if sizing her up. Did she know about the past relationship and worry Joanna might be here to pursue Lucas?

'I'm Bobbie's mum. And Cal and Mattie's. Lucas is my ex.'

Oh.

'None of my business of course, and he'd be mortified if he knew I was saying this. But he never understood what happened all those years ago. Why you turned your back on him.'

'Sorry, what?'

'I'm not trying to cause trouble but he once thought the two of you... okay, not my place. But you went away out of the blue, then came back a week later, then left again and I really believe you should talk to him, because he has lived all these years thinking he did something wrong.'

Joanna couldn't have answered, even if she knew what to say. Her throat constricted and her legs felt shaky.

Wanda tossed the paper towel away. 'I have to collect the kids as they're back with me for the next week, so there's nothing stopping you from knocking on Lucas's door to apologise. Anyway, nice meeting you.'

As the door closed behind Wanda, Joanna gripped the edge of the basin. What had just happened?

She couldn't stay here now.

Not at the wonderful Christmas party.

Not in Rivers End.

Joanna stepped out of the restroom and looked around. The front door was the quickest way out. She hurried across to it and pushed but nothing happened. It must be locked after a certain time. Nobody was in this vast lobby, with its water feature and long reception desk and sense of calm and welcome.

I'm not calm and I'm definitely not welcome. And I'm supposed to apologise?

She sank onto a chair.

Why would Lucas have thought for even a minute that she had left town just after their kiss? And why did it sound familiar?

All those years ago, on the beach in Willow Bay, Joanna had mustered up her courage to look for Lucas and ask what had gone wrong between them. Salina had been surprised to see her.

'*When did you get back, JoJo?*'

'*Back from where?*'

'*Queensland.*'

'*I haven't been anywhere.*'

Salina had frowned. 'Okay. We all thought you'd decided to move to Queensland with your parents. Roslyn told us so.'

'Roslyn told them that?' she whispered.

'Oh there you are! I was looking everywhere.'

As though summoned by Joanna's memories, Roslyn hurried over with two glasses of sparkling wine.

'I'm free now and thought we could sit with Lucas and properly catch up now Wanda and the kids have left. And I'm starving, so let's go eat dessert.' She stopped in front of Joanna, holding out one of the glasses.

'Did you tell everyone I'd moved to Queensland?'

Roslyn blinked, her face blank. 'Huh?'

'Does Lucas think I deliberately left without saying anything and effectively broke up with him by my absence? You told me that, in hindsight, you'd been a terrible friend, so is that why? You took advantage of me being busy helping Mum and Dad pack and made up a story so he wouldn't come looking for me, and then somehow twisted things until he thought I'd lost interest or something?'

What had he said on the beach the other day when she was walking away?

'*Leave, JoJo. You don't have conversations. You just leave, every single time.*'

Roslyn sat beside her. 'Have some wine, Joanna, and we can talk.'

'I don't want wine. I want the truth.'

After placing the glasses on a low table, Roslyn tried to take Joanna's hand, but she pulled it away.

'Alright. Here's the truth.' Roslyn had paled but she lifted her chin. 'I was losing my mother. On top of that, I was losing *your* parents, who were the closest thing I had to family other than Mum and because you were so close to them, this fear...' she put both hands over her heart, 'deep and constant fear, drove me kind of nuts because I really thought you'd decide to leave Rivers End sooner rather than later to follow them north. Then who would I have? Meanwhile you were so happy and full of yourself because a boy liked you. I just was hurting, and I wanted *one* thing to be good in my life.'

'So you went after the first boy I ever dated? How was that possible from my best friend in the world?' Joanna struggled to keep her voice low.

'What I did was horrible and I can never repair the damage. But you wanted the truth and I'm explaining where my head was back then. I didn't really set out to make you think he and I were an item and quite honestly, JoJo, we weren't. Certainly not from his side. We were friendly but he never returned a kiss. Never. Remember that night I came to warn you about Trent?'

'Of course I do. For a moment I actually believed you did care about me.'

'I was there intending to apologise for my lie about you going to Queensland. I missed you so much and by then I'd realised I was hurting Lucas as well because I'd mentioned how career-focused you were, knowing you'd told him about the internship. But then I saw the book on the counter. You'd folded the corner of the page for a university in Queensland.'

Roslyn had been flicking through it when Joanna caught up

in the kitchen. And that was when she'd seen the ring on her finger.

'You told me Lucas gave you the ring.'

'No. No, Joanna, I said Lucas was so sweet. And I get that it misled you and after you threw me out I went home and cried myself to sleep over it. Mum gave the ring to me. It belonged to her mother.'

Joanna stood and took a few steps away to stare through the large window into the dusk. The glass reflected Roslyn and Joanna watched her through a haze of conflicting emotions. The woman was still the same person she'd loved her entire life until that summer. She probably never stopped loving her, although the pain of betrayal overrode anything else. Yet Joanna had lost so much because of Roslyn's actions, no matter how compelling the motivation. Through this all came a realisation.

I was at fault as well.

She'd been so caught up in her feelings for Lucas and her parents' move that she'd not listened to her instincts that something was wrong in Roslyn's life. And now she had similar instincts and still had let it slide, so maybe she wasn't the friend she'd believed she was, either. And never once had she gone to Lucas and asked him, to his face, whether their short relationship was over. She'd been afraid of conflict and sorry for herself.

'JoJo? From the bottom of my heart I apologise for everything I did. These last few days I've had you back in my life and found a happiness I never thought I would feel again. I know you're leaving again soon and I guess this time it is for good and this is too much to ask...'

The reflection of Roslyn stood, swaying that little bit again like Joanna had seen before. With her hands clasped together, Roslyn took a step forward then stopped and her head dropped.

'Please forgive me.'

As the weight she'd carried for decades fell away, Joanna turned to face Roslyn.

'I do, Rossie. I do forgive you.'

TWENTY-SIX

'Please come back to the party,' Roslyn said.

They'd sat quietly together for a while, gripping each other's hands, with occasional smiles and a few tears. Nothing more was said. For Joanna, there was so much to say but not now. She was drained and Roslyn was pale. Tomorrow she'd ask what was going on to make her friend sway sometimes and lose colour. Tonight was not the time.

'I don't think I will, Roslyn. Between Wanda confronting me in the restroom and... this, I need a chance to process.'

'Wanda?'

'She said I need to apologise to Lucas for leaving him without an explanation.'

Roslyn's mouth dropped open and her eyes glistened again.

'Don't you dare cry any more tonight. Whatever Wanda believes, or Lucas, it won't affect us again. We've been apart for too long and I... I like having you back. I want you in my life.' Joanna gave her a quick hug and then got to her feet. 'Go and enjoy the evening and if you don't mind telling Marge, Bess and Annette I enjoyed meeting them?'

'Are you driving?'

'Walking.'

'I can drop you home.'

'Thanks, but the walk will clear my head. Goodnight.'

Joanna hurried out of the building, slipping around the outside to reach the footpath. Rather than go through the shopping area, she took the first street on the right, leaving behind the music and lights and laughter.

There were only a few homes along here, all on the town side. She passed the church with its graveyard in darkness, then the community hall which had its lights on. For a moment she paused at the driveway, tempted to see if the door was open and perhaps she could take another look at the flotsam.

You have enough to worry about tonight.

She kept walking, trying to keep those worries at bay until she was home and changed into something comforting to wear, with a cup of herbal tea and a chance to think about her future in the quiet of the beach house.

It was only when she turned into the road to Aunt Beryl's place that she hesitated.

Joanna stood still, listening to her surroundings and letting her eyes adjust to the darkness here where there were no streetlights. Lucas's house was the closest, but invisible through the forest, so she might have been miles from any habitation rather than a few hundred metres from home.

A car suddenly turned into the street and she moved to one side to let it pass, watching its taillights before it disappeared down a driveway.

She covered the rest of the distance quickly, breathing a quick sigh of relief when she was at the end of the road. Something had spooked her but there was no logic behind it. The sooner she was behind a locked door the better. She reached for the house keys as she passed the carport then abruptly stopped at the bottom of the steps. The overhead light wasn't on, yet it was activated by motion and solar powered. It never failed to respond.

Joanna dug around in her bag for her phone and was about to turn on the flashlight when a distinct footstep on the concrete pad in the carport froze her in place.

'I wouldn't do that. No, don't turn around.'

The voice was male. Almost snarling.

Her finger hovered over the app as he continued.

'Time to leave town if ya know what's good for ya.'

'What do you mean? Who are you?'

'Shut up!'

All she had were her house keys – hooked over a finger – and her phone. The latter might give her a second to get away.

'Be gone by first light tomorrow. Do ya hear me? I know what ya did. I saw ya kill a man. And I'll tell the police if ya don't leave.'

This can't be happening.

There was another footstep, closer.

Joanna touched the app and spun round as her flashlight turned on, pointing it in the direction of the voice. For an instant she saw a man, hands up as brilliant light shone into his eyes, and then he was moving away.

Headlights swept across the bushes along the driveway.

It was all she could do not to drop the phone. If this was someone else coming to threaten her...

She threw herself toward the steps, tripping on the bottom one, her phone going flying as she grabbed for anything to stop the fall. Both her hands found the top step and a piercing pain made her cry out.

'Joanna! It's me. Lucas.'

And then there were firm hands on her waist, supporting her so she could stand and when she did, warm arms enveloped her and held her tight.

. . .

'You should see a doctor.' Lucas had cleaned the glass out of the palm of her left hand and was closely inspecting it.

'I am. You're a doctor.'

'Not the right kind and you know that.' His voice was gruff in a way she'd never heard. 'Last tetanus shot?'

'Everything is up to date.'

'How can you be sure?'

'Because I travel a lot and need to know these things. Ouch.'

'Sorry. Will you please see someone in the morning?' He began to dress the cuts which fortunately weren't terribly deep, and were restricted to the fleshy part near her thumb.

But that man said I have to leave by first light.

Joanna made a weird sound which was from trying to control a hysterical giggle.

'Deep, slow breaths. You've had a bit of a shock, falling in the dark like that.'

He was so close to her she could easily have touched his face with her spare hand. Even moved her face enough to kiss his lips.

You really are in a state of shock.

The man in the shadows had terrified her. Not just by breaking the light bulb and waiting for her in the dark, or his dire warning to leave, but the content of the threat. She was sure she hadn't killed Trent but how did anyone else know a thing about the night she'd run for her life? And why wouldn't he simply go to the police? Why hadn't he gone to the police all those years ago?

'What frightened you, Joanna?'

Lucas had finished and was tidying after himself.

'I'll do that. But thank you.'

'Don't change the subject. Your aunt keeps a decent first aid kit and I'm returning it to order.' He glanced at her with a small smile. 'Come on, tell me why you were shining that flashlight all over the place when I drove in.'

There wasn't a chance she'd tell the truth. He thought badly enough of her already, quite apart from knowing what he'd do if she said someone just threatened her. He'd call the police himself but whether it would be to have her arrested or to find the man was anyone's guess.

'I thought I heard something. Probably a possum.'

'Did you see anything?'

'You did notice the light over the front door is smashed to pieces? Bit hard to see in the dark.'

'Except you had your flashlight on. I'll put this away.'

Lucas left the bathroom and after giving the bath a longing look, imagining it filled with bubbles, Joanna followed. He was in the kitchen, closing the cupboard where the first aid kit belonged. Her phone was on the counter and she checked the screen.

'Think it landed face up,' Lucas said. 'Shall I make you a coffee? Or tea? Or pour a brandy? That might help the nerves.'

Joanna glanced at her hands, one bandaged, both trembling a little. She hid them behind her back. 'There's plenty of red wine. Auntie prefers that. Would you like one, or...'

'Or?'

'I don't remember ever seeing you drink alcohol actually. You always offered to be designated driver.'

His eyebrows raised briefly. 'Now that is an odd thing to remember. I would love a glass of red, thank you.'

A few minutes later, settled on the balcony, Lucas poured two glasses of wine from the bottle Joanna had selected. She should have said no. For him to leave. There was so much more to factor in now. More than just her career. Or her rekindled friendship with Roslyn. A sinister threat added a dark element which needed her attention.

'Does the hand hurt much?'

'Hmm? Oh. Not too much. And thank you, gosh, how rude of me. Thank you for literally picking me up and then fixing me.'

And holding me against you until I could breathe again.

He lifted his glass. 'To fixing Joanna.'

'I guess I can drink to that. Cheers.'

His eyes were impossible to read. The overhead light was off so as not to attract insects but there was enough coming from the living room to see his face, albeit in a shadowy way. There was an air of mystery about him and it was surreal to be so close to Lucas after so many years. Joanna was still attracted to him. She ached to be in his arms again. And she could never tell him such a thing.

Lightning flashed in the far distance and they both turned to watch.

'A few hours yet,' Lucas said. 'It'll build for a while before landfall. Not nearly humid enough.'

It was good that the people of the community could enjoy their Christmas event without rain and make it home safely.

'Do you think more pieces will wash up? From whatever is submerged, wherever it is?'

'I do. And I hope something will identify the boat and put all the speculation to rest.' Lucas sipped on the wine, his eyes on Joanna again. 'Everyone has a theory, it seems.'

'And what is your theory?'

She held her breath. Surely he didn't feel the same as Roslyn and believe Trent's yacht met with disaster and was only now coming back to haunt the town?

'I prefer facts. Most likely it was deliberately scuttled and claimed under insurance as a stolen craft and we'll never know who was behind it. Have you been back to Rivers End beach since I saw you on the jetty?'

Where I refused to talk to you and dived into the sea?

Thank goodness the darkness wouldn't show the heat rising

in her face. She'd been so abrupt with him, yet he'd done nothing wrong. 'A few times. I talked to Mick Hammond late one evening and he showed me some of the pieces he'd collected.'

'Do you want to help look after the storm? Our team could use another set of eyes.'

Of course she did. What better way to see what, if anything, washed up? Unless something appeared which incriminated her.

'Don't feel pressured, Joanna. Not everyone is keen to wander along a beach straight after a storm.' Lucas had the smallest smile playing on his lips. He knew she loved the power of the sea and was unafraid of the weather. Or, he used to know.

'I'll be there.'

'Do you want me to call once we get things set up? The marquee is down in anticipation of the storm front.' He leaned forward a little, his eyes searching her face. 'That is if you don't mind me having your number.'

A little shiver went up her spine. A nice one. Had he not completely given up on her?

'Lucas? Why *are* you here? Why did you leave the party and drive here tonight?'

Their glasses were almost empty and Lucas refilled them both after a glance at Joanna resulted in a nod to go ahead. He held his, gently swirling the crimson liquid for a moment before giving her his full attention. 'I need answers, Joanna. I came for answers.'

For the longest time, Joanna stood at the balcony railing just staring into the night. Lucas hadn't moved or spoken since he'd said he was here for answers and his patience must be wearing thin. Yet he was still there at the table. She heard the small creaks from the timber boards as he adjusted his position and the quiet clink as his wine glass was lowered to the table.

All these years apart. Both believing the other had simply given up on their developing relationship while all along, someone they both cared for was manipulating the situation.

'I've forgiven her,' Joanna said.

'Forgiven who?'

Joanna returned to the table. Whatever needed saying, however this ended, was overdue and inevitable.

'Roslyn asked me to forgive her tonight and I did. Ask your questions, Lucas. But you may need to ask her some as well.' She pushed the wine glass away. No more tonight. Nothing could deaden the pain in her hand or her heart.

Lucas did the same with his glass. 'It was Roslyn who suggested I come and see you. Initially she said she was worrying about you walking home on your own, but then she told me that not everything she'd said all those years ago was true. That she'd made poor decisions and dragged you and me into her own world of pain.'

'She said that?'

He nodded. 'She also hugged me and said she'll understand if I never speak to her again. Have I been mistaken all this time? About you and me?'

Joanna's heart was going too fast.

'After our date... our perfect evening by the river and strolling around the town and talking about our hopes and dreams... and you kissed me... it was as though it never happened. I didn't see you again for days except once, at a distance, and you didn't wave back so I figured you hadn't seen me but then there you were with Roslyn.'

'But you went to Queensland the very next day.'

'No I did not. I was at home helping my parents pack.'

His visible confusion pulled at her.

'I came to your house the next afternoon to see if you'd like to go swimming because I was keen to get my confidence up in the sea. I knocked and nobody answered and then Roslyn came over from her place to tell me... oh.' Lucas slumped back in his chair. 'She told me you'd gone ahead to ready the new house before you officially moved. That you'd decided to go to a Queensland university and pursue your career alone. Why would she do that?'

'I didn't know any of this until recently, but her mother was terribly ill. I think she was an emotional mess and she wanted something good in her life.'

'Me?'

Joanna nodded.

Lucas ran a hand through his hair. 'When you appeared at Willow Bay suddenly and Roslyn denied saying you'd left town it made no sense. Good grief. Why didn't I question her? Or talk to you?'

Tears brimmed in Joanna's eyes but she kept eye contact with Lucas. 'Do you remember her kissing you on the jetty?'

'Sure and it was kind of weird. We'd hung out a couple of times, just talking, and she wanted to wait there. Said something about some sailboats going past she liked watching so I was looking for them when she suddenly kissed me. Then she laughed and said she kisses all her friends.'

A tear escaped and rolled down Joanna's cheek but she barely noticed.

Lucas leaned forward and reached over the table to touch the tear, so tenderly that another followed. And another.

'That day? Roslyn asked me to meet her at the jetty and when I arrived, I was so happy you were there as well. My two favourite people. She looked at me then kissed you. It was like sending me a message and I was shocked and hurt.'

'I'm so angry with Roslyn right now.' His hand shifted, cupping her cheek. 'So you didn't walk away from us, did you?'

Joanna's hand covered his and she moved her face slightly to kiss his palm. 'We were both caught up in Roslyn's lies. I left because my best friend betrayed me and I believed there was no hope for a future with you.'

There were no more words to say. Not at that moment. Lucas came around the table and when Joanna rose, he held her against his chest until both their hearts were beating in time.

TWENTY-SEVEN

29 JANUARY 2000

I hang up from a long phone call with Mum and Dad. They've met some of the neighbours and have decided to build a coop and get chickens for fresh eggs and to keep the vegetable garden free of pests. Dad starts at his new job in a few days and Mum plans to look for a job soon. It was so good hearing their voices now they've got over the worst of the move. They sound happy.

If I move there, then maybe one day I will be happy again.

It would be completely different living in Queensland where I can study and find like-minded people to fill the void left by Roslyn. And Lucas.

Thinking about this makes me sad and I go to find my camera so I can take the film to be developed and then send some of the photos to my parents. The camera box isn't in its usual place then I remember I had it in my beach bag. I hadn't even taken out my wet clothes and everything smells bad so I throw everything washable into the machine and put the bag in the late afternoon sun to air.

But the camera isn't there.

After half an hour of fruitless searching I have no option but to go to Willow Bay. It had to have fallen out of the bag. I have a vague recollection of setting it down for a minute on the sand to help Trent drag his dinghy high up the beach.

All the way there I tell myself off for being so careless. The camera means a great deal to me and I have to find it. Dusk is falling as I jog past the empty carpark and reach the sand. I have a carry bag over my shoulder because the box with the camera is too large to fit in my normal handbag, and my housekeys and wallet are in the bottom, along with a towel, in case I end up getting too sandy or even wet.

A dinghy is heading in, but it isn't Trent's and I don't recognise the two people inside. There's a man who looks a bit younger than Dad, and a boy. I guess he's nine or ten. I don't pay them much attention as I begin to search. It is only when they climb out of the dinghy and leave it barely out of the waves as they trudge through the sand that I notice the man is carrying a large backpack. The kid looks unwell and he stops and vomits near a tree. The man laughs at him and says something about being a poor sailor. I'm doing my best to look as if I didn't see a thing because that's embarrassing and don't even glance their way until I'm sure they've gone. The boy is out of sight but the man has his hands on his hips and is watching me. I slip between some trees and hide for a few minutes because the beach doesn't feel safe like it usually does.

I can see the outline of the boats in the bay, even Trent's, which is the furthest out. There's a light on and he's standing on the stern and I think he's looking this way. The sunset behind him makes it all a bit hard to tell.

The little boat abandoned by those people is at risk of being washed off the shore so after checking that I'm alone, I run down and drag it up as high as I can. I know who this belongs to and it certainly wasn't those two. How rude to use someone else's property and then not even leave it where they found it.

None of this is helping me find my camera. It has to still be in its box, which is bright yellow and about half the size of a shoebox. At least I had the presence of mind to bring a flashlight and when I can't locate the box where it is light enough to see, I turn it on and begin checking around the trees. Someone might have found it and put it out of the reach of the sea. I go up and down the length of the trees then right up to the rocks at the end of the beach but there's nothing.

The only other place it might be is either in Trent's dinghy or on *Spee-Dee-One*. I had my beach bag with me when I used the bathroom last time I was onboard, so did it fall out?

I'll have to come back tomorrow and I'm so cross with myself and almost ready to cry.

'Joanna?'

I've been so intent on the ground that I hadn't seen his dinghy approach. He's standing knee-deep in water with a hand on the little boat and I go to meet him. A few days have passed since I saw him last and I'm not sure what his mood will be like.

'What are you looking for? I saw the light flashing around from the boat.'

'I've lost my camera.'

'Is it in a yellow dry box?'

'Have you found it?'

He's grinning. He actually looks happy and more relaxed than in ages.

'Pretty sure it's below deck. Same as some of mine.'

As relieved as I am, I can't believe he hasn't let me know before now. He knows where I live... I think.

'Oh, that's great news. It was a gift from my parents and I thought I'd lost it forever.'

'Jump in and we'll go get it.'

I glance at the sky. In a few minutes it'll be night and there's a lot of big clouds congregating along the horizon. Quite honestly, I'd prefer to go home and finish reading a paperback I've been enjoying and eat chocolate ice-cream.

'Storm is hours away. Tomorrow even. Or I can row back and get it if you want to wait but I'd love some company for a while. If you're up for it?'

'I'll come with you. Just for a bit though.'

'Jump in. I've got a lot to tell you.'

The camera is fine. I inspect it thoroughly then return it to its box and lock all the clamps which keep it airtight and waterproof, should I somehow manage to drop it on the way to shore. This is a lesson in responsibility and I won't make such a silly mistake again. I put it into the bottom of my bag. Like Trent said, it is similar to some of his. For the first time though, his normally chained and locked boxes are scattered around with a few having their lids open and nothing inside.

'I'm making pizza if you're hungry?'

While I've been checking the camera, Trent has turned on the small oven and taken ingredients from the fridge.

'I made pizza dough earlier and even if I do say so, my pizzas are world famous.'

'World famous? I see.'

He waggles a rolling pin at me until I laugh and agree to stay for dinner because now I'm here, it feels nice to have someone to talk to again.

'How can I help?'

'You can sit on my bed and chat. Would you like a beer? Or glass of wine?'

This is the first time in ages he's offered me anything other than water or cola and I've rarely seen him drink anything else either. I have had wine sometimes when out at dinner in a restaurant with my parents or sometimes in Melbourne, Roslyn and I had a cocktail if we were with a group from university.

Trent has a bottle in his hand, holding it up. 'This is Chianti, an Italian wine which goes well with rustic pizza.'

'What is rustic about your pizza?'

'Excellent question. Perhaps the shape isn't quite round. But it deserves a nice wine so is that a yes?'

'Yes, please.'

Why not? I'm an adult of legal age to drink. I live alone in a big house and it is beside the point that it doesn't belong to me and is up for sale. Maybe if I begin to think of myself as independent and mature then the other stuff won't hurt so much.

Trent doesn't have actual wine glasses so pours what looks like a lot into normal water glasses. We tap them together saying 'cheers', then I sit, cross-legged on the end of his bed with my bag beside me.

As he rolls out dough and then chops up tomato and onion and capsicum, Trent tells me he is going to leave Rivers End within a couple of days because he's concluded his business here.

'I'm going to go up the east coast. I might stop in Sydney briefly to see someone I know then will sail all the way to far north Queensland. How about it, Joanna? Travel with me and I'll drop you close to where your parents live.'

I sip the wine and it warms me.

He is smiling so much. Whatever was bothering him is gone. I like watching him cook. He enjoys it and soon the smell of pizza is making me so hungry that I drink my wine too fast.

'Shall we eat on deck and watch in case the storm suddenly turns?'

'Great idea.' I'd rather not be stuck here if it arrives too soon to get to shore.

He has a big tray and puts our pizza and plates on it. 'Can you grab the wine and glasses?'

We eat sitting on the bow. It isn't the easiest to get to when carrying stuff but once we sit, the tray acts like a little table.

The sky has the occasional flash of lightning in the distance. The air is increasingly steamy and I stop drinking the wine and go grab us both some bottled water. But Trent keeps filling his own glass with wine and he gets funnier by the minute, telling me about some of the places he's visited and making it sound like one long party. Hopefully he can still row me to shore, otherwise I'll row myself and bring the dinghy back tomorrow for him.

'Did you see the man and little boy earlier?' I take the last piece of pizza and bite into it. Trent really did a good job with the crust.

'Where?'

'In a dinghy which belongs to Mr Campbell's boat. They left it in the shallows without bothering to get it to a safer spot, so I did.'

Trent gulps the last of his wine then immediately refills it.

'Actually the man was kind of creepy, he stared at me for ages.'

'Forget about them.'

'But don't you think it is odd? I hope they weren't stealing from the other boats.'

'I should row you to shore. Storm's close.'

'Now? Oh, okay. I'll help take these below and give you a hand cleaning up.' I stand, adjusting my stance as the boat rocks.

'Leave it, Joanna.'

His mood has changed again and there's a sharp note in his voice.

My throat closes up and I kind of freeze in place. It's just like with my biological father when I was young. He'd be so sweet and loving then suddenly his face would become angry and then he'd start yelling. This will be the last time I hang out with Trent.

At first I don't think the wine has affected him at all because he gets to the stern without faltering, but then he seems to be struggling to untie the dinghy.

'Oh, my bag is downstairs. Be right back.'

Thank goodness I keep a hand on the rail as the boat lurches suddenly. A long rumble of thunder is followed by lightning, much closer than before. I get below fast. I just want my bag and to go home.

Some of his dry boxes have slid across the floor. I start to put them back and when I lift one, it opens and I gasp. There's packages inside. Wrapped little logs with thick tape around them holding something white. One falls out and when I pick it up, a trickle of powder appears from a tiny cut. Are these... drugs?

'Hurry up, Joanna.'

I drop the box when he yells and then there are footsteps as he comes down the steps.

Trent stops, his mouth open. Then he reaches the bottom in a second and starts putting the packages back in the box, even trying to scoop up the small pile of powder. He looks at me and I have never been so afraid in my life. His eyes are wild and his mouth is formed into a snarl.

I race up the steps, gripping the rail at the top when another wave tilts the boat.

'Stop. Why, Joanna? You can't leave now.'

He is right behind me when I reach the deck and his face is enraged. His hands reach for me and I push him away. He loses his balances and topples backwards, rolling down the steps to land with a sickening thud.

'Trent?' I go almost to the bottom of the steps. 'Trent, wake up.'

His arm suddenly snakes out and brushes my ankle and I scream and stumble over my own feet to get away. The dinghy is still tied up but my fingers can't loosen the knot. I go to the side of the boat and dive.

. . .

The first few seconds are the worst.

A shock of cold water. Sea water stinging my eyes and filling my nostrils. Legs kicking, forcing my body down and away from sight as fast as possible.

Where I can't be seen in the blackness of the sea.

I'm close to the sea bed and stay down as far as I can, swimming along the bottom until my lungs are ready to burst. I have to get away. I have to save myself.

When my air is gone I surface, gasping too loudly. Trent might hear and find me.

The air crackles with electricity and the water swells and swirls.

I rotate, frantically paddling on the spot as I get my bearings.

Dark shadowy hulls surround me. Other yachts moored close by. After a few more deep breaths, I swim again.

The water is in turmoil, dragging me in the wrong direction, and the waves are huge. Lightning flashes across the sky and thunder rumbles. My energy is almost drained yet I have no choice but to swim. Nobody is going to save me if I get caught in an undertow.

I can barely believe the feeling of sand beneath my feet and I stagger into the shallows and flop onto the beach.

My body heaves and shudders as I draw air in and perhaps it is still the shock of what just happened. Not just the swim but the awful moments on the boat when he realised I knew his terrible secret.

He's a drug dealer.

On shaking legs I part walk, part crawl to the safety of the bushland. I lean against a tree, water dripping down my face. My bag is on the boat but I'm not going back to get it. So are my shoes. Keys. Purse. And my camera.

How could this have happened?

It wasn't supposed to be like this.

A fork of light illuminates his boat and I'm sure I see him there, standing on the bow.

My heart is pounding.

I have to keep moving.

I have to get to safety.

Of course he'd still been alive when she left. How could Joanna have forgotten Trent's attempt to grab her ankle?

A strong, hot wind blew Joanna's hair back from her face.

Dawn was accompanied by grumbling skies and dripping humidity and Joanna had driven to Willow Bay hoping to beat the storm. Her dreams overnight were vivid, replays of the night she'd fled from *Spee-Dee-One* mixed with a shadowy figure following her. She'd had no choice but to come to the beach, even before coffee.

She was at the same tree where she'd stood all those years ago. Had she overreacted? If Trent had come up the steps she would have heard while she untied the dinghy rather than throwing herself in the sea at night. She still wouldn't have got to her bag without climbing over him.

It was flight response on steroids, Joanna. Stop beating yourself up.

Easier said than done.

All the time she'd spent with Trent, on and off the boat, and never the slightest suspicion he was dealing drugs. Or smuggling them. There was enough in that one dry box to cause immeasurable harm, whether it was cocaine or heroin. Nine-teen-year-old Joanna had never seen either close up and looking back, was incredibly naive and trusting.

There was more she wasn't quite remembering... a blur created by her brain protecting her on the night and made worse thanks to the decades between.

Slipping her sandals off, Joanna walked to the tideline, stopping short of the waves which rolled in with increasing ferocity. Overhead, thick storm clouds hung and the air stilled. There was another scent. Impending rain.

What don't I remember?

There was a detail just out of reach and she was certain it was from that night. Something connected to the man who'd threatened her in the carport. Joanna gazed at the boats in the bay, all straining against their moorings. There were so many more here these days and the dinghies had a designated place along the tree line, unlike the past where they'd be dotted around.

'The dinghy.'

Thunder boomed and Joanna sprinted back to her car as the sky opened, making it behind the wheel seconds before heavy rain pattered on the roof.

There'd been two people on the beach that evening but much earlier. One had been seasick and the other had stared at Joanna for a long time. Had they just done some drug deal with Trent? Was the man watching her trying to work out whether she'd paid them attention?

It sank in that she might well have been in terrible danger on the beach.

More than that... was the man who'd stared at her the same person who threatened her last night?

. . .

From the balcony the storm was glorious to watch. Joanna had coffee and some fruit with yoghurt and she pulled the table and chairs hard against the wall to avoid the rain and worst of the buffeting wind. It made more sense to sit behind glass but there was something majestic about the wildness of a storm which spoke to her on a primal level. The opposite of who she was.

Her whole existence was about being calm and measured.

Impressions mattered in her fickle industry, at least for those on the buying side. Designers might get away with a hot temper but her job was to be neutral.

If I was a designer, would I be temperamental?

Doubtful. Joanna had always been the peacemaker and logical one when she and Roslyn worked together. Perhaps her career moving into the business part of fashion had served her better than her creative side. At home in Queensland she had a whole room filled with her designs but they remained without a label. Roslyn had the label and shop but didn't have the energy or business knowledge to build upon her success.

Her phone beeped with a message from Roslyn.

> Power is out in town so I'm going home for the day. Doubt if anyone will be shopping in this weather anyway. Come and have lunch today?

Joanna didn't respond, not yet. Everything was still raw and she had so much to process. Not the least being her time with Lucas.

After their hug, they'd moved to the living room and talked for ages. Lucas spoke of his marriage to Wanda and divorce more than eight years ago. His regret of the failed marriage and his pride in his sons. The relationship with Wanda was good and they shared custody of the boys, with never a harsh word spoken.

Joanna opened up about her career, from the excitement of fashion season in Europe to the multi-facets of her day-to-day work. She mentioned the company was being sold and that she had limited time to make her own offer.

'Will you? Is owning the company your end goal in life?'

His question made her think. He hadn't asked if she could afford it, or wanted it as a long-term investment. Lucas touched a nerve. Her end goal was never owning a company. It was owning a small and thriving fashion label and boutique.

She replied to Roslyn.

> Probably not lunch. I'm helping on the beach once the storm passes so unsure of my timing. But may I drop around later?

Close of business today was Ted's deadline. She had to make a decision.

> Sure. I'm settling in with a book then will spend the afternoon either baking or sewing so just turn up whenever.

Was there any chance she and Roslyn could find a common ground with Joalyn Designs? Joanna had so many ideas, now based on experience, if Roslyn was interested. The 'end goal' might still be possible.

Lightning snaked through the sky and crashed into the sea, sending a geyser of water soaring.

The real question was whether all the threads of the past would conspire against her, or bring a new start toward happiness.

Joanna found a latex glove to protect her bandaged hand from the elements, slipping it on before she left the car at the top of the cliff. Lucas had messaged to say the marquee was going back up and she'd left home almost immediately, sitting in the carpark trying to work out if she was making a mistake by helping. She really couldn't see another way to get any kind of control back over her life without knowing more about the shipwreck.

Although the storm was long gone, leaving growing patches of blue sky, it was still windy but warm enough to wear shorts.

The marquee was busy with volunteers. Mick Hammond was there as well as a few faces Joanna had seen before. And Lucas. He was writing on a clipboard and didn't notice her until she was almost at the marquee. When he looked up, his smile warmed her heart and messed with her senses. She pushed all of that away for now, unwilling to think too deeply about her feelings.

'Most of the town is without power so quite a few SES members are helping people with portable generators, not to mention clearing fallen trees and the like. But on the other hand, we've got extra help because people don't want to be in a house or shop without power.'

'Yes, Roslyn said she'd closed the shop for the day and gone home.'

'Good. She doesn't rest enough. Come and choose a spot to work in.'

Why does she need to rest?

That feeling of something not being right with Roslyn returned and Joanna stored it away for when she saw her later today.

A small whiteboard on an easel was beside the table with refreshments. The top half had instructions on how to handle different types of finds while the bottom was a rough map of the beach with dotted lines breaking it into eight zones.

'Do you have your phone, Joanna?' Lucas asked. He held out a cotton carry bag with a long handle.

'Yes.'

'Okay, if you come across anything, message me and I'll come and run you through the process. In the bag are more gloves if you need, as well as some large plastic bags for any small pieces you find.'

Joanna accepted the bag and slung it over her opposite shoulder.

Lucas lifted her gloved hand. 'How is it?'

'I redid it this morning and it looks a ton better.'

'Still should have a professional opinion.'

She just smiled and pointed at the whiteboard. 'Where do you want me to start?'

His eyes told her hadn't given up the subject but for now he tapped a spot on the board. 'I'm taking that zone to the left of the jetty, so how about you take the right?'

This was harder than Joanna expected. Underfoot, the sand was either too soft and powdery from the wind, resulting in her sinking and sliding with every step, or else rock-hard along the tideline, which then forced her to keep stepping back to avoid the waves.

Lucas had spent a few minutes walking with her and said to stay out of the sea unless she absolutely had to wade in to collect anything. The water was foamy and murky and he warned there might be sharp objects carried by the unpredictable currents. Once he was satisfied that she understood what to look for, he moved to his own area.

For a man who'd been nervous about any body of water bigger than a swimming pool, Lucas's confidence was a credit to him. He understood the sea and respected it, while admiring its power. Same as Joanna.

For the next hour she focused on watching the waves curl up then smash onto the beach, all the while slowly wandering a couple of feet away from their reach. Up and down the hundred or so metres she was responsible for, wind on her face and sun on her skin. She'd slathered herself in sunscreen and wore a hat but planned to go under the marquee for a while once she'd returned to the jetty one more time.

All the water was looking the same and her mind was drifting when she saw it.

She stopped, then hurried to the jetty and ran along its length.

'Joanna?'

'There's something here!'

Not taking her eyes off the water, she began to go down the ladder at the end, just enough to get closer to the surface, which was only a few feet from the top of the jetty. Holding on to a rail with her good hand, she leaned as far as she dared, arm outstretched to reach the yellow box bobbing nearby. Her gloved fingers grazed it but it drifted infuriating inches away. She went down another two rungs, her legs now in the ocean. She couldn't see more than a foot down and the current pulled hard at her.

'Come up!'

Lucas ran toward her carrying a long pole with a hook. His face was as tense as his tone and as soon as she was within easy reach, he helped her up – firmly. 'What part of staying out of the water didn't I make clear?'

He didn't wait for an answer, turning away and extending the pole over the edge of the jetty.

Was I just scolded?

There wasn't time to be affronted because Lucas had the hook through the handle of the dry box and was carefully pulling it closer. Joanna went to the edge as it came within reach of his longer arms and he leaned down and used the hook to bring it to him. The choppiness made it tricky and for a moment the box was at risk of disappearing beneath the jetty, but then with a grunt, Lucas grabbed and got it. He straightened and deposited the box on the timber.

Is it mine?

The size was the same, but so had been some of Trent's. Were any of his yellow, though?

She'd never had a name on hers so there was only one way to find out.

Lucas got to his feet and stared at her, eyebrows raised. 'I wasn't far behind you. I just wanted to get the pole first.'

'It was floating away.'

'And if necessary we have the lifeguard helping out, who has a boat. Now that this is free of wherever it was caught, it isn't about to sink.'

But it might be mine. Or it might be drugs.

Joanna wanted to scream it out. This dry box might hold the answer to whether it was Trent's boat at the bottom of the sea. Her future might depend on the contents.

'Okay, sorry about getting carried away.'

'Let's take it to the marquee.'

'And open it?'

He scooped it up, brushing off seaweed and showing her some barnacles on the bottom. 'Not here. This will go somewhere out of the elements and we'll get Mick to supervise. Just in case.'

'In case what?'

'Hopefully there's something inside to identify the owner.'

She followed him to the marquee, trying not to look desperate but her heart was thumping heavily in her chest. The commotion had attracted some of the other volunteers and when Lucas put the box on a table, they gathered around. Someone took photos from every angle. Another person put on gloves and lifted it to inspect.

This felt like a forensic unit rather than a group of enthusiasts who liked retrieving stuff from the ocean.

Mick Hammond had puffed his way from a distant part of the beach and was gulping water but hadn't taken his eyes off the box. Snippets of conversations reached her, speculation on the age of the box and how this find must mean there was about to be a huge discovery.

This was terrible.

Inside was either her camera, with photographs which would identify her as its owner, or drugs, assuming they were still intact within their layers of wrapping. Drugs would be better. For her.

What am I doing? Why am I not stepping forward?

She'd left Trent at the bottom of the steps on his yacht instead of phoning an ambulance or the police. Even though he'd tried to grab her ankle, it might have been a last attempt to get her to stop. To help him. Trent might have been mortally wounded in the fall and she had abandoned him.

Her chest was tight.

Joanna had made a terrible, awful mistake all those years ago. She'd believed he was just winded. He'd been moving, enough to scare her a second time. And he'd been furious because she'd seen his haul of drugs and told her she couldn't leave now. Her fear of him overwhelmed her logic.

Pulling the handle of the cotton bag over her head, Joanna left it on a table and stepped out of the marquee. Nobody would notice because the whole lot of them were drawn to the new thing in their midst. She walked as fast as the heavy sand allowed and climbed the stone steps quickly. It was only at the top she looked back.

Away from the marquee, unseen by the volunteers, a man stood. Legs apart, hands in his pockets, he wore a cap and was staring at Joanna.

TWENTY-NINE

Turning into an amateur sleuth hadn't been on Joanna's bingo card for this year. But neither was returning to Rivers End, facing the end of her career, and having Roslyn and Lucas back in her life, and those had all happened.

Joanna left Aunt Beryl's car parked at the end of a lonely road and walked half a kilometre up a hill along a narrow track so she could take a look at the property belonging to the notorious Hammond family. The man who was on the beach this morning looked like the person she'd seen skulking around the community hall the other day and although she had no proof he belonged to the family, an uneasy feeling brought her here.

The computer search she'd done on Mick Hammond had led her to information about his family, with several of them having criminal convictions and jail time for theft, some with force.

I might be misjudging them. Stereotyping them.

People made mistakes in life and some paid for them by going to jail. It didn't mean they would repeat those mistakes. Except theft with violence wasn't a mistake. And whoever visited her last night had broken the overhead light and waited in the dark before making a deliberate threat. Not even close to a mistake.

She reached a fork at the edge of the hill and stopped, panting slightly from the climb. The scrub was dense but she managed to get close to the edge of a fairly steep drop and keep herself out of sight. This was probably the only vantage point overlooking the Hammond property, which was directly below her. The house was set back against the foothills and was surrounded by perhaps fifty acres of barren land. The only trees were around the boundary, inside a high fence topped with a row of barbed wire. It was like a cult compound.

Dozens of rusting cars and boats littered the area close to a massive shed.

There was no livestock or other sign of life.

Joanna shuddered. There was an aura of evil coming off the land below.

The front gate was pushed open by a figure who held it for a black ute to drive in. It looked like the one which had followed her the other day. They closed it and climbed in to the passenger side. At the house, the ute parked out the front and two men got out. The driver was the man from the beach and Joanna drew in a sharp breath. She had been right.

As though he'd heard her, the man's eyes roamed the hill-side. She slowly backed away and once on the path, hurried to the car, slipping a bit on the track made muddy from the storm.

She drove toward the town and was on the outskirts when a ute barrelled up behind her at speed. In seconds it was hard on her tail and if she braked, she knew without a doubt it would hit her. There were spotlights on its roof and when they suddenly turned on, their glare prevented her from seeing who was driving but the ute looked exactly like the one she'd just seen at the Hammonds' place.

Was the driver trying to run her off the road?

Her hands gripped the steering wheel tightly as she looked

for a place to safely pull over and let him pass. But then what? Would he stop too and get out and approach her? Joanna's heart was in her mouth.

A police car turned onto the road, coming in Joanna's direction from town. As it neared, the spotlights behind Joanna abruptly turned off and the ute slowed. Tyres squealed as it slid into a side street. The police car passed Joanna and she locked eyes with Mick for a second before he put on his siren and followed the direction of the ute.

Was he going to do something about what just happened? He was a Hammond, and from what Bess said at the Christmas party he was the only decent one, but that didn't mean he wouldn't take the side of a family member.

This was becoming serious.

Joanna drove to the only person she knew would have her back.

Her legs were still shaky when she tapped on Roslyn's door and it was taking a lot of self-talk not to hightail it back to Queensland.

'It's unlocked.'

Roslyn's voice was so quiet Joanna almost missed it. She opened the door and peered in.

'It's Joanna.'

'I'm in the living room.'

The house was quite dark, with most of the curtains drawn and no lights on. Had the power not been restored yet? At the doorway of the living room, Joanna paused.

'The light switch is to your left.'

Joanna obliged. That answered her question about the power. Roslyn was on one end of the sofa, sitting with her legs up and a blanket wrapped around her.

'Oh, are you not well?'

'Feeling a bit cold.'

The house seemed a comfortable temperature to Joanna. She perched on the other end of the sofa, worried by how pale Roslyn was. All thoughts about talking about the Hammonds vanished.

'Do you want me to arrange a doctor?'

Roslyn smiled faintly. 'All I do is see doctors. I decided to sleep rather than read and now I feel a lot better. Having a forced day off isn't a bad thing.'

'Lucas said it was good you were getting a rest... or something like that. What's going on?'

Roslyn adjusted herself to sit straighter and faced Joanna. 'On?'

'Since the first day I saw you in the shop I got a sense that something isn't right with you. Physically. You get shaky and go pale, like now.'

With a deep sigh, Roslyn nodded, then held out one of her hands for Joanna to take. Without thinking, Joanna extended the one with the bandage, then switched.

'What happened to your hand?'

'I'll tell you later. I want to hear about you. Please, Rossie?'

'My mother... she had breast cancer and didn't get diagnosed until there was almost no chance of long-term survival. Sadly, she passed more on to me than good looks.'

No. Dear God, please no.

'Seven years ago I had a lump removed and chemo for the same cancer which took Mum from me, but I'd caught it much sooner than she did, poor soul. All looked positive for a long time but then a few months ago I became increasingly exhausted and checked in with my specialist and the damned thing was back.'

Roslyn's hand gripped Joanna's but her voice was steady and her eyes didn't waver as she spoke.

'This time I had a double mastectomy and a mix of treatment and what you need to know, JoJo, is that the doctors feel they got it all. There's never a guarantee, but early signs are promising.'

'But you're so pale...'

'The after-effects of the treatment hit me later than normal but apparently it isn't uncommon to get tired easily and have shaky moments for some time. I tend to live my life as usual, which means too many hours on my feet for my body's preference. That's why I have some help in the shop and I don't do much sewing now.'

'You should have told me.'

'I *am* telling you.' Roslyn's smile belied the news she'd delivered.

'No. The first time. Why on earth didn't you let me know then? Did Aunt Beryl know?'

'What would you have done, JoJo? Seriously, how would you have responded?'

'I would have come here...' Her voice trailed away. Would she? In all the years she'd been away, had Joanna once considered Roslyn might need her? 'I'm sorry.'

'Stop it. You protected yourself the best way you could. And I had family and friends here who supported me, so feeling guilty is wasted emotion.'

It didn't matter that the logic was sound. Joanna had a well of tears ready to spill over and she bit her lip hard to stop them.

'I'd like to show you something. Will you come and see?' Roslyn released Joanna's hand and threw off the blanket. 'And I still want to know what you've done to your poor hand.'

After a stop in the kitchen for a welcome glass of sparkling water, Roslyn led the way through the house to a door leading outside. There was a covered walkway which took them to a second, smaller building. Roslyn pushed a door open. 'Come on in to sewing central.'

They were in a small kitchen with a bathroom leading off it and then, after a few steps along a hallway, a large room opened up.

'Oh my goodness. This is wonderful!'

Joanna didn't know where to look first and her eyes darted from several cutting tables to industrial sewing machines to a row of mannequins. There was a large corkboard on a wall with colourful pins and work orders. Along the far end was a number of wheeled hanging racks, most filled with clothes in bags. And fabric. So many rolls of fabric.

'Do you like it?' Roslyn grinned. 'Everyone has today off thanks to the power outage earlier, but several days a week this place is buzzing. I have three staff who work around their commitments such as school or caring for elderly parents. Two of the racks down there are filled with school clothes because I have contracts with different places as well as keeping the shop stocked.'

'I love it. I am so impressed, you clever woman.'

Roslyn clapped her hands in glee. 'It is my happy place. Here and with my family, because grandkids make everything better.' She suddenly sobered. 'I didn't mean to be insensitive, JoJo. I know you wanted a big family. You never found anyone who gave you the love you deserve?'

What a sweet way of phrasing it.

Joanna shook her head. 'Some things aren't meant to be. My career has been my focus. Until now, anyway.'

'Meaning?'

'The night I got your letter, my boss told me he wanted me to be the one to buy out his company when he retires in the future. But while I've been in Rivers End, he's negotiated with a competitor who is offering more than I ever could.'

'Oh, I'm so sorry. What an idiot.'

That made Joanna laugh but Roslyn remained serious.

'No, really. We talked a lot about your career the other day and it's obvious you are a driving factor in the success of the company. You always had incredible talent as a designer, and have applied that to the business side of fashion. In fact, how dare he?'

'Hey, calm down. I appreciate the lovely words, but Ted isn't a bad guy.'

'He's a poop-head.'

Joanna laughed until tears ran down her cheeks. Roslyn looked affronted, until Joanna gave her a big hug and then she too laughed as they rocked side to side in mirth. When the moment passed, Roslyn stepped back and reached for a tissue box on the side table, offering them to Joanna and taking a handful.

'My grandies say that. No idea where they heard it but it seemed appropriate for this Ted person. So, now that we've established that you're facing a career change, why not stay in Rivers End? Why not...' Roslyn took a quick breath. 'I mean... would you like to work with me? Oh, I'm being silly because this little business wouldn't be fulfilling enough and the money wouldn't be anything like you're used to, and—'

'Roslyn, slow down,' Joanna said. 'There's a lot I have to sort out before I can make a decision about moving back here but, actually, that was something I was going to ask you. I mean, yes I'd love to explore working with you.'

'You would?'

More than anything in the whole, wide world.

When Roslyn threw her arms around her, it felt like coming home.

For the first time in days, Joanna felt she had real purpose. Maybe even the first time in years. She and Roslyn talked at length in the sewing hub, looking at some patterns designed for a more formal range. There was limited demand for ball gowns and evening wear here but Roslyn's designs were beautiful and Joanna began writing up a plan for them.

'We can create an online platform, as well as get some samples into a few high-end boutiques I know.'

'You can do that?'

'I can try. There's no guarantees. But legally, yes. There's nothing in my contract with Ted to stop me, because all the fashion I've purchased has been international. And speaking of Ted, I'll need to contact him soon.'

The afternoon had got away from Joanna. The opportunity still hadn't arisen to talk about finding the dry box or being pursued by a Hammond, let alone what happened to her hand. After the bombshell about Roslyn's health, nothing else seemed important. And the excitement of a potential partnership blitzed everything.

They were back in the house when the doorbell rang and Roslyn asked Joanna to answer while she checked the fridge for dinner options. Joanna swung the door open to find Lucas holding several plastic bags and smelling delightful. The bags. Not him.

'Good thing I over-ordered.'

'Oh.'

Remarkable use of the English language, Joanna.

Lucas was grinning but hadn't moved.

'Are you moonlighting as some kind of delivery person?'

'Apparently.'

'Hmm. Perhaps you should come in and we can see what Roslyn has to say.'

Roslyn was delighted. 'Oh, thank goodness. I really need to go shopping, so this is nice. Thank you.'

Lucas put the bags on the counter and kissed Roslyn's cheek. 'How are you feeling?'

'Best I've felt in years.'

He looked from her to Joanna, curious.

'I have to send an email, if you'll excuse me.'

Joanna went into the garden. It was time, and although she knew she didn't want to make an offer on the company, her fingers still shook and it took several tries to get the email written.

Hi Ted,

Thanks so much for giving me the opportunity to buy the business. After much consideration I've decided I'm not going to make an offer. Once I'm back, may we have a conversation about me exiting my employment please?

Joanna.

She read it back then sent it. She'd need to formally resign when she got back, but she owed him the chance to begin looking for a replacement. A moment of sadness disappeared as she joined the others in the kitchen. Both were laughing as Lucas unpacked what looked like a dozen takeaway containers and when they saw her, their smiles reinforced her decision.

After dinner, talk turned to the events at the beach.

'One minute you were in the marquee, Joanna, and then I noticed you at the top of the cliff. Was I too bossy on the jetty?' Lucas settled on an armchair.

'Why were you bossy?'

'Don't worry about it, Roslyn. And no, it had nothing to do with you.'

He gave her a look of disbelief but said nothing.

'Did you find more dry boxes?' Joanna asked.

'Actually, yes. Another washed up a bit later, almost in the same spot. There's also heaps more broken planks and a number of personal items, but so much deterioration from the seawater that they probably won't help identify the craft. However, there's now a theory about the rough area all of this flotsam is originating from and a boat with divers is going out tomorrow to take a look.'

This might all be over soon. One way or another.

'Has anyone opened the dry boxes yet?'

'No idea. They went off with Mr Fairlie.'

'Joanna, how *did* you hurt your hand?'

If Lucas wasn't here, Joanna might have told Roslyn about the man waiting for her last night. But how would he react if she told the whole truth? She'd minimised what happened, the way she downplayed most things. He'd probably insist they got the police involved and Joanna wasn't at all certain about Mick Hammond. No, she had to work out what happened with the yacht first because if Trent had died that night and she was culpable, then her friends wouldn't be dragged into it.

'Oh, the porch light had broken and I cut myself on some glass. Lucas cleaned the wound up for me.'

'Broken how?'

'Dunno. Overheated and exploded? But I'm healing up nicely so there's nothing to worry about.'

Lucas and Roslyn gazed at her so intently that Joanna almost folded and told them everything. Her concerns about Trent. The man who'd threatened her. Being chased by the ute. All the lies she'd kept to herself and the fears which kept building.

'Why do you look so upset?' Roslyn sounded worried. 'What's really going on?'

Lucas's phoned pinged and as soon as he read a message he was on his feet. 'Sorry. I'm needed.'

In the distance, sirens began wailing.

'Looks like the community hall is on fire.'

THIRTY

Joanna and Roslyn followed Lucas in Aunt Beryl's car. He'd torn out of the front door after delivering the chilling news and they both grabbed their handbags without even a word.

All the pieces of the shipwreck are in there.

'Park along here, Joanna. We need to keep out of the way of the fire trucks.'

After pulling over almost a block away, they climbed out, the stench of smoke reaching them before any sign of fire. Once they reached the corner, they stopped, arms around each other's shoulders in shock.

The community hall was alight, flames billowing into the sky and heavy smoke forming a trail in the air. Two fire crews were unrolling hoses and Lucas ran from wherever he'd parked to join them, climbing into the back of a fire truck first to get protective clothing. More sirens approached and in minutes there were four crews working on the blaze, while Mick Hammond tried to get onlookers further away. He was flapping his arms around and eventually, another two people wearing SES vests joined him to help.

They weren't alone on the corner for long as residents ran

from their homes in the immediate area and passing cars stopped. What filtered through the sounds of the fire and water and engines echoed Joanna's thoughts.

'Our hall... all the years of memories.'

'Will it spread to the sports club buildings?'

'The church. Somebody needs to phone the priest.'

'What about the assisted living centre?'

'We should evacuate.'

Some people were crying and Roslyn faced them, her palms up in front of her.

'Listen, please listen. Maybe we all need to go back over the road and give the fire crew plenty of room. They *will* contain it.'

'Should we pack our belongings ready to leave?' One man kept staring at the flames. 'All it takes is an ember in the wind to set a house alight.'

'How about you go home and listen to the local radio, Pat. There's bound to be regular updates and you can see from your window. Go on, check on your family.' Roslyn gave the man a smile and he nodded and ran in the opposite direction. She got onto her phone and called a number.

Joanna stepped a few feet forward, away from the anxious voices behind her. The fire trucks were close to the hall, using its driveway and the carpark. Beyond was the police car, parked on the verge, and Mick and his helpers were now setting up a barrier using police tape. A second and then third police car arrived, one taking each end of the street to stop vehicles driving down. There were several groups of onlookers and standing a little bit apart from the one nearest the hall was a man who had a terrible smirk on his face.

'You!'

She found herself running, weaving onto the road to avoid the service vehicles. Someone yelled at her to get off the road. Joanna lost sight of the man for a second and then he was gone.

'Hey, you can't be here!'

Mick Hammond held a hand up for her to stop, which she did, panting and pointing.

'Is there another fire?'

'No, but that man was creeping around the community hall the other day and then you saw him almost ram my aunt's car today! He probably set the fire!'

'Wait… where?' He looked in the direction she still pointed. 'There's no one. It's Joanna, right?'

'Yes. You followed his ute a few hours ago and I'm pretty sure he is a relative of yours so what are you going to do about it?' Joanna began to shout. 'He's getting away, but I know he's behind the fire!'

'Hang on, no. Uncle Ray wouldn't do that.'

But Mick no longer looked sure and he glanced around, then gripped the top of Joanna's arm and moved them both across the road where there were less people.

'Take your hands off me, Senior Constable.'

'Then stop yelling.' He dropped his hand. 'When exactly did you see him here before? And what did you observe?'

She rubbed her arm and told him the day and approximate time. 'Mr Fairlie might remember my visit because we spoke about the shipwreck. And I saw your uncle circle the hall then try to open the front door.'

'Using force?'

'Well, no, but—'

'But what? Anyone can access the hall when it's unlocked. Or they could.'

An almighty crash came from the hall as part of the roof collapsed. Sparks flew across the grounds. Despite this, the fire-fighters were winning and the flames were reducing in size and intensity.

'Did you speak to him? Your uncle, after he tailgated me with his floodlights on?'

'I wrote him a ticket.'

She hadn't expected that.

'Why were you here at the hall, Joanna? Seeing Mr Fairlie? And you were on the beach at almost midnight one time talking to me about the shipwreck, then Lucas had you helping after the storm today.' He folded his arms, staring at her. 'What is your real interest in the shipwreck?'

Is this it? Will my world come crashing down like the roof just did?

Joanna's mind searched for a cohesive answer and the longer it took, the more Mick's eyes squinted at her. Then a blur of movement appeared in her peripheral vision and Roslyn stepped between them.

'Really, Mick? Instead of hassling an innocent visitor to the town, why don't you get on with the job of finding whoever just destroyed our beloved community hall!'

'Ray Hammond,' Joanna muttered.

'Be careful who you say that to, or he could sue you,' Mick warned.

'Joanna is coming with me to help settle the assisted living residents, so go do police stuff and let's all get through this awful thing.' Roslyn had hold of Joanna's hand and tugged at her. 'We're going right now!'

The message finally got through and Joanna reluctantly went with Roslyn, who wouldn't release her hand until they were back at the car.

'We'll drive around the block to get there. Come on, there's fewer ears in here.' As if to prove her point, Roslyn slid into the passenger seat and closed the door.

The minute Joanna was behind the wheel, Roslyn turned to her.

'Right, spill it. What the heck was that all about? Running off like that down the middle of a road around fire trucks and then having words with a police officer. This is about Trent, isn't it?'

Joanna started the car and carefully drove away, wary of people randomly crossing. 'We're going to where the Christmas party was held?'

'Yes, but talk while you drive. Since when do you even know Ray Hammond, let alone accuse him of starting a fire?'

'A few days ago I was at the hall speaking with Mr Fairlie about the shipwreck. We left at the same time and I went to the church graveyard briefly, then saw a man acting weirdly at the hall. Circling it, then yanking on the doors. Anyway, I saw him again on the beach this morning, after the storm. He was staring at me.'

'What? Why?'

'I had the strongest feeling he was one of the Hammonds; don't ask me why I did but I went up the hill behind their place and saw him.'

'Joanna! Are you completely out of your mind? Those people are dangerous!'

'I know.'

'Okay, what does that mean?'

'There's no way he saw me, but when I was almost back in town, his ute hurtled up behind me and I thought he'd push me off the road; but then Mick came the other way and he turned off. Mick just told me he gave his uncle a ticket for it.'

As good as it felt to tell Roslyn about it, Joanna knew she had to stop there. Any more and she might put her friend at risk.

'Where shall I park?'

'There's a visitor carpark just after the main driveway. Mick is braver than I gave him credit for if he's ticketed that awful man. The only good thing is that Ray has no kids, so that whole criminal side of the family will die off when he does.'

The car parked, they climbed out. From here the fire was obvious. Not anywhere as fierce but still going and the smoke was now settling above them, making the air uncomfortable to breathe. More cars came to park and there were people rushing to check on their loved ones.

'We'll go and help, but JoJo? I want you to stay at my place tonight and we can talk more, because I feel it in my bones this fire has something to do with the shipwreck. And if the Hammonds are involved, then you might be in danger.'

What would make Roslyn believe Joanna might be in danger? The words played over and over in her mind. She'd never directly told Roslyn about the events on board *Spee-Dee-One*. Yet Roslyn had written to her when the parts of a broken yacht began to surface, assuming Joanna needed to know.

She must know more than I think. But how can I raise it after all my lies?

Less lies than withholding information. Keeping things to herself.

'Dear, is everyone alright? There wasn't anyone inside the hall?'

Joanna blinked as Bess appeared on the quadrant of grass, followed by Annette and Marge. There was no sign of the little dog.

'I think it was empty.'

How do you know? Where is Mr Fairlie?

'It is awful. Terrible. We all have so many memories of the hall.'

'I don't,' Marge stated. 'Still dreadful.'

'Where's James Regal?'

'With my ex. We have a custody arrangement.'

Joanna almost burst into laughter, not so much because of the concept but the monotone it was delivered in, and a roll of Annette's eyes from just behind Marge. Most likely there was a heavy dose of adrenaline and panic mixed in Joanna's emotions as well.

'Do you have family you'd like me to call? Any of you?'

'My son Brock is on his way,' Annette said. 'I told him I am perfectly safe but he wants to sweep me up and take me home for the night.'

'And you will love that! Being in your matrimonial home again.' Bess was so earnest that Annette hugged her.

'What about you, Bess?' Joanna asked.

'No, I'm fine here with my friends. Well, any who stay.' She smiled at Annette.

'The fire won't reach us and our rooms all have filtered air so the smoke shouldn't upset our lungs too badly.' Marge looked from Bess to Annette. 'You should both go with Brock and get some mountain air for a change.'

'Marge? Anyone you want me to call?' Joanna felt she'd get a quick negative response but wasn't prepared for the sudden grief which filled Marge's normally stoic face.

'Thank you, but no. James Regal is safe, which is all that matters.'

Oh, there is a story with you.

Joanna's phone rang and she was about to cancel the call when Bess touched her arm. 'We're all fine here, dear. Answer.'

It was Lucas and he sounded exhausted.

'Where are you?'

'At the assisted living community with Roslyn.'

'Good. Fire is all but out. Nobody inside, thank goodness.'

'Oh, that is good news. Are you alright?'

'Me? A bit grotty, but nothing a shower and a glass of wine won't fix.'

Joanna didn't know how to respond. She longed to ask Lucas to meet her at the beach house. Run him a bubble bath. Bring him a glass of wine and let him take however long he needed to unwind from the difficult job he'd just done.

'Roslyn wants me to stay with her tonight.'

'Good idea. Listen, once you are both there, would you phone me? Please?'

'Of course. Are you really alright? That fire was terrible.'

'I really am. Gotta go.'

'Talk soon, then.'

'Yes.'

Finger over the 'end call' button, Joanna hesitated. She needed to tell Lucas everything. But he'd ended the call and she put the phone away.

Joanna was back at the beach house. Like Lucas, Roslyn's son-in-law was one of the volunteer fire crew and was staying overnight to monitor what was left of the community hall, so rather than leave her daughter and grandchildren alone, she went to stay with them. There'd been considerable discussion about Joanna joining them but tonight wasn't the time. She wanted to phone her parents and Aunt Beryl.

And avoid answering more questions from Roslyn.

When she'd driven in, she'd left her headlights on to let her open the door to the house, and collected a flashlight. After locking the car, she'd checked around the house; then each room, closing curtains. The house was secure and she even locked the sliding door to the balcony. With so much attention on Ray Hammond, Joanna hoped he'd keep his head down and leave her alone but if he was responsible for the fire, then what else had he done in the past? Was he the man who'd seen her on the beach at Willow Bay all those years ago?

She jumped when her phone rang. Her nerves were shot after today's events, from finding the dry box, to the fire and everything in between. She answered without checking the caller and immediately wished she'd left it to go to voicemail.

'Joanna, why on earth do you want to resign? I can't have that!'

'Good evening, Ted.'

She took the phone into the kitchen to pour a glass of wine. 'This message of yours is upsetting me a lot.'

'I'm sorry. That wasn't the intention.'

'Then why send it?' Ted was worked up and wasn't stopping there. 'The negotiations I'm in specifically include you as part of the deal so I'm sorry, but you need to stay in your role for at least a year. That's what I already promised them.'

Joanna sank onto a stool.

'Ted, you gave me until close of business today to make you an offer yet you've just said you've already offered me to another buyer as an employee for a year? You never had the intention of letting me buy the company.'

A kind of numbness descended on Joanna. All these years growing Ted's company, putting up with his demands and worse, his wife's crappy attitude.

'Let's be real, Joanna. You can't afford to buy it.'

'Maybe not, but then again, my parents and my aunt offered to help finance an offer along with my own ability to borrow, which is considerable.'

'Then why didn't you meet my deadline with an offer?'

'My priorities have changed.'

'Change them back!'

Joanna placed the phone on the counter and sipped the wine as Ted ranted for a few minutes. When he'd calmed down and asked if she was still there, she tapped the speaker.

'My contract is out of date, Ted. This is the first annual leave I've taken in years. I'm overdue long-service leave. And most importantly, I'm not a commodity for you to sell.'

'Okay, okay. Sorry. Please reconsider.'

'This isn't how I imagined we'd part ways but I don't deserve to be yelled at, particularly not this late at night. I'll write you a proper letter of resignation and be back in a couple of weeks to pick up any personal items. Goodnight.'

His voice was spluttering as she ended the call.

She wouldn't cry. Not over Ted or her job.

The phone rang again and she started to laugh, a bit hysterically. It was Lucas and when she answered, she must have sounded odd.

'Did I wake you?'

'Nope. I just quit my job.'

'O-kay. Want to talk about it?'

'Not even a little bit. I forgot to phone you.'

His low chuckle finally pushed the numbness aside.

'You did. Roslyn just rang and said you were home.'

'She needed to be with her family and I had some things to deal with here.'

'Like quitting your job.'

Joanna's earlier thoughts about running a bubble bath for Lucas drifted through her mind. Instead of voicing them, she wandered to the living room.

'Lucas, was everything destroyed in the fire? Everything collected from the shipwreck?'

He sighed. 'Sadly yes. Still a bit too soon to see all the damage but everything on the tables was burnt, some more than others. The reason I wanted to talk to you was about the dry boxes.'

Putting down her glass, Joanna straightened. 'What about them?'

'Mr Fairlie took them both to his house earlier and locked them in his safe. He didn't want to leave them in the hall where more people had access and had arranged to open them tomorrow with Mick and some others, in case there's anything important inside.'

'So they're not destroyed?'

'No, far from it. Between the boat going out in the morning to search the area that's been pinpointed, and whatever might be inside those boxes, we might finally find the mystery shipwreck. Whatever made it sink, or whoever, will be discovered.'

THIRTY-ONE

29 JANUARY 2000

I'm not even halfway home when the storm makes landfall.

There isn't a soul around. No cars have passed me since I stumbled onto the rough bitumen road, whimpering with every step from the pain in the soles of my bare feet. At least this road is better than the track from Willow Bay, which was a nightmare of stones and prickly weeds when I'd tried to find grass to walk on.

The rain is like a sheet and there's no point even trying to find shelter because I'm already soaked to the skin from the swim. I just want to get home and lock myself in and cry for a week.

Trent is a drug smuggler.

Why else would he have so much in that one dry box – and there'd been others which weren't open, so who knows how many packages he had. That late-night meeting on the jetty at Rivers End beach had to be part of it. Perhaps even the people in the rowboat earlier tonight, although who would take a child to a drug dealer's meeting?

The way he'd turned on me when he realised I'd seen the

drugs scares me so much I keep checking behind in case he's following.

Unless I really hurt him? He wasn't dead because he reached for my leg and I am certain I saw him on the stern looking for me. I need to calm down. I didn't kill him. But will he want me silenced? I stop at a corner and brush the rain from my eyes, gazing back to the main road. A flash of lightning shows only houses.

I still don't know if Trent has my address but it wouldn't be hard to ask around and find out where I live. My only hope is to tell the police. And it is the right thing to do.

Instead of going home, I follow a different road to get to the police station. There's only one officer in Rivers End and he lives in the house at the back of the station but no matter how many times I ring the bell or pound on the door, nobody appears. I finally notice the police car is missing from where it is always parked. I'll come back in the morning and maybe he can help me get my bag from the yacht.

From here it is two blocks to home and the rain is even worse. Thunder crashes overhead and I'm terrified lightning will strike me. I like storms but being out in this one is horrible. It is only when I'm shivering at my front door that it hits me. How on earth can I get inside? I have no keys. The pot plant we used to keep a spare key in has gone to Queensland. I could break a window. But then I'll have to get it repaired and anyway, what if Trent comes to find me and climbs through it?

Roslyn's mother has a key.

I peer through the rain at the house next door. There's a light on downstairs.

'Oh, why?' I clench my hands in frustration.

This isn't what I wanted to do but in a minute I'm tapping quietly on their door and when it opens, it is Roslyn on the other side.

'Joanna? What on earth? Come in.'

'I need my house key.'

'Oh... I think Mum has it on her keyring and she's not here tonight.' Roslyn reaches out and takes my arm. 'Oh my gosh, you are frozen.'

None too gently she pulls me inside and closes the door.

'Why are your feet bare... oh, is that blood? Oh my god, did someone... were you assaulted?'

I shake my head because I wasn't, not in the way she means, and then stupidly start crying. She helps me take off my clothes there and then, running to get towels when I'm down to my lingerie.

'Here, put on my slippers to walk to the bathroom. Mum will have a fit if we get blood on the carpet.' She wraps a big towel around me. 'Come on, you can get into a bath and warm up.'

'I just... need... to go home.'

'You just need to get warm and dry. Stop arguing with me.'

She guides me upstairs and gives me her own fluffy bathrobe to sit in while she runs a bath. Steam rises and I'm beginning to warm a bit and manage to stop crying and being pathetic. Roslyn adds bubbles which smell nice and once the water is ready, leaves me to climb in, warning me she'll be right back.

The hot water stings but feels oh-so-good and I shuffle down so all of me but my head is under the bubbles.

I let my mind drift and don't hear her come back in but then realise Roslyn is sitting beside me holding a cup of hot chocolate. She looks so worried that for the first time in weeks I see how much she still cares about me. And that makes tears drip down my face.

'Come on, JoJo. It's only hot chocolate. Nothing to cry about.'

That kind of makes me giggle and I sit up more and take the cup.

'Can you poke your feet out and let me take a look?'

I manage one at a time and she inspects both thoroughly.

'You didn't do this crossing between our houses. Where on earth have you been?'

What am I supposed to say? If I tell her about Trent being a drug smuggler then she'll probably go and confront him and put herself into danger. If something happened to her I couldn't forgive myself because she warned me he was trouble.

'I was out walking and got caught in the storm.'

'Oh, sure you were. Walking where?'

'Why isn't your mother home?'

Roslyn's face falls and for a second, I'm sure her lips quiver. But she stands and goes to the door.

'I'm going to make up the spare bed for you and get the first aid kit. Let me know when you're dry and I'll have some pyjamas for you.'

With that she leaves, pulling the door almost closed.

I long to call out for her to come back so I can tell her about Trent's terrible secret, which is now mine. And once I've seen the police tomorrow and know Trent is being arrested then I'll explain everything to her. Nothing will stop me.

I wake up early, just as the sun is rising. The storm is long gone and the clear sky makes me wonder for a minute if I dreamed last night.

But my feet still hurt when I stand.

Roslyn did a good job applying some soothing cream and bandaging both feet after my bath and when I fell into bed, I slept deeply.

I strip the bed and put the sheets into the washing basket. Roslyn had hung my dress to dry in the laundry and it is, along with my lingerie. I borrow a pair of her shoes – runners – which are slightly big for me but go over the bandages. I write a note saying thank you and that I'm fine and will return her shoes and be back later to pick up the key.

Letting myself out, I say a silent *thank you*. Roslyn was my friend again last night. She was amazing. I can't wait to be able to tell her the truth and find a middle ground for us both. No boy is worth losing a lifelong friendship, nor our future plans. We'll work it out.

The walk to Willow Bay takes longer than usual because my feet hurt and my muscles are sore from swimming under-water for so long. I reach the beach in full daylight and stop at the top of the sand to catch my breath. How can the bay be so calm again after such a storm?

And where is *Spee-Dee-One?*

I check and double check the yachts which are moored.

Trent is gone.

But his dinghy is still here, upside down high on the sand.

Last seen, it was tied to the stern of his boat.

How on earth did it get back to shore and be in its usual position?

Then it all makes sense.

Trent must have come looking for me last night. He rowed in and stowed the dinghy as was his habit. He'd searched for me but not found where I lived. Or had he? Had Trent gone to my house during the night? I hadn't checked it after I left Roslyn's.

Except... how did he get back to his yacht?

I walk up and down the row of upturned rowboats. Mr Campbell's is the only one missing and when I gaze out at the boats bobbing gently in the bay, can easily see the yacht it belongs to is still moored, without the rowboat. Was Trent so drunk that he took the wrong dinghy?

Heading to the police station, I pass Mr Campbell's beau-tiful jewellery store which is one of my favourite shops to visit. It doesn't open until ten, so I can't let him know someone stole his dinghy.

I wish I had a car right now. Walking hurts and takes so long. I couldn't run if I tried and might need to redo the bandages soon. When I finally reach the police station, nobody is here. Again. There's a bench on the small porch and I sit for a while, leaning back with my eyes closed. Maybe I doze for a while because I suddenly jump and look around. I feel like I'm being watched but can't see anyone nearby. There's a phone number written on an information panel to contact the police officer if the station is unattended and I memorise it to call from home.

I'm almost at my street when Roslyn drives past, heading for her house. Her mother is in the passenger seat and they don't see me because they are talking. By the time I catch up, the car is in their driveway and the front door is closed but then Roslyn hurries out.

She looks upset and pale and I think for one ridiculous minute that she's been worrying about me, and I'm about to hug her and say I'm doing better when she holds out the key.

'Mum took it off the keyring. Keep it, Joanna. We don't want to be responsible for you anymore.'

Did I hear her correctly? I take the key. 'About last night—'

'No more knocking on the door, okay? If something is going on with you and Trent then that's your business, but I've warned you about him and don't want you bringing that kind of trouble here.' Roslyn's eyes are red and puffy. 'My mother doesn't need to deal with your issues. Don't come over again.'

This isn't my friend from last night. My mouth is so dry I can't get a single word out and I try to take her hand so I can squeeze it. But she snatches hers away and stares at me with that same cold expression I've got used to.

'Why don't you just go to Queensland for real?'

She spins around and runs to her house, slamming the door.

. . .

I stand outside my house for a while, crying so hard I don't even bother trying to get the key into the lock.

Between Trent last night and Roslyn, this feels like my biological father all over again. Hot and cold. Kind then cruel. Loving then frighteningly angry. Her mother has always been so kind to me and is friends with my mother so it doesn't even make sense she'd tell Roslyn to stop me visiting. I need to phone my parents because this has all got too big for me. I can't do this alone any longer.

Someone has slid an envelope under the door and I scoop it up, locking the door and gripping the key. I leave the envelope on the kitchen table and run upstairs. In my dressing table drawer I have keys to the back door and garage and slide the house key onto the ring. I kick off the shoes – Roslyn's – and slide soft socks on my feet. Stripping everything else off I toss it all into the washing basket and put on fresh clothes.

I'm going to phone my parents and ask for advice and just hope Dad doesn't think he needs to come straight back. Or should I call Aunt Beryl?

In the kitchen I gulp down some water, trying to work out what to do. Aunt Beryl is a better idea because she lives here and will let me move to her place sooner. And she might be able to help me work out who to contact to report Trent because I don't feel right about calling the police using the emergency number.

I notice the envelope and my heart speeds up. Is this a note from Roslyn? She might have left it for me in case she wasn't the one to give me the key. I really, really don't want to be upset again but then I wonder if the real estate agent has a buyer they want to show through.

At first I'm confused. There is a single sheet of lined paper which looks ripped out of an exercise book. The handwriting is messy and the spelling poor but the message sends a terrible chill through me.

Leve and never come back.
Ya aunt and friend will suffer if ya say a word. I have places to burry them.
This is ya only warning.
Run for ya life.

I scream aloud and rush around the house checking every door and window is locked. And then I phone my parents.

'Daddy? I miss you and Mum too much. I'm moving to Queensland.'

THIRTY-TWO

NOW

Joanna opened the diary which she'd hoped to never read again but this time she turned to the last page.

An envelope, folded in two, was taped on all sides hard against the back cover.

'I knew I kept you for a reason.'

Wearing lightweight gloves and using a sharp knife, she sliced through the tape. Opening the flap of the envelope, Joanna slid out the single page she'd had the presence of mind to keep. All those years ago, terrified and distraught, she'd had the strangest need to hide it rather than throw it away. And over time, she'd forgotten its existence.

Back then she'd believed the threat and felt completely helpless.

Not now.

Reading the note brought a rush of emotion – but unlike the fearfulness and confusion of her youth, this one was powerful and productive. Joanna was angry. And quite able to focus the fury where it belonged and put right old wrongs.

The man who'd been with the boy at the beach was the most likely person to have written the note but she could only speculate about who he was. Who the child was. She could probably offer a description, but where was her proof?

Last night she hadn't fallen asleep until almost dawn, continually checking the local live news channel for updates on the fire. Once she did sleep, it was deep. She woke late in the morning and took a long shower while she processed the thoughts and memories which plagued her after Lucas had spoken about the divers going out.

The dry boxes were going to be opened, or perhaps already had been. Would anything have survived decades of submersion? It was possible that one of those waterproof and airtight containers held her camera and assuming the serial number was still readable, there was every possibility it would be identified as hers. This fear had controlled her for decades. It drove her away from Rivers End, that and the breakdown of her friendship with Roslyn, and clouded her life in so many subtle ways.

Not anymore.

Joanna was going to find Mick Hammond and tell him everything. It was a risk, because if he was corrupt or controlled by his uncle, then it could easily backfire. She'd just have to trust him.

If Aunt Beryl were here she'd ask her to accompany her to the police station. She couldn't ask Roslyn. Not with their history back then and her current health. Lucas was out of the question. Their reconnection was real but a long way from asking favours about such serious matters and anyway, if Joanna ended up in legal trouble she didn't want him involved. The only person in Rivers End who might be impartial and had no shared history was Christie. Joanna turned her phone on to look up the number for the beauty salon but then changed her mind and put it down. It wasn't fair to ask someone she barely knew.

The phone began to ping as messages arrived. She stared at it, not wanting to lose momentum. But ignoring messages made her twitchy so she picked it up again.

Two missed calls, two voicemails, and an email from Ted in the space of two hours this morning. Those would wait until she was ready.

A missed call from Roslyn. No message.

Missed calls from Dad and Aunt Beryl. Voicemails from both.

Joanna listened to them. One of Aunt Beryl's friends had phoned about the community hall fire and everyone was worrying. She quickly sent them both the same text message that the fire was out and nobody was hurt and that she would call a little later today.

Throwing everything she needed, including the diary, into her bag, Joanna headed to the door but then stopped. She took the diary out, unfolded the threatening note, and took photos. These she emailed to herself. Whatever happened today, she couldn't afford to lose this vital piece of the past. At the car, Joanna glanced at the beach house. Was she about to be arrested and never see it again?

She'd just pulled up outside the police station when Lucas rang. There was no immediate sign of the patrol car as she answered.

'There's news, Joanna.'

'About the fire? It *was* started by Ray Hammond?'

'Ray Hammond? What makes you think he was involved?'

Oh, crap. I never mentioned it to him.

'Is it about the fire?'

'Joanna... okay, we'll circle back to him. Not the fire. The divers have had success. A very deteriorated yacht is caught in submerged rocks between Willow Bay and Rivers End. Surprisingly close to the coastline, in a deep pocket renowned for being dangerous.'

Every part of Joanna froze.

'Early reports are that it matches what was washed up.

Divers have recovered more dry boxes as well as personal effects, or what remains of them. They are taking photographs of what is left in the hope of getting an identification of the boat, assuming it was registered.'

'I see.'

'Mick was here at the marquee when the news was coming in but he disappeared in a hurry.'

'To where?'

'I'm a bit worried, actually. He kind of glazed over and said he had to check something. Probably at the station.'

'No. No, I'm here and he isn't.'

'Hang on, why are you at the police station?' Worry laced Lucas's voice. 'Joanna, what is going on?'

She longed to tell him. To pour her heart out and share her history from that awful night but then his role in all of it might come to light. Not that any of it was his fault, but he was a sweet and kind person and would feel bad for contributing to her friendship with Trent because of his behaviour with Roslyn.

And there I go, fixing everything for everyone even if they don't ask or need it.

This was how she'd lived her life.

Protecting her aunt and Roslyn from the threats from that man.

Protecting her parents from the truth of why their daughter changed her future plans overnight.

Protecting Trent by not following through with a police report about the drugs.

And ultimately, protecting herself from dealing with the fallout if she'd have phoned the police instead of running away.

Joanna dropped her forehead onto the steering wheel. She'd never seen herself so clearly.

'I'll come and find you. Stay at the police station, please.'

She lifted her head. 'I'm okay. I promise. Lucas? Do you ever remember seeing a boy at Willow Bay? And a man?'

'I've seen plenty of kids at Willow Bay. When?'

'Oh, sorry. Back when we were... the summer we met. He might have been with his dad or alone. About ten. Didn't like the water.'

Lucas chuckled. 'Apart from the last bit you might be describing Bobbie or a hundred kids. What did his father look like?'

'Kind of scruffy. Maybe wearing a cap of some kind.'

'Not really visualising them. Can you hold for a minute?'

Lucas must have moved the phone away as he spoke to another man for a minute. Two words made Joanna's heart thump in her chest.

Body. Police.

When he returned his voice was serious. 'Are you able to come to the marquee?'

'Why? What's happened?'

'Best to talk in person.'

If he wanted to tell her a body had been found then she needed to find Mick first.

'I will. Soon. I have to make a quick phone call and there's something else I have to do.'

The police car was the only vehicle in the carpark at Willow Bay. Joanna pulled in near it. As she climbed out, the sound of an approaching motor made her pause, watching to see if it was the ute because her gut screamed that Ray Hammond hadn't given up. But the sound stopped and she figured it had come from the main road.

Joanna jogged down to the sand, stopping in the tree line first to see where Mick was. He was sitting on an upturned dinghy, staring out at the water. Coming here to look for him was a gamble. Yes, he was a Hammond. And might turn on her.

But it was his half-memory when they met the first time which had stuck in the back of her mind.

She'd asked if he'd ever heard stories about a yacht disappearing and his eyes had gone blank before he shook his head.

'Moment there I thought there was a memory of something. Talk about watching a boat as a kid but jeez, that's so long ago it could mean anything. Never liked being on the beaches when I was young so it would have been strange to go and watch one.'

Had Mick been the boy in the rowboat all that time ago? The age fitted. He'd been uncomfortable around the beach. Well, he was here now, the way she'd been drawn back to Willow Bay time and again. She crossed the sand and when he noticed her, he stood, his face so distraught she thought he'd been crying.

'I'm so sorry to intrude... there's something terribly important I need to tell you.' Joanna said.

He nodded. 'Feel like a walk?'

They wandered in the direction of the rocks at one end of the beach, staying close to the tideline for the harder sand.

'I heard divers found the remains of a yacht, Mick. I know which yacht it is and I know who owned it.'

He glanced at her but didn't speak.

'The last time it was moored in Willow Bay was the twenty-ninth of January 2000 and I was on board. For a little while.'

'And you swam back to shore very late at night.'

Joanna stopped dead, blinking at him in surprise.

'I was a kid. Got dragged to places no kid should ever go,' Mick said. 'Put it all out of my mind once I left home. Had a new life. A career where I did good stuff. People who saw me as Mick, not a Hammond. Not gonna lie, Joanna. It hurts, dredging this all up.'

'I know it does. But you remember things about that yacht? *Spee-Dee-One?*'

'Yeah.'

They started walking again.

'Are you not on duty?' Joanna had suddenly noticed Mick wasn't wearing his uniform.

'I took my uniform off. It's in the car. Once I heard about the divers and some of the stuff they found, I got a flashback or whatever you'd call it. Felt so ashamed for my part I couldn't wear the uniform.'

'Oh, Mick. No, you were a child. And I imagine you had no choice.'

'Generations of criminals, my family. Some were only petty thieves but others... violent, nasty men. Only one left now and he's the worst, I reckon.'

Mick's phone rang and he looked at it for a long time before answering. 'What's up, Lucas?' He listened, his face showing nothing although he nodded a couple of times. 'Might pay to get Green Bay police to head down to the beach. I'll be along soon, mate. Just chatting with Joanna.' He rang off and pocketed the phone. 'Divers found a body in the wreck. Virtually a skeleton. Water police are gonna take over from the team out there and I reckon we need more help here to catch the killer.'

He turned and stared at Joanna.

Do you already know what I did?

'This is what I need to discuss with you. But in your official capacity as a police officer.'

'Still am.'

'In that case—'

'Wait!'

They both turned as Roslyn ran across the sand, waving her arms. She caught up, chest heaving as she drew in breath.

'You shouldn't be running.'

Still gasping for air, Roslyn grabbed Joanna's arm. 'Mick... she was... Joanna was with... me. That night.'

'What night in particular?' Mick crossed his arms. 'Slow breaths.'

Roslyn's face was red from the exertion and it took a minute for her to speak more coherently. 'Joanna stayed at my house the night that Trent sailed away in *Spee-Dee-One*. We were together the whole time.'

'Stop it,' Joanna whispered. 'There's no need.'

'But I... why? What have you said?'

Joanna removed Roslyn's arm from hers and led her to one of the rocks to sit on.

You came to give me an alibi. I can't believe you'd go out on a limb like this.

Wanting to hug Roslyn, instead she gave her a quick smile. 'A lot has happened since I phoned you.'

'Yes, I heard at least some of it. From Lucas. So you really, really need to come home with me.'

'Not just yet, Roslyn,' Mick said. 'And you don't need to alibi Joanna because I know where she was that night, because I saw her swim back from Trent's boat. She dragged herself out of the water, shivering and terrified. I'm so sorry I couldn't help you.'

'And ya still can't help her, ya little fool.'

Ray Hammond stood a few metres away, loosely holding a revolver at his side. His voice sent a shiver through Joanna – he was definitely the man who'd been in the carport. And he looked ready to kill them all.

'Oi, that's mine. My service revolver. Hand it over.' Mick walked toward his uncle with one hand outstretched and the other behind his back, gesturing at Joanna and Roslyn... as if telling them to go.

There was a way between the taller rock formations which would lead to the cliff and from there, to the little beach beneath Aunt Beryl's house. But it was a risk going where there was nobody to help. Perhaps there was a way to circle back to the car. Roslyn grabbed her hand as Ray Hammond spoke again.

'Nah, might hang on to it. Seeing as ya left it sitting there in ya car, might be mine now.'

'It was locked in the boot, Ray. Why break into a police car?'

'Why become one of them?' The older man sneered. 'Sold out, didn't ya? Not a step closer.'

Mick stopped, legs apart, making himself as big as he could. Shielding the women.

Joanna couldn't see the other man's face and she tugged at Roslyn and once their eyes met, slowly slid between two boulders. Roslyn followed, not that she had a choice, so tightly was Joanna holding her hand.

'Thing is, Ray, the boat was found. And guess what? There's a body in it. Bet it has a bullet hole in the front of the skull where you shot Trent.'

You shot him?

Almost stumbling in shock, Joanna put her free hand over her mouth. The need to scream almost overwhelmed her but then Roslyn squeezed her fingers and nudged her forward. She hadn't killed Trent. She hadn't left him to die. He was murdered.

'Knew I should have locked ya in the shed instead of taking ya with me but I was trying to teach ya skills, Mick. Teach ya how business works.'

'By selling someone a stash of drugs then going back to rob them of it? Not that it worked out for you, did it, Ray?'

'I got enough. Hadn't expected him to fight back.'

The path through the rocks curved back toward the bushland. 'Stop for a sec.' Roslyn pointed out past the moored yachts to the channel into Willow Bay. 'Police boat.'

'Go into the trees. Quietly,' Joanna whispered. 'Phone for help.'

'Come with me.'

'I won't be far behind you. Go. Hurry.'

Although Roslyn looked terrified and reluctant to go, she nodded and wove through trees until out of sight.

Joanna turned her phone's video camera on and snuck back the way she'd come. She hid the best she could between the boulders, recording the terrible scene playing out on the beach. Mick had moved about ninety degrees so that he was facing the sea. It had forced his uncle to turn away from the bay.

'Told ya to stop moving.' Ray raised the gun. 'Had a thought, mate. Those two women ya like hanging out with so much? Telling them our family secrets? Time for them to die and it'll be this gun which does it.'

'Sure, Ray. Hand it to me and I'll track them down.'

'And then ya can put one in ya own head.'

'Just give me my gun, Uncle Ray. Please.'

The police boat was much closer to shore and Mick glanced at it for a second. Ray's head jerked around to look and Mick lunged forward.

'This is the police. Put down your weapon and get on your knees.' The loudspeaker boomed across the distance.

Mick was almost on Ray when the other man fired and he crumpled onto the sand. Ray raised the gun again and moved closer, aiming at Mick's head.

Joanna flew out of her hiding spot, scooped up a chunk of driftwood and slammed it against the back of Ray Hammond's head. For a terrifying second the man simply stood there and then, like a house of cards collapsing, he fell.

THIRTY-THREE

'Mick will be fine, JoJo. Surgery on his leg and some time to heal and I'll even help with the physio at no charge.' Lucas sat on the sand beside Joanna, holding her hand. 'He's one of the reasons you're still alive. Safe.'

'What's the other reason?' Joanna had finally stopped trembling from shock.

'A certain someone who stepped up and saved her own life with the help of some driftwood. And Mick's and Roslyn's lives. You were so brave.'

I don't feel brave. I don't feel... anything.

The last hour had been a blur.

Once Ray Hammond was face-down on the ground, Joanna had dropped the timber and carefully collected Mick's revolver. A police dinghy was powering in and she stood at the edge of the water and placed the gun on the sand and her hands in the air. Mick was moaning in pain and the other man was out cold.

'Please arrest the older man. He just tried to kill a police officer.'

'Take a few steps away from the gun, ma'am. We saw what happened but need you away from it.' A young female officer was first to jump out of the boat as it came almost out of the low waves.

Joanna walked back several paces.

'You can drop your hands. Are you hurt?' The officer slid the gun into an evidence bag from her pocket.

'No. Not me. Mick is. The police officer. The younger man.'

'We know Mick and more help is coming. Can you go and sit up under a tree for me? Stay in sight, please.'

She didn't think she'd make it all the way going past Mick and Ray, circling them as several police rushed to handcuff Ray. Her legs were jelly and it was only when Roslyn appeared from the direction of the carpark and put an arm around her waist that Joanna managed the last few metres.

Paramedics arrived. More police, this time from the carpark. The hive of activity faded from Joanna's view as she leaned against a tree trunk and closed her eyes. She felt Roslyn move away at one point and another arm go around her which gently pulled her against a muscular body. A nice-smelling body with a heartbeat close to where her head rested. A warm hand brushed the hair from her face and when she opened her eyes, Lucas was watching her.

'Roslyn's just being checked at the spare ambulance and you should go as well.'

'Spare?'

'There's three and Mick and his uncle have gone separately. Roslyn rang emergency and I did too, asking for police and ambulance on my way here. I saw the police boat...' His voice trailed off.

Joanna straightened to see him better. There were worry lines around his eyes.

'When did you arrive?'

'Not in time. I knew something was wrong and when Mick said you were with him I phoned Roslyn and she just about gave me heart failure, saying you'd come here to talk to him about the night Trent's boat disappeared. I had no idea, Joanna. None.'

'About Trent?'

'About you turning up at Roslyn's house in a storm at midnight. I can't believe she never told me you'd escaped from him, and that he was a drug smuggler.'

'She didn't know anything about Trent until I told her, just after I spoke to you earlier.' Joanna took his hand, loving the feel of his fingers curling around hers. 'Nobody knew... at least, I thought nobody did but as it turns out, Mick was there that night with Ray Hammond.'

'Okay, this is getting complicated. I might ask the police if you can leave and get you somewhere away from here. Or did you walk?'

'No, I have Aunt Beryl's car. Oh... you came around the cliffs?'

He grinned. 'Ran the entire way and almost ended up falling into a huge rockpool. Now, sit tight and I'll be right back.' He kissed her forehead and got to his feet.

It was early evening before Joanna was able to phone her parents. There'd been a long interview at Green Bay police station and more to come as further information about the body discovered in the wreck came to light.

Lucas stayed at the station the whole time. He'd driven her there in Aunt Beryl's car and then home, before leaving on foot again with the promise of being a delivery man once again when she was ready to eat. Having him there stopped her from falling into a heap. He knew she'd been caught up with some-thing dangerous and illegal – although without her knowledge until the last few minutes – yet he hadn't turned his back on her.

Roslyn was cleared by the paramedics but went to her

daughter's house to sleep for the afternoon. They'd spoken briefly and Joanna was concerned by how exhausted her friend was. And incredibly thankful she'd alerted the authorities.

Taking her phone onto the balcony, Joanna dialled Dad.

The ocean stretched out beneath a sky filled with evening colours of gold and pink and hues of blue. How wonderful to sit quietly and watch until the velvet darkness of night fell.

'Joanna? We're all here on speaker. Can we put it on video?'

She tapped a button and the three people she loved most in the world came into view. Dad was closest, with Mum and Aunt Beryl leaning toward him from either side. They all waved madly and she waved back.

'Young lady, we are never letting you out of our sight again!' Mum tried to look fierce but her face crumpled and she began to sob.

'Good grief, Molly. She's fine. Look at her sitting out under the beautiful evening sky!'

But Aunt Beryl's eyes were glistening and even Dad busied himself hugging his wife rather than look at the phone. Joanna was still too numb to cry but it hurt so deeply seeing her family distressed.

'Auntie is right. I'm fine and I'm sorry you've heard snippets of news without all the facts. Today was stressful and bizarre but everything is okay now. And I have so much to explain to you all. And need your forgiveness.'

Joanna took them back to the summer where everything changed. She chose her words carefully because upsetting them further was the last thing she wanted. At long last she unburdened the grief of losing her first boyfriend to her best friend. And then losing the best friend whom she'd planned an entire future with. She glossed over the details but Dad leaned forward.

'Roslyn deliberately made you think this young man was no longer interested in you, while telling him that you had already decided to move away from Rivers End? She manipulated both of you?'

'She did. And she's regretted it ever since. Because I'd forced you, Auntie, to never tell me a word about the town again, specifically anything to do with Roslyn, it got worse than it needed to.'

'I saw Roslyn grow up. It is hard hearing her duplicity, love,' Mum said. 'I knew her mum passed away and I would have come for the funeral but it was when I'd broken my leg.'

'That's right. You got on a horse for the first time in decades and promptly fell off.'

Mum burst into laughter.

'She was lucky she only broke a leg,' Dad said. 'Fell off the horse and rolled down a steep hill.'

'I do remember, Dad. It was me who was at Mum's beck and call for three months.'

Everyone laughed and the tension about Roslyn dissipated.

'So, Joanna,' Aunt Beryl said. 'What now?'

'Unsure. I've not made an offer on the company and after discovering Ted tried to sell me as part of his package, I resigned.'

'We know. And I'm sure I'll play golf with him again but he'd better watch out in case I accidentally run him over with a buggy.' Dad's face was so serious that Joanna had to peer at the screen to see the twinkle in his eyes.

'I have a feeling Hazel will keep him occupied travelling the world on an ocean liner for some time. I'm happy not to worry about flying overseas for a while and... I'm thinking of staying in Rivers End. I'm sorry, Mum and Dad, because I know you moved next door to be near me.'

'Ha! Not even close. Your father only wanted access to the little pier you have at the back of your house for fishing and kayaking. We'll be fine, honey. As long as you visit and let us visit.'

Aunt Beryl sat forward. 'Let's have a chat about the beach house. Another time?'

There was a tap on the door.

'I think my takeaway is here.'

'Go eat, child. And open one of my bottles of wine. A good one.'

The tide was low and the little stretch of sand below the beach house was pleasantly warm beneath a picnic blanket.

Joanna and Lucas had finished the fish and chips he'd brought them for dinner and each held a glass of red wine. Their backs were against a rock at the base of the cliff. The waves gently whooshed, quieter than the seagulls who'd hung around while they ate but had gone to bed with the coming of night. The last of the light faded and Lucas flicked on a battery-powered lantern they'd brought with them.

'This is nice,' Joanna had hardly spoken in the last hour. Physically she was unharmed but her senses still reeled. 'Thank you, Lucas.'

'I always like fish and chips.' He grinned.

'For everything.'

'*Everything* is a pretty wide statement.' He still smiled but his eyes were serious. 'There's a lot I messed up. From before.'

'There's a lot we all messed up. Lucas, you were caught in the middle and had no more of an idea of what was going on than me. I wish back then I'd had the courage to have stood up for myself with Roslyn. Maybe if I had, she'd have found a way to tell me about her mum's illness and I could have been her support instead of us losing so much. And I'm not blaming myself. Just thinking aloud.'

'You put others first all the time. Do you remember the first time we really spoke?'

I've never forgotten. Your gorgeous blue eyes stole my heart.

'I brought you a soda because I thought it was a good way to break the ice. You looked a bit lost.'

Lucas nodded. 'Quite lost. New town and new job. Salina insisting I go everywhere she did was sweet but I was nervous meeting her friends. And that's my point. You saw someone who needed a friendly face, and made the effort even though you were pretty shy yourself back then.'

Joanna sipped her wine. Between it and the food and the proximity of the sea and this man, she was breathing again. There was much still to happen before her future was settled, but the weight of holding on to guilt and fear for decades had lifted.

After his phone beeped, Lucas read a message. 'Okay, so this is from one of the team, just an update on a few things. If you'd prefer not to know tonight—'

'I do. Prefer to know, please.'

Even if it is bad. No more secrets. Not ever.

'Mick is out of surgery to remove the bullet from his leg and should fully recover.'

'Thank goodness.'

'Ray Hammond is concussed—'

'Oh no!'

Lucas chuckled.

'No, seriously. I've injured him.'

'Did you ever take a proper look at that lump of timber you hit him with? I did and whether you believe in karma or not, there has to be a reason you picked it up.'

'I don't understand.'

'It came from Trent's boat.'

Joanna almost dropped her glass. 'No!'

'Yup. The boat which Ray Hammond sank came back to haunt him in the shape of a washed-up beam which stopped him killing again.'

She gazed out to sea. Somewhere between this beach and

Willow Bay, *Spee-Dee-One* was a home for barnacles and seaweed. Nobody would ever have known, had a minor earthquake and series of storms not disrupted its resting place. She would have gone through the rest of her life wondering what really happened that night and a killer would have stayed free.

Lucas went back to reading from the message. 'Hammond has been charged with a number of offences relating to the events of today and as the fire brigade found evidence of arson at the community hall, police are investigating him for that. Once Mick gives his statement about what he remembers about Trent, there'll be further charges.' He looked up. 'He's going to go away for a long time.'

'I'm so relieved. I hope Mick will get some counselling about his upbringing and what he was forced to do back then.'

After putting the phone away, Lucas took Joanna's hand, playing with her fingers. 'I spoke to Mick briefly when the paramedics had given him a pain shot and were prepping him for transport. That night, after Hammond and Trent did their deal and you went to his boat, Mick and his uncle waited in the trees at Willow Bay until you emerged from the sea, hours later. Then Hammond rowed out to steal the drugs back, leaving Mick as a lookout on shore. Mick heard a gunshot. A lot was blurry afterwards but he's sure he climbed under a dinghy during the storm and his uncle returned at dawn. Trent's boat was gone.'

'So he killed poor Trent, then took the boat out of the bay and scuttled it.'

'Good a guess as any. Then rowed back. Dangerous, and he could easily have been drowned.'

Joanna shivered.

'Cold?'

'I think today has caught up with me.'

Lucas lifted her hand to his lips and kissed it. 'I'll pack this all up and let you settle down for the night.'

. . .

Alone again, Joanna unlocked the sliding door and pushed it open, then did the same with her bedroom windows. There was nobody threatening her now. Lucas was only at the end of the road and had made her promise to phone if anything worried her.

She slid between cool sheets, no longer shivering.

The beloved sound of the ocean washed over her and she closed her eyes and slept.

THIRTY-FOUR

Joanna pushed open the door to Joalyn Designs, juggling a large bouquet of highly scented flowers. As with the first time she'd visited, she'd sat in the car over the road for a while but this time, she wasn't building the nerve to go inside. Instead, she was building the nerve to ask Roslyn if after the recent events she still wanted them to work together in the future. Their future.

There were no customers in the store and also, no Roslyn. A big box of Christmas decorations was behind the counter, ready to hang.

In the week since the arrest of Ray Hammond, Joanna had visited Roslyn twice at home, with her friend coming to the beach house once as well. Roslyn had taken a few days off and her part-time staff member was only too happy to fill in. The stress of the events of the beach had taken a toll on Roslyn. Her tiredness was through the roof and she'd arranged an appointment with her local specialist.

'About time you came back! How many clothes are you buying today?'

Roslyn was smiling as she came through the door to the back rooms. Her curls were more-or-less controlled behind a floral headband and she wore a stylish white pantsuit. Her eyes moved to the flowers.

'Heading up to the graveyard next?'

'Actually, these are for you.'

Eyes widening, Roslyn accepted the bouquet. 'JoJo... these are gorgeous.'

'So are you.'

'Aw, that is so sweet. Thank you. Let's get them in a vase.'

Roslyn headed back the way she'd come. 'Do you have time for coffee?'

'I'd love one.'

Through the door was a small hallway with a room off either side and a kitchen straight ahead.

'Come through. I have monitors so we'll see if anyone comes in.'

Roslyn took a vase from a cupboard and filled it with water. 'Gosh, these smell so good. How lucky are we to have such a terrific florist next door?' She played with the flowers for a minute. 'Do you mind if I keep these in the boutique? They'll look lovely on the counter.'

'I'd like that. Can I help make coffee?'

'No, you can sit and talk to me, please. I want to know if the police are giving you any grief about anything.'

Joanna perched on a stool as Roslyn set up her coffee machine.

'They've been wonderful. Hours of interviews about Trent but at no time have I felt as if I am to blame for his death, or been asked why I didn't know he was a drug smuggler. They encouraged me to talk about those weeks when I'd hang out with him. The night I dived off the yacht. And even about the camera and, did I tell you? They managed to get the film developed and later today, I'm collecting the photos.'

'After all these years and from the bottom of the ocean?'

'Being waterproof and airtight preserved the film, at least to a degree.'

The coffee machine got noisy for a minute or two then Roslyn handed over a cup. 'I've already had too many today, which is one of the downsides of having a machine at work on a quiet day.'

'Oh, I hear you. If I'm working in the office I over-consume and if I'm in France or Italy... I really over-consume!'

'But are you going back to that world?'

Joanna sipped coffee to consider her words.

'I'm not. Ted is furious, but I've given him my resignation and as he's made it hard for years for me to take any kind of leave, I'm using it all up in lieu of working out my notice.'

Roslyn's eyes flicked to the monitor which showed live footage from four cameras. One outside the shop and three within. A customer had just walked in and was browsing.

'I should go and look after them, but why don't you do it?'

'Me?'

'All of a sudden I fancy a cup of herbal tea. It might take a few minutes. Go on. I'll be there before you need to touch the till. See how it feels to work here.'

This is a test, right?

Putting a big smile on her face, Joanna went in search of the customer. It was Christie and the women embraced.

'I'm so happy to see you, Joanna and I'm so proud of you for being so brave! One less criminal on the streets, thanks to you, and I have no doubt Mick Hammond is thankful for you being there.'

'Pure instinct. Mick needs a lot of praise, though. He tried to protect Roslyn and me from his uncle.'

'Then you both are brave. Are you working here now, in the shop?' Christie's eyes were warm. 'Please tell me you're staying in Rivers End?'

'I'm going to move back here, yes.'

'And she'll be working here as well.' Roslyn approached. Her voice was quiet and almost tentative. 'At least, I hope she will.' She stopped close to Joanna and took both her hands. 'Isn't it time we got to work on our dreams?'

Sudden tears stung Joanna's eyes and made everything blurry.

'Oh Rossie, yes. Yes, I think it is time.'

Aunt Beryl stood at the edge of the garden. She'd barely moved in the fifteen minutes since she'd suddenly insisted she wanted to pick some flowers for the kitchen table.

Joanna had checked her a couple of times through the window, sensing her aunt was struggling with the idea of leaving her home of so many years. After arriving back in Rivers End last night, she'd done nothing but talk about how much she loved seeing her sister again; but then she'd gone quiet this morning.

Carrying two cups of tea, Joanna wandered down to join her aunt.

The weather was beautiful with a light sea breeze heightening the smells of summer. The sky was clear and the ocean was its serene mirror.

'Oh, I was just coming in, dear.' Aunt Beryl accepted the cup. 'I got distracted from picking flowers because there's really nothing on earth which matches this view. The canals are nice and Broadbeach is so pleasant to walk along but this... well, it stays in your heart.'

How I longed for this view, and sea spray.

'Are you set on moving to Queensland? I'm happy to find my own house here and give you your privacy again.'

'I guess you could always move in with Lucas.'

'Auntie!'

With a chuckle, Aunt Beryl finally turned to face Joanna.

'Teasing aside, he's a good man and one who cares deeply for you, and I hope you find a way to finish what you started so many years ago. My one true love is still the only man for me, but not everyone gets a happy ending.' On that surprising note, her eyes returned to the view.

Joanna had never heard about any true love, and for the first time she realised she knew little about her aunt's younger years.

'But as for your kind offer, I'd like to keep to the arrangement we've discussed in the past few days. We'll each continue to own our homes but effectively swap our addresses. I'd rather not go through the hassle of selling and buying with all its associated costs and besides, one day, this beach house will be legally yours.'

'One very, very distant day,' Joanna said. 'I've booked a flight to Queensland next week to pack up my personal belongings. And a couple of pieces of art I'm fond of.'

'And while you are gone I shall do the same here. My collection of teapots is coming with me.'

Joanna grinned. 'You'll need a small removalist truck for those alone.'

'Or I could leave them.'

'Don't even think about it. I'm going to begin my own collection.'

Joanna was asked to attend a meeting at the Rivers End police station and when she arrived, only Mick was present. He shuffled around with a walking cane and made her a coffee after offering her a seat at his desk which had a miniature Christmas tree on the corner.

She'd only seen Mick once, at the hospital, taking him flowers and chatting about anything other than the events in Willow Bay.

'How is the healing going?'

Mick carefully carried her coffee across then sat opposite with a grunt. 'Yeah, not bad. Bullet missed the bone but still hurts like hell sometimes.'

'Are the detectives coming to see me?'

'Just me. Official stuff first – there's still a while before forensic testing proves we found Trent but it's pretty damning toward Ray. Hole in the skull apparently matches the same kind of gun found on his property, along with a stack of other weapons. All illegal. My recollections have become sharper after working with a therapist and I'll be testifying against him. You and Roslyn will have to at some point.'

'We expected that. I guess I always thought I might be the one being charged.'

'Only thing you might have done better was phone triple zero that night, given the police station was unattended. But nobody holds you accountable for what happened to Trent. He might have fallen down the steps, but I guarantee you he was alive and well until Ray got to him.'

It truly is over.

'On to less official news. The station is going to have an overhaul. Rivers End and the region is too big now for one cop so there'll be some changes. Two officers here full time with one living here and the other coming from Green Bay to begin with.'

'Probably a good idea. You'll be the one living here, though?'

He shook his head. 'I've put my notice in.'

'I'm sorry to hear that.'

'Nah. Had some time to do a proper think about my life and I reckon I've proved I'm not a typical Hammond. Always had an idea about running an online shop – even talked to Harriet and Olive at the bookstore about their set-up now they sell online. Going to do a couple of courses and find something more to my liking than chasing down criminals.'

His eyes lit up as he spoke.

'In that case, I'm very happy for you. And Mick, I'm very

grateful. You did everything you could to protect me and Roslyn from your uncle.'

'You saved my life, Joanna. I'll never forget that.'

The sun had barely risen above the cliffs behind Rivers End beach when Joanna ran across the sand and onto the jetty.

Later today she was flying to Queensland to begin the relocation process and have her last Christmas living in her home on the canal.

In less than a month, she and Aunt Beryl would have swapped homes and Joanna would begin to work with Roslyn. At long last. There were already plans in place for new lines and designing together brought exactly the same energy as in their younger years, only now they both had a lifetime of experience.

She stripped off shorts and top and shoes and pulled a towel from her bag for after her swim. The water called to her and it was only the creaking of the timber behind which made her pause before diving.

'Last time we were both on this jetty, you dived into the sea rather than talk to me.'

The words might have been serious but Lucas was smiling. He only wore board shorts, his sandals were in one hand and a towel in the other.

'Not at all. I could barely remember you.'

He made a kind of spluttering sound, then put the towel and sandals down. 'Sure, JoJo. That's why you looked like a startled bunny and kept changing the subject.'

'I was not startled. And I'm hardly a bunny, although they are cute.'

Lucas closed the distance between them and loosely dropped his hands around her waist, as he'd done so many years ago in the tunnel beside the river. Before he'd kissed her. Joanna's hands had a mind of their own, winding up his body to entwine behind his neck. The scent of him played havoc with her senses but she didn't care. She had nothing to hide from him now.

'You're cute. Even cuter than a bunny.' He kissed the tip of her nose. 'When you come home... here, to Rivers End... would you come on a date with me?'

She'd finished the dress in the sewing room and it fitted perfectly.

'A proper date?'

He pretended to think about it. 'I could collect you in a limousine and we could borrow a yacht and sail to an island where there's a waiter and chef and string quartet.'

'Or, I could ask *you* for a tour of the town, seeing as its grown so much, followed by takeaway sitting by the river and a walk on the beach.'

Lucas's eyes smiled as much as his lips. 'And then I'd kiss you. And walk you home.'

His smile dropped. Joanna knew he was remembering how horribly wrong everything had gone straight after their first date so long ago.

She leaned closer, her face tilted up. 'I think that sounds perfect. Except I'll want more than one kiss. And more than one date. But—'

Lucas kissed her and she melted against him, letting her fingers run through his hair and feeling both their hearts beating in time.

When he lifted his head, his eyes were filled with a passion she'd never seen and longed to explore.

'But?'

'But... ' Joanna gently slipped from his embrace and turned to stand on the edge of the jetty. '*More* than one kiss. *More* than one day. But you need to catch me first.'

In a graceful arc, Joanna dived into the Southern Ocean.

EPILOGUE
NEXT SPRING

'And that, wonderful people, is the end of the evening! Thank you all for attending, and remember to collect your goodie bags on the way out. Shall we have one more round of applause for the models?'

Roslyn had a microphone in her hand and stood on the stage of the newly rebuilt Rivers End Community Hall. Wide timber steps led down either side onto red runners of carpet forming a border around the hall. Tables and chairs were set up inside the red border with people having just finished the last of the meal served by a local caterer.

Applause rang out as fifteen models, aged from five right up to seventy-five, paraded down one set of steps, all the way around the outside of the tables and back up the other set. They waved the whole way, every person enjoying their moment of fame as part of Rivers End's very first fashion show. When each model was lined up on stage, Roslyn reached from behind the curtain and tugged until Joanna came with her to the middle of the group.

'Couldn't do any of this without the Jo part of Joalyn Designs! Our very own Joanna Johnson is the driving force behind this stunning new community hall, so please remember that every dollar you've spent to be here tonight is being donated to support its ongoing maintenance and future free programs for old and young alike.'

As much as the applause and being in the spotlight embarrassed Joanna, she carried a deep sense of pride in her part – along with Roslyn – in getting the community behind a quick rebuild. She'd worked hard behind the scenes with other traders and a few of the wealthier families in the region to raise money and organise working bees. The local builders had donated their time and efforts as had other tradies, and the result was a purpose-built building which would serve the community for decades. She and Roslyn had already started a sewing basics class which was well attended and a lot of fun.

The models gathered around Roslyn and Joanna. Bobbie was one and he threw his arms around Joanna's middle. At one of the tables below, Lucas sat with Cal and Mattie as well as Wanda with her husband and daughter. Everywhere Joanna looked were people she knew, some, like Christie and her husband Martin, now close friends.

'You did very well, Joanna. And you, Roslyn.' Bess kissed them both. She'd been the most senior model and was a wonderful ambassador for the brand with her gentle smile and obvious enjoyment of showing off a range of designs tonight. 'I'm going to change, then Marge and Annette and I are going to Rivers End Food and Wine Co. for a nightcap if you'd like to join us.'

'Let's see how long it takes us to pack up,' Joanna said. 'Thank you a million times for being part of this.'

'Not often I get the chance to dress up, and in such lovely clothes.'

In minutes the hall was empty apart from half a dozen helpers who were dismantling tables, stacking chairs, and clearing the last of the plates to pile up for the caterer. In the changing rooms, clothes were returned to racks and gradually the babble of excited voices disappeared and it was just the two of them, again.

'I could never have done this a year ago,' Roslyn said. 'I wouldn't have dreamed of being part of such a big event or running a fashion show and dinner.'

'And seeing you with so much energy again makes me happy.'

'Last check-up came back normal.'

'There's nothing even remotely normal about you, my darling. But you look absolutely stunning tonight.'

'We both do.'

In front of a large mirror, they hugged, then looked at their reflections.

Joalyn Designs had expanded into three lines: Natural – the original affordable day wear; After Dark – evening and special occasions; and New Gen – children and teenagers. There was a long way to go to fully develop the latter two but between Joanna's business flair and contacts, and Roslyn's passion for the boutique and the increasing team of women who helped bring the designs into reality, they were making positive inroads.

Joanna leaned the side of her head against Roslyn's as they gazed in the mirror. 'We really are living our dream.'

'And about time. I meant to say how pleased I am you took my advice and wore this dress.' Roslyn straightened and adjusted the neckline of Joanna's dress... the one she'd started sewing all those years ago. 'I still don't think you have the neckline quite right.'

'You do know I created this design when I was barely out of school? And I didn't take your advice. You told me I could wear this or swimwear.'

'And you are beautiful in either.'

Joanna spun around. Lucas stood in the doorway.

'Sorry to startle you... may I steal you away once you are finished here?'

'Oh, you can have her now, Lucas. We've got the hall until lunchtime tomorrow, so once the caterers leave I'll head off and come back in the morning to do the rest. Go on, shoo.'

'Do I have any say in this?'

Lucas and Roslyn both said no at the same time.

'Just let me change.'

Holding his hand out, Lucas shook his head. 'Not a chance. If you hadn't noticed, I have a suit on, so we can be fancy together.'

'Where are we going?'

It wasn't as though the town was overrun with high-end venues.

But he just smiled and Joanna collected her purse.

It felt a bit strange strolling around the town at night in a custom-made evening gown. The blue fabric was soft against Joanna's legs and despite Roslyn's comment about the neckline, she loved how it fitted. Her hair brushed her shoulders now, and when she glanced at her reflection in a shop window, she looked happy.

'Have you eaten tonight?'

'Six outfit changes for fifteen people, including a five-year-old? Not even anything to drink other than a few sips of water.'

'Let's fix that then.'

They were close to the wine bar and Lucas stopped them outside. 'Can you give me a minute? Look, the ladies are waving.'

Sure enough, Bess, Annette and Marge had a table near the window and while Lucas went inside, Joanna waved back with a grin. He was back in under a minute, carrying a cooler bag.

'Whatever are you up to?'

'Being romantic.'

He held out his arm and she slid her hand onto it.

They'd been on many dates in the past few months. Sometimes out for dinner or a picnic or else homemade meals and board games in front of a roaring fire on icy winter nights. There was no doubt in Joanna's mind that her heart belonged to him. If anything, the older version of Lucas was even more attractive and their life experiences brought new richness into their conversations.

Tonight felt different.

Lucas was quiet as they walked, reflective.

He must be tired, as he'd not only worked today but helped ferry a lot of the clothes across to the hall and had taken on the role of seating everyone.

'Bobbie was amazing tonight,' Joanna said. 'He's a natural.'

'He told me he's going to be a movie star.'

'And they've gone home with Wanda?'

'Yes, still another week of school and then my house will become a riot of boy noise, smells, and mayhem. Perry loves it.'

So do you.

They'd reached the bridge and wandered to the path along the river. These days there were nice benches set every so often for people to enjoy the water and at the third one, they stopped.

'It isn't a yacht to an island with a chef and waiter and string quartet, but would you care to have some refreshments?'

Lucas opened the cooler bag and unpacked three small plates covered with foil, two glasses, and a mini bottle of French champagne. 'Hang on, ah, there's bottled water as well so shall we sit here a while?' He waited for Joanna to sit before joining her.

'These smell so good, and I can't believe how hungry I am now!'

'Good thing that Leo knows your favourites, after us eating there so often.' Lucas put the plates between them on the bench and began removing the foil. 'Most of this is for you because I ate at the event, but I would love a nibble of each.'

The offerings of different tapas were typically delicious. As they ate and talked, a canoe glided by in the dark. The couple paddling waved and called out good evening. Joanna knew them. Dan was one of the builders who'd worked so hard on the hall and Sadie's mother owned the inn.

'I should have borrowed a canoe.' Lucas was gazing after them.

'You do know I have two kayaks.'

'No offence, but they are nowhere near as romantic.'

'Gondolas are romantic.'

The meal was finished and Lucas packed the empty plates way. 'I guess you've been on gondolas. When you've visited Italy for fashion shows? Do they have fashion shows in Venice?'

'I've never once had time to ride on one.'

'Would you like to?'

All of a sudden, Lucas was closer, his eyes unreadable in the darkness, which was only broken by the light of the moon.

'I would love to.'

'Then come with me.'

I am so confused.

'To Venice? For a romantic evening on a gondola?'

'For our... oh my lord, this is harder than I expected.' Lucas shuffled until he wasn't sitting on the bench but had somehow gone down on one knee. He tapped his pockets, grinning. 'Don't ever ask me to do this again.' He found what he wanted, a small box.

'Lucas...'

'Joanna. JoJo. My love. The girl who I fell for more than twenty-five years ago and never really forgot. And the woman who sits before me like a dream come true. Will you come to Venice with me? For our honeymoon? And marry me?'

He opened the box, his hands shaking and she cupped them

with hers. The ring was one of George Campbell's creations and a perfect solitaire.

'How beautiful.'

'Yes. Yes, you are beautiful and I'd really like to kiss you and open the champagne and put this on your finger so...'

'I will come to Venice with you.'

'Joanna!'

She leaned forward to brush her lips against his. 'And yes, a million times, yes. I will marry you.'

A LETTER FROM THE AUTHOR

Many thanks for reading *The Secrets of Willow Bay*. I hope you enjoyed meeting Joanna, Lucas, and Roslyn. If you want to join other readers in hearing all about my new releases and bonus content, please sign up for my newsletter.

www.stormpublishing.co/phillipa-nefri-clark

If you enjoyed this book and could spare a few moments to leave a review, that would be hugely appreciated. Even a short review can make all the difference in encouraging a reader to discover my books for the first time. Thank you so much.

With Joanna and Roslyn I set out to explore the dynamics of a true friendship which got lost for a long time. Many people lose contact with dear friends thanks to time and circumstance. What happened with these strong young women was a sudden shift from being unbreakable to being broken, partly through outside circumstances and partly because they forgot what mattered. The foundation of their friendship was shaken to its core.

At what point is a relationship beyond salvation? Can shattered trust be rebuilt? Does the wisdom of life experience see past mistakes through clearer eyes? I wanted the reasons they were friends to shine through regardless – their love of fashion, their genuine admiration for each other, and the humour which survived the pain.

Joanna's journey was complicated by the weight of the night

she discovered Trent's terrible secret. By not reporting what happened on the yacht, the drugs, and the threatening letter, she lost her power. I believe coming home to face her demons regained it and much more.

Thanks again for being part of this amazing journey with me and I hope you'll stay in touch – I have so many more stories and ideas to entertain you with! From my heart to yours.

Phillipa

www.phillipaclark.com

facebook.com/PhillipaNefriClark

instagram.com/phillipanefriclark

tiktok.com/@PhillipaNefriClark

ACKNOWLEDGEMENTS AND A NOTE

As ever I want to give much love and thanks to Emily Gowers and the entire team at Storm Publishing. This is book four and I am so delighted to continue our work!

Sometimes my enthusiasm for an idea outweighs my knowledge about a subject (actually, often) and having a shipwreck which was suddenly washing up after decades is a perfect example. What was likely to wash up and what condition would the pieces be in? Would clothing and other materials still exist? And what would even cause it to suddenly break apart?

Thanks to the expertise and sound opinions of a number of people, I have learned much and had a few surprises along the way! A particular shout out to Simon Michael Prior, an Aussie coastguard who patiently answered my questions (he writes coastguard mysteries), and fellow Storm author Gregg Dunnett who helped at the beginning of my research.

I have enormous respect for the Australian Coastguard, who save many lives and work tirelessly to keep our waters safe. The SES, State Emergency Service, are another wonderful group who attend emergencies from a fallen tree to major flooding.

My readers make my work joyful, as do my friendships with many and with like-minded authors.

Because I write mostly Aussie-set stories, I sometimes forget our terminology and spelling is occasionally different from other countries. An example is my use of the word 'ute' which is the same as a 'pick-up truck'. A utility vehicle, sometimes four-wheel-drive, either with a tray at the back or a canopy. Or 'Esky' being the Aussie word used the most for a cooler or chill box. Our seasons are opposite the Northern Hemisphere so the festive season is during summer. School holidays over summer are long, from mid-late December through to late January. I do hope the context helps identify any anomalies but please always feel free to reach out to me if you'd like more information on anything in my books.